A GRIEF AGO

The two sisters Gaynor and Kathleen
were complete opposites: Gaynor was
impulsive and friendly, in love with her
childhood sweetheart Gary whom she
planned to marry after finishing her
degree. Katherine, on the other hand,
was lovely and remote, still yearning
night and day for the dead man she
loved – even though she had since
married her first boyfriend, the playboy
son of a wealthy businessman.

But Gaynor was soon to have her
dreams shattered when Gary, who came
from the poorer end of town, cruelly
left her for someone else. And
Katherine's coldness was to force her
husband Paul into a foolish affair, which
was to have tragic consequences for
them all . . .

Also by Nan Maynard

A CRUMB FOR EVERY SPARROW
LEAF IN THE WIND
THIS IS MY STREET
THE BAWDY WIND
WEEP NOT, MY WANTON
RED ROSES DYING
IF YOU CAN'T CATCH, DON'T THROW

and published by Corgi Books

A Grief Ago

Nan Maynard

CORGI BOOKS
A DIVISION OF TRANSWORLD PUBLISHERS LTD

A GRIEF AGO

A CORGI BOOK 0 552 10597 x

Originally published in Great Britain by
Robert Hale and Company

PRINTING HISTORY
Robert Hale edition published 1976
Corgi edition published 1977

This book is set in Intertype Plantin

Corgi Books are published by
Transworld Publishers Ltd,
Century House, 61–63 Uxbridge Road,
Ealing, London W5 5SA
Made and printed in Great Britain by
Cox & Wyman Ltd., London, Reading and Fakenham

PROLOGUE

THE snowdrops would be out again, around the cottage, by now almost certainly growing in careless profusion in the long-untended, tiny garden. Once, she remembered, there had been big clusters of snowdrops each side of the porch, blazons of simple purity, in odd contrast to the atmosphere of intrigue and earthiness inside the cottage. The cottage that her father had refused to let again after David had died in it.

'We want no sensation hunters offering exorbitant rents,' Hugh Scarlett had said. 'I wasn't exactly perceptive in my choosing of its last tenants. It shall stay empty from now on.'

'It never was much more than a reinforced summerhouse anyhow,' mother had said in her thin, tight voice, 'I always felt there was something evil about it.'

Never evil. My beloved cottage, lonely now beside the silent river, the dark woods behind you, whispering with ghosts, the boathouse dark and sinister, still cradling the secret of its crime of murder while the water slaps accusingly against its walls. How are you looking now, my lovely cottage? You waited a long time for him, then he came and he never left you again alive. Loving you, how have I kept away from you all these years? Yet, loving *him*, how could I go to *you*?

'The snowdrops are out now around the cottage,' Gaynor said suddenly.

Katheryn raised her head and stared at her sister.

'You've been there?'

'Of course. Katie, we have to talk, we have to decide what we're going to do with the estate, the house and . . .' She looked into the blankness of her sister's eyes and stopped from saying 'the cottage'.

'Later,' Katheryn said. The sadness was swamping her again, her mind had become blinded with thoughts of a time long ago, of snowdrops and a strange, forbidden love and the sweet agony that was David.

CHAPTER ONE

DOROTHY TRENT was half Chinese. Her Chinese mother had died of cancer when Dorothy was nine. The Chinese woman had seemed to welcome death thankfully and the girl knew it was not just because of the pain of her illness, but because of the strange western world to which she had never grown accustomed. When Dorothy had later mentioned this to her father, he had replied, 'Nonsense. I lived for years in China and I soon got used to it. It's just a matter of adjustment. Unfortunately your mother didn't live long enough in England to get adjusted.'

Dorothy's father married again soon after her mother's death, an English woman this time. By the time Dorothy was eighteen, she had three step-sisters. In this sturdy, essentially English family she was the odd one out, the cuckoo in the nest, with her slant oriental eyes, dark hair, slightly sallow skin and petite figure. Now, at the age of twenty-two, she had lost her earlier look of frailty and had become a startling beauty. Taken by her first lover, a married man, Reggie Gunner-Cartwright, a rich, notorious lecher, when she was almost eighteen, Dorothy became obsessed by a crazy love for him and an agonizing need for the delights he taught her body. She was, from the first time his skilful hands touched her, his absolute slave, but Reggie Gunner-Cartwright soon tired of a faithful mistress. He whispered erotic suggestions to her of widening her sexual horizon. 'Try others, my darling. You will always come back to me in the end, more desirable and experienced than ever and I shall love you for it.' So besotted was Dorothy with this man that she went with other men, even finding pleasure in them, but always her heart and her body stayed exclusively the property of her satanic tutor.

Her position of secretary to Paul Earnshaw, the young managing director of Digby-Meade Tyre & Rubber Company, had been obtained for her by Reggie Gunner-Cartwright, who had a controlling interest in this and many other firms.

'We have to lie low, my darling,' he had said, 'cool it for a few months. My wife is becoming a threat. Be kind to Paul Earnshaw while you're waiting, teach him what I taught *you* and tell me all about it when we're together again.'

Dorothy knew that Paul Earnshaw found her attractive, but so far, his attitude to her had been strictly that of boss to secretary.

'His wife will come into money of her own now,' Dorothy said to Anthea, the girl who had the flat at the top of the large Victorian house in Bayswater where both girls lived.

'Katheryn Earnshaw's mother died a year ago,' Dorothy continued, 'and now her father's been killed in a car accident. He was in the detergent and washing powder set-up, semi-retired.' She shrugged. 'There's money all round the Earnshaws. Paul's father has his own business, flourishing. Katheryn Earnshaw's father owned Marbrook Manor down on the Thames at Marbrook. Now Katheryn Earnshaw and her sister stand to inherit the lot.'

The other girl sighed.

'To them that hath, it shall be given. To them that hath not, it shall be taken away. Me, I'm a hath-not, always have been, always will be.'

'Me, too.'

'Don't be funny, with *your* looks?' Anthea Potts' eyes enviously appraised the luxury of Dorothy Trent's room. 'This isn't exactly a slum. It's bloody Mayfair compared with my garret up aloft.'

Ignoring her friend's remarks, Dorothy went on, 'Don't you remember, Anthea, Katheryn Earnshaw figured in that scandal of the riverside cottage. You remember, the case of that David Lloyd who was accused of murdering his sister who turned out to be his wife.'

'Yes, I remember,' said Anthea. 'That was some scandal. He was ever so dishy, wasn't he, from his pictures in the papers?'

'Yes, and as corrupt as they come, blackmail, drugs, procuring. The cottage he lived in with his sister-cum-wife was on the estate of Marbrook Manor – Katheryn Earnshaw's home. She had to give evidence at the trial Katheryn *Scarlett* she was then. They reckoned it was her evidence that got him acquitted.

I remember seeing his picture in the papers and Katheryn Scarlett's once. The murdered girl was lovely.'

'Ah yes,' Anthea sighed. 'Sometimes I think it's safer to be plain and homely like me.'

Dorothy laughed. 'You don't have to be murdered just because you're good looking.'

'No,' Anthea said reflectively, sipping the drink Dorothy had poured for her, 'but you stand a better chance.'

'What happened to that man, Lloyd, after he was acquitted, I wonder?'

'You remember,' Dorothy said, 'he shot himself, in the cottage, by the river. Very dramatic, it was.'

'Ugh! Definitely, sin doesn't pay,' Anthea said.

'Lots of high ranking gents must have breathed sighs of relief,' Dorothy said, 'I remember my father saying he reckoned there were lots of exalted names in David Lloyd's little black book.'

Anthea tut-tutted. 'So much corruption in high places. God, I wish I could get in on some of it – enough to keep me in comfort for life. Beats bashing a typewriter any day. Trouble is, I've got nothing anyone wants and I don't know anyone to blackmail.'

'I would be content with just one man,' Dorothy said, her eyes stark, '*the* one.'

Anthea sat back and picked up her drink.

'I wish you'd stop thinking of him. It spoils you for other men.' She gave an exaggerated sigh. 'Why, with your looks you could have anyone, someone young, handsome . . .'

'I don't want someone young and handsome. I want Reggie.'

How could you explain to a girl as normal as Anthea Potts about the black delights of that first love, the baring of two erotic demon souls, going down into the depths of lovely depravity together, bound always by the intimate knowledge of each other's desires.

Anthea shook her head despairingly.

'Silly girl. Say, wasn't he, your Gunner-Cartwright, mixed up in that Lloyd scandal, and his wife – the Lady Tabitha?'

'Only on the edge of it,' Dorothy replied, 'they lived near and were in the same set.'

Yeah, I bet he was on the edge, Anthea thought sourly, I bet that one was right in it with his collection of twigs and whips. To Dorothy she said:

'And was Paul Earnshaw in that crowd, too?'

'I shouldn't think so. He'd have been too young. He was with a firm in Windsor, studying accountancy, and should have gone into his father's business when he qualified, but Reggie came along and lured him into the Digby-Meade company.'

But Anthea didn't want to hear about Gunner-Cartwright. She couldn't understand this snake-rabbit set-up between him and Dorothy Trent, anyway. Made you feel a bit sick, a pretty girl like Dorothy and that middle-aged lecher.

'You may fall in love with Paul Earnshaw.'

Dorothy smiled bleakly. 'I shall probably sleep with him.'

So that's the set-up, Anthea thought. Dear Reggie's orders, make Paul Earnshaw happy and get off *my* back.

As if sensing her friend's thought, Dorothy said:

'Reggie and I agreed not to see each other for a while. Lady Tabitha was getting restive about us. She has a hold over him in some way, she must have.'

'She's his wife,' Anthea commented dryly, 'or weren't you thinking of that?'

'No, I was not,' said Dorothy coldly. 'Reggie and Lady Tabitha have gone their separate ways for years. She stopped being a real wife to him years ago.'

'Yeah?' said Anthea. 'I reckon Adam composed that pretty ballad when he sneaked out of the Garden of Eden and all the bastards have been singing it ever since.'

Seeing the stony expression on Dorothy's face, she added softly, 'Don't mind me, pet. I'm just a sour, repressed bitch, eaten up with jealousy.'

Dorothy relaxed, smiling.

'I think you're nice.'

'Yes, they all do, the women. You see I'm no competition. The men like me, too, I'm a good shoulder to cry on and ever so grateful for a quick feel.'

'Oh, Anthea.'

'I suppose I'd better blow. You'll be wanting to get ready.'

'Paul Earnshaw's entertaining some German buyers. I'm to

12

go along to take notes. Also, my knowledge of German will be useful.'

'Always married men,' Anthea said, 'look love, with your looks, you could go places. I know it's none of my business, but there's seldom any future in it when the man's married, so watch yourself.'

'My future is Reggie's,' Dorothy said, 'one day . . .'

In your heart you don't believe that, Anthea thought, any more than I do.

'I dunno,' she mourned, 'you attract married men like you carried a welcome sign lit up on your 34 C cups. Remember Faversham?'

'Faversham was never serious,' Dorothy said, 'he came along when Reggie was in California for three months.'

Sent to me by Reggie. Quickly Dorothy rejected the torturing memory. I used Faversham to try to get Reggie out of my system. It didn't work. Faversham could never be Reggie. Paul Earnshaw, for all his charm and good looks, could never be Reggie either. No other man can give me what Reggie does. His silky voice crept into her memory. 'My lovely baby Chinkee schoolgirl, my adorable little one.' Those soft, creeping hands, those warm, insatiable lips, so weak I am with longing for you, Reggie, so ready, so weak . . .

'This wife of Paul Earnshaw's, this Katheryn,' Anthea said.

'What about her?'

'Just what is she like?'

'I've never seen her, except her picture that time in the newspaper.'

'No photograph on his desk?'

'No, only his children. They have twin girls.'

'Funny,' Dorothy said, shutting Reggie from her thoughts, 'she never rings him at the office. He rings *her* and afterwards he always looks sort of frustrated, a look almost like despair, just for a second. I've noticed it so many times.'

'Do they quarrel on the phone?'

'Oh no, it sounds as if the conversation's ultra-polite, but it's his look after he's put the phone down that bugs me. Also, she never comes to the office. Wives usually come to the office some time, if it's only to look over the opposition.'

'I'd say he was in love with her,' Anthea said, 'if she never rings him and he comes away from the phone looking like you said.'

'Yes, well,' Dorothy said. 'Perhaps he is.' She put down her glass and rose from her chair. 'I'll have to throw you out now, love. I have to get ready.'

'Where are you dining?'

'The Hilton. We have to start early because the Germans are flying back at eleven o'clock tonight.'

'And you'll be sent home by taxi when the dinner's over?'

Dorothy's delicate eyebrows shot up a fraction, her almond eyes narrowed.

'Will I?' she said. 'No, I don't somehow think so. Not tonight.'

In her bath Dorothy Trent ran her hands up and down her smooth slim body. Am I a bad girl because my body craves for a man? Isn't it the natural primitive urge? Only one man can really satisfy me. Reggie is mine and one day I mean to get him.

She got out of the bath and scented her body all over before she dressed and went out to meet Paul Earnshaw.

CHAPTER TWO

THE gardener watched the two sisters as they strolled through the garden towards him, the three-year old twins, Lucy and Linda, skipping ahead of them. Both sisters were dressed in dark jeans and thick sweaters. Katheryn Earnshaw was very tall and willowy, slim to the point of thinness. Her shoulder-length dark brown hair was looped back from her face with a black ribbon. Her sister, Gaynor, was nothing like her, short and inclined to plumpness. She was, nevertheless, very pretty. Her straw-coloured hair was cut short and curled naturally. Her manner was always open and friendly, whereas you never felt you really knew the other one. Sometimes Katheryn Earnshaw was friendly, at other times she was very much the mistress of the house. The gardener could never forget the brush he'd had with her over the snowdrops.

'Dig them up.' she'd commanded. 'I want none of them left.'

'But they's allus bin here,' he'd protested, 'proper pretty little things, they is. Makes you think of new birth, new life.'

'Or death,' she'd replied stonily.

'Don't you like snowdrops then, miss, madam?' He'd always had difficulty in calling her madam, she seemed so young.

'I don't want them here,' she'd replied, 'dig them up at once please.'

He had been forced to obey. After all, it was her garden and she was the missis.

The two sisters stopped beside him.

'Hello, Parsons,' Gaynor Scarlett said, 'you're looking younger than ever, I do declare. Must be this lovely country air.'

He smiled into the bright young face of the girl.

I feel about a hundred some days, miss,' he answered, 'rheumatism, you know.' He turned to his mistress. 'Should have a wonderful show of roses this year, madam.'

'I like roses,' she said.

'It's a big garden for you to do, Parsons,' said Gaynor Scarlett.

'Oh, I has help, miss. My young nephew from the village, he come in when I want him. His mum keeps the shop, she glad to get rid of 'un occasionally. Them darned little sycamores'll be poking through soon, comes up in their thousands every spring, they do, from them trees there.'

'You'll have to train the twins to pull them out for you,' Gaynor said. She was regarding affectionately the two little girls who were racing each other to the wall where the peaches grew in the summer. Katheryn, too, turned to watch them. Although she smiled her eyes seemed to go beyond the children to some secret place. Looking at her, the gardener thought, she don't look old enough to have a husband and two kids and a bloomin' great house like this. She has the quiet, he thought, of a woman of sixty, as if she'd seen it all before. In the village they said she was a bit odd, racing off sometimes in her sports car as if all the demons in hell were after her. And Arthur Smith from the pub had seen her once or twice in an all night coffee bar on the motorway when he'd been returning from jaunts with the boys.

Yes, up in the village they weren't too keen on Katheryn Earnshaw because she was something they couldn't understand.

Parsons didn't understand her either. Often he would watch her as she played with her children. She played their games, tended them, yet he felt there was something missing in her attitude towards them, like, you might say, she was looking after someone else's kids.

Katheryn called the twins now and she and her sister walked on towards the house.

Gaynor looked up at the lovely house, Monk's Folly, as they approached it.

'This is the sort of house I always wanted father to buy. I never really liked the Manor House.'

'Well, you'll probably be able to buy your own now,' Katheryn said.

'Tonight,' said Gaynor, 'we have to sort things out, Katie. I must go back tomorrow.'

'Oh, can't you stay?' Katheryn said, 'It's the Gunner-Cartwrights' silver wedding house party this week-end. Reggie and Tabby insisted that we take you if you're still here.'

Gaynor pulled a face.

'Bang-bang C and his lady-wife are hardly my scene. Besides, should you go to parties so soon after father's death?'

Katheryn turned with a movement of irritation.

'That's absurd. Not going to a party won't bring him back, if I wanted to, and, after all, Paul and father didn't exactly get along. I owe it to Paul to go to Reggie's party.'

'You know,' Gaynor said unemotionally, 'you really are a prize bitch, Katie, aren't you? You always have been.'

'Thanks.'

'Well, you didn't give a damn for father, but you could at least be a little less cold-blooded about it. And, while we're on the subject, I haven't noticed you exactly prostrating yourself before Paul, yet now, for his sake, you have to go to the nasty old party.'

'I want to go to the party.'

'What for?'

'What does one usually go to a party for?'

Gaynor nodded. 'Of course, for kicks, like you use your sports car, your marriage to Paul. Gosh, you've changed, Katie, since . . .'

'I've grown up,' Katheryn interrupted coldly.

'Oh, I see,' Gaynor said, with a ghost of a smile, 'that's what it is, is it?'

'Well,' Katheryn said, 'if you really do have to leave tomorrow, we can talk tonight after dinner. Paul won't be home, he's staying at his flat in town. He's got to entertain some German buyers. He doesn't want to drink and drive back afterwards.'

'Very wise,' Gaynor said. 'Do you ever go on these business dinners with him, Katie?'

'Me? No, of course not. Why should I?'

'Some wives do.'

'What do I know of tyres and rubber?'

'You could learn.'

'Why on earth should I?'

Gaynor shrugged. 'I dunno. I just thought . . .'

'I entertain here if Paul wants me to,' Katheryn said, 'beyond that, I don't interfere.'

Because you don't care, Gaynor wanted to say, but she knew the futility of trying to break down Katie. She might as well save her breath. Suddenly Gaynor was swamped with a feeling of depression, of foreboding. She wished desperately that she and Katie were children again and there had never been David.

That night, after dinner, the girls sat together in the study, sipping brandy with their coffee.

'You won't carry on at University now, will you?' Katheryn asked, 'I mean, we shall have money . . . you needn't . . .'

'Yes, I shall carry on. I want to teach history eventually.'

'You'll probably get married.'

'I *shall* get married, but I still don't want to be a cabbage.'

Katheryn looked up sharply.

'You've got someone?'

'The one I've always had,' Gaynor replied coolly. 'Gary Thompson.'

'Good Lord,' Katheryn said wearily, 'don't tell me that silly affair is still alive.'

'Why shouldn't it be?'

'Well, you were just a kid, then, and he . . .'

'And he came from the wrong end of town?'

'I didn't say that.'

'You didn't have to, it's written all over your ladylike phiz. He's articled to a firm of solicitors in Harlow New Town, Marvin, Marvin, Marvin and Bales. David,' she paused, then almost defiantly she added, 'David got him his chance with their London office. They drafted Gary to a new office they've opened in Harlow. He's doing very well. He's only got his finals to take now.'

'You've never had a chance to meet anyone else,' Katheryn said, 'I wish you'd come around with us for a while, broaden your horizon.'

'With *that* crowd? I hate the Gunner-Cartwright set — they're all so false. I want Gary and truth, and I want university. I can't just sit back and live on what father left me. I'd become a moron in no time.'

'I'd hate university life,' Katheryn said. She shuddered delicately, 'so communal.'

'What's wrong with that? Anyhow,' Gaynor said, 'I'm what they call a sugar plum student. I don't have to rough it like some of them. I try to atone, though. I have people in to super posh noshes. I do them on my new cooker.'

'I don't see why you should have to atone,' Katheryn said, coldly.

'Gosh!' Gaynor said, 'if you saw the conditions some of the students live in.'

Katheryn shrugged. 'That's *their* hard luck.'

'It could have been mine, too,' Gaynor replied, 'if father hadn't had money. I try to keep my rooms as austere as possible so as not to rub it in.'

'More fool you,' Katheryn said, 'have as much comfort as you can get.'

Gaynor smiled.

'I've still got that lovely purple circular rug, though, in the middle of my room, you know, the one . . .' She stopped. 'Of course, I was forgetting, you haven't seen my rooms, have you?'

'No.'

'Paul came once.'

'Paul?' Katheryn showed her surprise.

'Yes, that time I had flu. He brought me some wine and fruit.' Gaynor grinned as she had used to do as a child. 'He's not half bad when you get to know him, you should try it some time.'

'He's my husband,' Katheryn said curtly.

Gaynor eyed her sister obliquely. 'Yes, well?'

Katheryn busied herself stirring her coffee.

'University doesn't seem to have done much for you, you're still given to silly juvenile remarks.'

'And marriage hasn't done much for *you*, except maybe made you even snootier.'

'Thanks.'

Gaynor sighed and smiled. 'We always got at each other, didn't we? I suppose we always will. If we weren't sisters we'd probably hate each other.'

'I don't see why,' Katheryn said. They were silent a while, then Gaynor said:

'Poor father! He only went to a board meeting once in a blue moon. I wonder if he went to sleep at the wheel.'

19

'Or was tight,' Katheryn said evenly.

'That's mean.'

'Why is it? He always drank a lot, you know that. If he'd lived, he'd probably have married again,' Katheryn said, 'Paul told me there were already rumours, a young woman somewhere. If he'd married her, you and I would probably have got nothing.'

'And you'd have minded?' Gaynor said.

'Of course I'd have minded. The money was mother's originally, anyway, so we should have it. I like money.'

'More than father's happiness?'

'Rot,' Katheryn said contemptuously, 'father was a pompous fraud, and a lecher. Before mother died he had women . . .' she paused, then quietly she added, 'He had Harriet.'

'Harriet?' Gaynor's voice was low, her eyes widened, '*Harriet*?'

'Yes, after that fête – in the boathouse.'

'How do you know?'

'I saw them. It was horrible.'

'Oh gosh!' Impulsively Gaynor put her hand out to her sister. 'Oh, Katie, poor you.'

Katheryn leaned back from her sister's touch. 'I'm just glad it was me, and not mother. The shock would have destroyed her. She hated sex.'

Gaynor stared abstractedly in front of her for a long time. She looked as if she wanted to cry, then, in a small voice, she asked, 'Did David know?'

David, his deep, wonderful voice slaying Harriet that awful, obscene night. Then, later, comforting her as if she were to be pitied. Would that hateful jealous memory never fade?

'Yes,' Katheryn said now to her sister, 'David knew.'

'Ah,' Gaynor said, almost in a whisper, 'at last you've spoken his name.' She leaned again towards Katheryn, tears standing unashamedly now in her bright eyes.

'David loved you,' she said slowly, 'I think I knew it right in the beginning when we used to be with him by the river. The way he looked at you, a special yearning kind of way as if you were out of reach, and you knew it too when you lied for him at the trial.'

20

Katheryn's eyes widened, she opened her mouth as if to speak, but no words came.

'Oh yes,' Gaynor went on triumphantly, 'you lied. You knew he loved you, didn't you? David, the bad, the cheat, the lecher,' she paused and her voice softened, 'the beloved. Oh yes – I'd have lied for him, too. I loved him too, in a different kind of way, but because he loved you, you're living on that, aren't you? Dead to everyone else. You don't even see your lovely kids, really see them.'

'What on earth are you talking about?'

'Sorry. Forgive me,' Gaynor said with a little smile. 'Maybe I'm letting my imagination run away with me.'

'I think you must be,' Katheryn said coldly.

'That's how I see it, though,' Gaynor said, 'just you and the memory of David, your own precious little world, you and him locked in it together. It's unhealthy. It can't go on, Katie, he's dead, stone cold dead, and, even if he'd lived you could never have had him. You know it. Face up to it.'

There was silence between them. Katheryn had lowered her head and was shielding her eyes with her hand.

Presently Gaynor said, 'I wake up in the night sometimes and wonder who murdered Harriet.'

Katheryn looked up then, 'It wasn't David.'

'No, it wasn't David.' But it *could* have been, Gaynor's heart told her. Swiftly, for the hundredth time, she rejected the thought. Much as he might have had reason to, David couldn't have killed Harriet.

'About the house,' Gaynor said to Katheryn.

'It will have to be sold,' Katheryn said, 'won't it?'

'Of course. I've always hated it, it sounds so bloody pompous – Marbrook Manor. Mr. Rowbotham says a research institute are interested in it. The grounds would be ample for extra buildings and a car park.'

A look of pain flashed across Katheryn's face. She shuddered.

'How ghastly!'

Gaynor waited a moment, then softly she asked: 'and the cottage?'

Katheryn's voice was sharp. 'The cottage?'

'I want you to have the cottage,' Gaynor said, 'it's always been yours, ever since you used to go down there and talk to its ghosts when you were a child. Remember how you used to try and keep me out.' Gaynor smiled. 'Well, now it's yours as far as I'm concerned. You won't have to tell me ghost stories to keep me out any more.'

Katheryn was silent a while, then evenly she said, 'I don't want it. It'll have to be sold as part of the estate.'

'No it won't. We could make a separate access to it through the woods at the side of the manor grounds.'

'I don't want it. What would I do with a tiny, damp, riverside cottage?'

'You could take the children there to picnic and swim like we used to.'

'The river's too dirty for swimming now,' Katheryn said. 'I shall buy a villa in Spain with my money and take the children there to swim in the sun.'

'All right,' Gaynor said resignedly. 'That's really what I came down about.' She sighed. 'It's a stark thought, isn't it? I mean, mother and father both gone. There's only you and me left of our family now.'

'I have my own home and children,' Katheryn said.

'And Paul.'

'Of course, and Paul.' The merest shade of disdain crept into Katheryn's voice as she added, 'and you'll presumably soon have your own husband.'

'I know,' Gaynor said. 'It'll be wonderful, but I just feel, now and then, a tiny twinge of fear. If anything should go wrong, we've got no kith and kin except each other.'

'Go wrong?' Katheryn queried, 'what could go wrong?'

'Forget it,' Gaynor said, 'I just felt a bit depressed, I suppose, for a minute. After all, we have lost both parents in a fairly short space of time.'

'You never wanted to live with them,' Katheryn said, 'you couldn't wait to get away.'

'I know. I said forget it. It was maudlin. I had a moment of panic. I suddenly felt lonely. I'm all right again now. Well, I'm for bed. I have to be up early tomorrow morning. It'll probably take me half an hour to start my car.'

'You'll buy a new one now, surely?' Katheryn said.

'Yes,' Gaynor replied, 'that's one reason why I have to go back, I'm taking delivery of an M.G.B.G.T. tomorrow. Old Daddy Rowbotham has advanced me the money.' She smiled softly. 'Gary will be surprised. He's so used to seeing me in my old banger, he'll love the new car, all zippy and smart.'

'No doubt,' Katheryn said dryly.

Gaynor sighed heavily. 'You don't understand, Katie, he's not like that. I wish you'd meet him.'

Katheryn shrugged and Gaynor sighed again. Then with an abrupt change of subject she said sharply, 'If you don't want it, I do, Katie, the cottage. We mustn't let it go.'

Katheryn stood tense for a moment, her hands clenched, then she said,

'What on earth do you want it for? You couldn't possibly live there when you marry, it's too remote.'

'I wasn't intending to live there,' Gaynor said, 'I just want it. I shall keep it in repair and look after it and one day . . .'

'One day what?' Katheryn queried frigidly.

'One day, you never know. It can come out of my share of the estate.'

'There's no need for that,' Katheryn said, 'I expect it's derelict now, anyway.'

'No, it isn't.'

'How do you know?'

'I looked after it every time I went home. Mother couldn't have cared less, but father approved of keeping it from decay. He paid for everything I needed to have done to it.'

'All right,' Katheryn said evenly, 'Consider it yours.'

'And yours too, Katie,' Gaynor said quietly, 'any time you care to see it.'

Before Katheryn could reply, she had gone.

Gaynor Scarlett lay sleepless in her bed in the luxurious guest room allotted to her in her sister's elegant home. Depression swamped her again. So many things were wrong. Katie and Paul, for instance. Paul had been Katie's first boy friend and she had seemed to like him until David had come along. Gaynor remembered how fearful she'd been for her sister when David Lloyd had killed himself, but Katie had gone about, calm as ever and if her eyes were dead, then only those very close to her would have known it. Then, suddenly, she was a dynamo, no party was complete without her, the fast young set of Marbrook became too slow for her. So many things were odd about that time, like wealthy Reggie Gunner-Cartwright's sudden adoption of Paul Earnshaw into his gay, top-layer set. If Katheryn Scarlett was a swift goer, then the new, slick Paul Earnshaw came a close second. And it had seemed as if, in the midst of the dizzy whirl of parties and social functions, they stopped and saw each other as if for the first time. Then, before the snowdrops came out again round the cottage, Katheryn Scarlett and Paul Earnshaw were married.

So many things you'll never understand, Gaynor Scarlett, so don't try. Think about dear Gary instead. If only he were nearer and not bogged down with swotting. If only we could meet more often. But now, she consoled herself joyfully, there's nothing to stop us getting married. Oh Gary! How handsome he'd grown, so mature, so different from that insecure, immature boy who'd held her, sobbing, in his arms when David's trial had revealed the dreadful truth about Gary's sister. If it hadn't been for me, Gaynor told him silently, you would have given up then, my Gary. You'd never be where you are now, on the road to a successful career. Oh Gary, I love you. Gary. The beloved name on her lips Gaynor Scarlett at last fell asleep.

In her room, Katheryn Earnshaw pulled her curtains back to the stars. There had been so many stars that night, that night David had acknowledged his love, so many stars that the sky had been closely studded with them like a big black cloth strung with diamonds. She opened the window and leaned out. It was very cold tonight, and silent, with just the faint night rustlings in the garden below. And lonely. Like that other night had been lonely for her, even though David's love had blazed out of concealment – love – bitter, despairing, wonderful. She closed the window and, leaving the curtains wide, went to her dressing-table drawer. From under some lingerie she drew out the pictures. She looked at them briefly and put them all back, save one. That one she held close to her heart. The lady in the

Edwardian dress, high at the throat, wide puffed sleeves, parasol poised daintily over one shoulder, smiled dreamily back at
her from the frame. Behind the lady the steam launch waited at
the landing stage of the cottage garden.

'The lady in David's picture has your face, Katie.' Gaynor
had said, all that long time ago. 'I want Katie to have my
pictures' David had said. David, David. Her curtains still
wide, Katheryn Earnshaw got into bed. The picture she put
on Paul's empty pillow beside her, like a child taking a doll to
bed for comfort. She lay for a long time in her precious loneliness before she dropped off into a troubled sleep.

CHAPTER THREE

'Do you think you should drive Mr. Earnshaw—' Dorothy asked.

'Paul,' he said.

'Paul then.'

He gazed around him. 'I like airports at night.'

She smiled. 'I just like airports.'

He was more than a little tight. He turned and looked down into her face.

'Why do you like airports, Dorothy—'

'They promise escape, romance, adventure.'

'You shouldn't lack any of that with your looks. Those Krauts loved you tonight. I thought I was going to lose you to old Otto Gunther, trying to bribe you like that, lecherous old bastard.'

'No bribes would get me to work away from England now,' she said.

Not while there's the remotest chance of getting Reggie back, but this nice Paul Earnshaw wouldn't know she meant that. He would think it was because of him. He took her hand.

'A very successful evening,' she said, 'you got your terms tied up without any difficulty.'

'Thanks to your German and the way you dazzled Otto and that other Kraut pipsqueak, Willi, he brought along.'

'Ah Willi,' she said, 'he put his hand on my knee under the table.'

'What did you do?'

'Nothing for a minute, I thought it was you.'

He looked down at her quickly.

'Boss man's privilege?'

'When I found it wasn't the boss man,' she said, 'I moved.'

They were nearing the car park now. Again she said, 'Do you think you should drive?'

'I drove here.'

'Yes, but that was before you helped Otto empty his flask.'

'You don't miss much do you? I thought you were busy chat-

26

ting Willi up about the merits of Berlin and London shops.

'I'm trained to be observant and I'd hate you to lose your licence.'

'I'd hate it too.'

'Perhaps we might have a coffee,' she suggested, 'before we get the car.'

He made a grimace.

'I hate airport coffee.'

'Sorry. Just a suggestion.'

They were almost at the car when he said, 'What kind of coffee do *you* make, Dorothy?'

They stood facing each other, a new intimacy between them.

'Good,' she said simply.

He fished in his pocket and handed her his car keys.

'Care to prove it to me then?'

She swung the keys on their chain. Would this one blot out Reggie for her? She knew the answer already. No one could.

'I'd love to prove it to you,' she said.

He seemed to be dozing on the drive to her flat in Bayswater. She parked his Mercedes in the large courtyard at the side of the house which was used by the flat dwellers as a car park.

Inside the living-room-cum-lounge on the first floor of the big house he looked about him with interest.

'It's a big room. What very high ceilings.'

'Yes,' she said 'this house once belonged to a lordship in Victorian times.'

'I never pictured you in an old place like this,' he said, 'somehow I associated you with chrome and trendy custom-built furniture, a sleek apartment accessed by a swift silent lift.'

'Like a secretary in a Hollywood film.' She slung her hand-bag on to a chair and handed him his car keys.

'Take those before we lose them. I'll make the coffee. If you'd like some brandy with it, help yourself. The booze is in the cabinet over there. I'd like one too.'

His hand touched hers briefly as he took the keys.

'If I have another brandy, how do I drive back to my flat?'

She met his gaze steadily.

'We'll talk about that later. Relax now. You've had a tiring evening.'

'So have you.'

'No, I enjoyed it. It was nice to air my German. Besides, you were in the pilot's seat. I was only along for the ride.'

'You're my navigator. I couldn't get along without you.'

'Oh, Mr. Earnshaw,' she mocked him, 'you've brought your violin.'

'I thought I told you my name was Paul.'

'Old habits die hard. I've always called my bosses mister.'

'We're not in the office now. A lovely girl called Dorothy was just about to make a drunken bum called Paul a cup of coffee.'

Left alone he strolled over to her cocktail cabinet and got out the brandy. The cabinet, he noticed, was very well stocked. Maybe she had private means or a boy friend or lots of boy friends. He realized then that he knew very little about her, apart from her work in the office, except that she had a Chinese mother who was dead now and that she didn't go home much to her father. Paul found two brandy goblets and took them, with the brandy, to a small table set before a long chaise-longue. Tonight he felt high and ready to take on the world, but he knew it wouldn't last. By morning his mouth would be furred, he'd be gulping Alka Seltzer and sucking indigestion tablets and sloughed down with depression. A few more years of high living and rich business dinners and I'll be like Reggie, he decided, stomach like a distorted football, blood pressure that constantly needs checking and the only kick left in life making more money and pulling birds. I'll end up a bloody pervert like Reggie. Maybe I should have gone into father's business, but then, would I ever have got Katheryn? He knew the answer to that. No. The new Katheryn Scarlett who had emerged after the trial of David Caradoc Llewelyn Lloyd played high in exalted circles. There had even been a rumour once that she was about to marry old Phelps-Craven, the oil millionaire, who was all of sixty, had been through four wives and had the biggest yacht in the Mediterranean. But she had come back from the South of France where she had been staying with a school friend, sun-tanned and apparently un-committed and he, the intrepid Paul Earnshaw, had stepped in and won her. Like a bloody trophy, he told himself, and just as much life in it, yet the feeling of triumph still remained with him, triumph at getting Katheryn Scarlett after all that had happened. Sometimes, when he was very drunk, he would wish her dead so that he could be free of her and then, in the morning, he would know how empty his life would be without her.

If she knew that he was here tonight, with Dorothy Trent, would she care? But there was no fear of her finding out because he knew that nothing short of a dire emergency would make her ring their London flat to check if he were there. Never once had she approached him, he had to make all the advances. He picked up one of the brandy goblets and fondled it. Like this glass she is, he thought, warms with fondling, but it could be any man doing the fondling. Sometimes the frustration almost choked him. If Katheryn took little excursions into adventure to keep even with a randy husband, he felt he could take it better, but he couldn't imagine Katheryn having clandestine affairs. She had just the one big affair and that was locked in her heart. He was interrupted in his bitter reverie by Dorothy coming in with the coffee. She had changed from her long dress into an open-necked shirt and slacks. She looked very young and very desirable. She was far lovelier than Katheryn, but even that knowledge didn't ease the ache inside him.

She poured the coffee into gold cups and they sat down together on the chaise-longue.

'Real gold?'

She shook her head, smiling. 'Gold painted china. I'm only a working girl, remember.'

'I remember and I'm very glad that you work for me, oh Lotus.'

She grinned, showing delightfully white even teeth.

'No one has called me that since a boy at school. "Chinkee-Lotus" he used to say. I hated it then.'

'I won't call you that again.'

He took a sip of the coffee, then put the cup down and took a bigger sip of the brandy. She got up, went to the cabinet and brought back the brandy bottle which she put on the table in front of them.

'I'm sorry,' he said, 'once I start, I can't bloody stop.' He patted her hand. 'I'll get you another bottle tomorrow.'

She moved a little away from him, folding her hands primly on her lap.

'That offends me.'

He drank before he answered her, then he said, 'I'm sorry, darling. I daren't offend you, you're too important to me.'

'This is very sudden, Mr. Earnshaw.'

He took her hands from her lap and kissed the palms.

'You know it bloody isn't. You've seen me watching you in the office, leering at your breasts and legs.'

She laughed. 'You've never leered. In fact, I sometimes wondered if you were a machine. Other men where I've worked . . .' She stopped and spread out her hands expressively.

He took another sip of brandy. 'Yeah, I bet. I can imagine it.'

'Your coffee is getting cold.'

He lifted the cup obediently and drank.

'Would you like some more?'

'No thanks. I'll stick to the hard stuff.'

A trace of coldness in her voice now she said, 'I see. You want to get absolutely stinking. Are you celebrating or drowning sorrows?'

'Neither, sweet, I told you. Once I start . . . Vino Collapso, that's my family crest.' He laughed tipsily. 'Tell you something funny, Lotus, my father-in-law, he invented his own family crest. Came from some punky little cottage in Wales, he did, but when he got to be a big boy he got this bloody crest, his initials intertwined with leaves. Christ, it was funny, but not so funny as the way it got up my old man's nostrils. Hated each other, they did. Old Scarlett with his new Rolls-Royce every two years with his blasted crest on the door, and my old man strutting about in the glory of his one time commission, like bloody puppets . . .

'Mr. Scarlett is dead,' Dorothy said, 'you shouldn't speak ill of the dead.'

Paul laughed. 'Yeah, you suddenly get precious when you're dead, don't you? People say nice things about you and refer to you as poor old so-and-so, or dear old so-and-so. I wonder if she'll . . . they'll say things like that about me when I'm dead.'

'Dead drunk if you don't watch it.' Dorothy said.

He laughed. 'Takes a lot to make me dead drunk, Lotus. Slur my words a little I may, but I can prove to you . . .' He reached for her, but she moved a little away.

Soberly he said, 'I've hurt you.'

'Disappointed me.'

Still without signs of tipsiness he said, 'I should still be making passes at you even if I hadn't had a drink.' He reached again for her hand and this time she let it lie passively in his.

'It was my lucky day when Reggie Gunner-Cartwright brought you into my office, sweet.'

Reggie! He had no place here in this boy and girl romantic stuff. Romance isn't Reggie's scene. I want you, Reggie, how I ache for you!

'It was lucky for me, too,' she said. 'Reggie impressed that on me, an up and coming young business brain he called you, said girls were falling over themselves to work for you. It was like auditioning for a star part in a play, legs, bust-line, hips, face and then, of course, last but not least, my secretarial ability.'

Paul's grip on her hand tightened.

'He's a bastard, a ruthless, selfish, lecherous bastard.'

Her eyes widened. 'I thought you liked Reggie?'

'Most of the time I hate his guts.'

'Then why do you appear so friendly?'

He laughed curtly. 'Most people would appear friendly if the biggest, richest merchant banker in London deigned to smile on them. Besides, I like money, Lotus. If I'd worked for my father I'd have done quite nicely, but I didn't want to do quite nicely, I wanted to do bloody well, so I tagged along saying "yes sir" to Reggie.'

'And your father, wasn't he upset?'

Again the hard little laugh.

'No, he was flattered. You see my old man's a snob. He's delighted to have a son in such exalted circles. Christ! What a circle.'

'You're young to be so cynical.'

'I'm a hundred years old, darling. The things I know would shatter you.'

And you, my young innocent, Dorothy thought, the things I know would shatter *you*. This place where you are so crudely fumbling me is Reggie's temple of sex, and I would give a dozen men like you for one night with Reggie.

'The things I know would shatter society, too,' he was saying, 'secret, evil things . . .'

She was suddenly alert.

'What do you know, Paul?'

He moved impatiently and released her hand.

'That I talk too bloody much when I'm on the drink.' A sudden thought seemed to strike him. 'Did Gunner-Cartwright extract an agency fee from you in your bed?'

She looked into the fine unhappy eyes turned on her with sudden intensity. She knew she had to lie. He was nice, this Paul, even if she couldn't love him, and he was a man and Reggie had taught her body to need men.

'No.'

'He didn't need to sell you to me,' Paul said, 'the first moment I saw you . . . Dorothy . . .'

She turned to meet him and their lips clung, his tongue moved inside her mouth, she responded to him in almost desperate passion. Eventually he released her. His voice was shaky as if he were drunk again.

'I want to go to bed with you.'

She smiled although her eyes were still desperate with desire.

'Before you've finished the brandy?'

'All right, so you don't sleep with soaks.'

'Did I say that?'

'No, but there's something wrong isn't there?'

She put up a hand and stroked his face.

'Not once have you mentioned love.'

'Right at this moment,' he said, 'I love you very much.'

'And tomorrow?'

'I think so. I'd be a fool if I didn't, but I'm not trying to talk you into it, Dorothy. I want you and just now I thought you wanted me.'

'I do,' she said, 'let's go to bed.'

He opened his eyes and regarded her approvingly. She lay naked beside him outside the bed covers. His fingers touched her breast.

'Little Chinese golf balls.'

She smiled sleepily. 'You play a lot of golf, sir?'

'I'd rather play this.'

She settled herself sensuously against him, snuggling her face against his shoulder.

'Not now. Let's go to sleep. We can do it again in the morning.'

'All right, it's your pad, you're the boss, but get inside the covers, eh, or we'll be cold.'

She laughed as she obeyed him.

'Cold the man says, after what happened just now.'

He pulled the bedclothes up over them both and took her in his arms.

'That was only a sample. After we've slept I'll show you some more.'

'Good.' She released herself gently from his embrace. 'Can't sleep like that,' she murmured drowsily, 'I'd suffocate. Let me put my back to your front and you put your arms round me and we'll sleep like that, babes in the wood.'

He obeyed, putting his arms round her, his hands on her breasts, but he wasn't sleepy now.

'Lotus,' he said, 'what's with the double bed in a bachelor girl's flat?'

She was silent a moment and he thought she was asleep, but presently she said, 'If you're thinking I had it for this purpose, you're wrong. The flat was partially furnished, this bed was part of the partial.'

It was true. He didn't have to know that the partial furnishing was done by Reggie.

'I'm sorry, I shouldn't have asked. Darling,' he said, 'what if anyone sees me leave in the morning? Will it be bad for you?'

She snuggled closer against him. 'No. I have nothing to do with the other tenants except Anthea on the top floor.'

'She entertains too?'

'Not like this,' Dorothy said, 'Anthea has short legs and freckles and has set her sights on a wedding ring.'

He laughed lazily. 'I'm glad you haven't got short legs and freckles.'

She seemed awake now. 'And that I don't want a wedding ring?'

'Do you?'

'I learned when I was very young,' she said, thinking of Reggie, 'that a wedding ring was not what I wanted.'

His hands tightened round her.

'Just think, darling, no more lonely beds when we go away on

33

business trips. What a lot of time and chances we've missed, darling, Paris, Amsterdam, Milan . . .'

He was thinking ahead, no more sleepless nights in strange cities, thinking about you, my Katheryn, torturing myself, now I shall have the delights of this lovely body to distract me, a sweet antidote to lonely hours and troubling thoughts. Beside him Dorothy lay silent, remembering other hands on her body.

'Darling,' Paul said suddenly, 'is there anything you'd like? Clothes, jewellery or something new for the flat maybe?'

'No. You don't have to pay me, Paul.'

'I wasn't intending to. I just wanted to give you something to show my feelings for you.'

'You're sweet, but I have all I need in that way.'

She wondered what he'd say if she told him that almost all the sumptuous trappings of this flat had been paid for by Reggie. He might be disgusted, but never jealous. He's trying, like me, she thought, to forget someone else. It won't work, but it's better than nothing.

They slept and woke again, both together, at seven o'clock. They made love with mutual passionate abandon and lay afterwards smoking and talking.

'I'll make some coffee,' Dorothy said, but he held her back.

'Not yet. Plenty of time. You needn't go into the office today, anyway, because I shan't be going in. I have lawyers to see for my wife about her father's will'

'I know,' Dorothy said. 'Remember me, I'm your secretary. I put it in your diary.'

'Of course.'

'Then you're having a day or two's leave,' she said.

'Yes, I shall miss you.'

'I shall miss *you*.'

'But there are things I have to see to at home,' he said, 'my wife has arranged for an army of builders, electricians and plumbers to come and see me about some alterations and improvements she wants done to the house.'

Dorothy was silent, wondering about this remote girl who stayed so much in the background.

'I'll go in anyway,' she said, 'even if I don't stop all day. There are things I have to do.'

34

Gently he stroked her cheek.

'You're a good kid. I'll never cease to be grateful to Reggie for finding you for me, even though I do hate his guts at times.'

'You hate him, yet you're going to this silver wedding house party of his, aren't you?'

'Of course, I couldn't miss seeing Reggie and Tabby celebrating their godless union.'

'If I hated someone,' Dorothy said in a low voice, 'I wouldn't go to their party.'

Paul laughed.

'We go to all Reggie's parties. He and Tabby come to all of ours.'

His thoughtless words had shown her just how shut out she was.

Boldly she said, 'And your wife likes Reggie?'

Paul shrugged. 'Does she? I wouldn't know. I don't think Katheryn – particularly likes anyone, but she likes parties.'

'Who stays with your children?' ·

'We have a resident maid-cum-nanny called Mabel, very capable.'

'A luxurious home, a beautiful wife, lovely children.'

Paul drew on his cigarette and closed his eyes as if in pain.

'What future is there in it, for any of us? What future for the kids? Atom bombs and pollution. So do we do anything positive about it? No, we booze and fornicate, declare dividends and stick our stupid heads in the sand and, when the end comes, we shall take our little loved ones, if they aren't registered drug addicts or alcoholics by then, and we shall cradle them in our helpless arms, seal the doors and windows and turn on the gas.'

She shuddered. 'What ghastly things you dream up.'

'I look at the kids sometimes,' he said, 'and I shiver with fear.'

'They mean a lot to you, don't they, those two little girls?'

'Of course. They're flesh of my flesh, obscene as it may sound.'

'And woman is the rib of Adam,' Dorothy said lightly.

He grinned at her, his serious mood dropping from him.

'Well, Adam made a bloody good one-off job of you, my darling.'

He took the cigarette from her finger, leaned over her and stubbed it out in the ashtray beside the bed. He put both hands on her breasts.

'I was going to make coffee.'

'Make love, darling,' he said, his mouth going down on hers. 'Can make coffee any time.'

Just before lunch, as she was about to leave the office, a small parcel was delivered to her by a messenger from a Bond Street jeweller's. She opened it to find a gold bracelet set with diamonds and pearls. The note with it said. 'To Lotus from Paul, for coffee and sympathy'. Once Reggie had sent her many gifts like this. She stood a moment staring at the pretty bracelet, then she slipped it on her wrist and put the case at the back of a drawer.

She went in and tidied Paul's office. Gold framed pictures hung on the wall showing the modern buildings of the firm's depots in Oslo, Essen, Amsterdam and Milan. She had been to Milan with Paul — boss and secretary — separate rooms. Next time it would be different. Although she could never love Paul Earnshaw, he had personality. The office seemed cold and soulless without his presence. She gave a little shiver and went through her own office into the big general office beyond, where the typists worked. She spoke to the nearest girl:

'I'm going now, Maureen. Mr. Earnshaw won't be in any more this week. He's going to a house party on Friday until Tuesday, so I'm taking time off, too.'

'O.K., Miss Trent,' the girl replied with a grin. 'He's lucky, isn't he? The kind of parties I go to don't last that long. It's all right for some, isn't it?'

'Yes,' said Dorothy, 'I suppose it is. If there are any messages, log them for me, won't you? Good-bye everyone. Have a nice week-end.'

As she walked out to her car, a splash of sunlight lit the gems studded in her bracelet. They shone cold and beautiful — fitting payment, she thought, for a high class whore.

CHAPTER FOUR

EDITH BRIDGES sighed as she folded the last shirt and replaced the iron on its stand.

'There,' she said complacently, 'he couldn't have 'em done
any better if they was to be done by 'is own mum.'

Diana perched on the edge of the table, painting her nails,
said tersely:

'You spoil him rotten.'

'No, I don't. I don't believe in havin' lodgers and not takin'
proper care of 'em.'

'He should take his laundry home or do it himself in a laun-
derette.'

Edith regarded her daughter with indignation.

'How can he, poor love? He don't get time and he don't get
home all that often, either, with all that swottin'.'

'He could if he didn't waste his spare time with her,' Diana
replied, 'Miss Gaynor Fitzwaller Scarlett, heiress student de
luxe.'

'Gary don't see her all that often,' Edith protested, 'in fact,
he hasn't seen her half so much lately since he's bin doin' all
that intensive swottin'. Anyway, he owes her a lot. He told me
he nearly flipped when all his family's terrible trouble came,
and if she hadn't persuaded him to go in fer the law, he'd
probably be servin' in a shop now. Poor little thing, she's just
lost her dad in a car crash and lost her ma a while back, that
makes her an orphan.'

'You make my heart bleed,' sneered Diana. 'Besides, she's
got a sister, the rich Mrs. Earnshaw.'

'Well money e'nt everything,' Edith said. 'Besides, he's got
his pride, has Gary, he'll want to make his own money.'

Diana shrugged.

'Who's arguing? Who cares anyway? I still say you spoil
him. After all, he's only the flippin' lodger.'

Edith folded up her ironing stand and placed it against the
wall.

'He's always seemed more like one of me own. I s'pose it's because I was sorry fer him, that poor sister of his being involved in that scandal when that David Lloyd man was on trial, and her dying, all tragic, like that. It must have bin dreadful for them all. I always felt more sorry for Gary and his mum and dad than for her. After all, she chose a life of sin and shame and she paid for it. If we embark on a life of sin, others gets hurt, and we . . .'

'Oh Mum!' Diana said wearily, examining her painted nails, 'get out of the pulpit, will you? The lecture's wasted on me. I'm not having a life of sin, worse luck. All my debauchery tonight's gonna consist of going down the Club for a bit of a dance and a giggle, if I'm lucky.'

Edith sighed. 'Can't think why you give up young Jimbo Edwards. You've done nothin' but moon about ever since. Why don't you sink yer pride and ask him back?'

Diana's eyes grew stormy.

'Because I don't want him back. Why do you think I sent him packing in the first place? Silly little berk.'

'I dunno,' Edith mourned. 'I said to yer dad only yesterday, I said, I can't understand our Di, I said. She was that keen on young Jimbo at one time, I said. I mean I know he works for Bunny Akers now, but you never know, he might in time get his own plumbing business like Bunny did. I mean, there's always plenty of work fer good plumbers, I said to dad, I said . . .'

'Oh Mum, for Gawd's sake!'

Diana Bridges was a dark girl of medium height. Although not a beauty, she had, nevertheless, a fleeting look of beauty when she smiled. Her eyes were dark, rather melancholy and she had a clear pale complexion and wide mouth. Her legs were long and very shapely and the mini dress she was wearing now showed them to perfection.

'Well, I don't understand you young folk, I'm sure,' Edith said.

'Then don't fret yourself trying.'

Edith smiled. 'Gary says I remind him of his mum. I say the same sort of things. Dad and me's gonna visit Gary's parents one of these days. Gary said his mum's never got over the shock of their Greer dying an' the disgrace an' all, but he says he thinks she'd like to see us, him tellin' her all about us, like. Dad says when he gets a day off he'll run me over to Marbrook. Yeh, I feel I'd like to meet Gary's mum, me bein' like a mother to him since he's bin here. Poor soul, I bet she never thought when she named them kids for film stars, Greer and Gary, how one of 'em was gonna end. Lovely names.'

'Rubbish,' Diana scoffed, 'I think they're daft names, both of 'em.'

'Oh I know romance is old-fashioned,' Edith said huffily, 'and film stars e'nt what they used to be neither.'

'Good job,' Diana said, 'get that Clark Gable!'

Ignoring her, Edith went on, 'Dad'll no doubt get on well with Gary's dad if we visit, both of 'em bein' staunch Labour like. Although Gary's dad left the Council after the scandal, Gary says he's still an active member of the party.'

'Gary isn't Labour,' Diana said.

'No, well,' Edith smiled tolerantly, 'kids is seldom what their parents want 'em to be. Take you, now, always brought up staunch Labour . . .'

'I'm nothing,' Diana said in a bored voice, turning the top on her varnish bottle. 'I never wanted the vote. I certainly shan't use it.'

'Women's Lib would scrag you for that,' Gary Thompson said, coming into the kitchen.

The girl and the young man stared seriously at each other for a second, then the girl turned her eyes away.

'That scares me.'

'Thought you was in your room studying, young Gary,' Edith said, fondly reproving.

'I was, but I heard voices down here and I got suddenly lonely.'

The boy gazed round the cosy kitchen. Like mum's at home, it was, bright pans hanging on the wall, comfy warmth exuding from the boiler, the meaty smell of cooking lingered. The room might be small, but it was very inviting. It only wanted Mr. Bridges in here spouting about the Labour party and it would be just like home. At one time, Gary thought, I couldn't wait to get away from it all, now I often find I'm missing it.

'I just remembered somethin',' Edith said. 'I woke up at half

past one this mornin' and your light was still on, young
Gary. You won't do yourself no good swottin' till all hours like
that.'

'I wasn't swotting all the time. I just couldn't sleep.'

Edith looked at him critically.

'At your age you shouldn't be troubled with sleeplessness.'

'I'm not usually.'

'Worrying about the exams?'

'No, not more than usual.'

Diana eased herself off the table.

'Well, I'm going down the club, Mum. Shan't be late.'

'Could you give me a lift?' Gary asked.

She stopped and stared at him with eyes that were faintly
hostile.

'Where to?'

'Where you're going – the club.'

'No swotting tonight?'

'No, don't want to get stale. I feel like a night off.'

'That's nice,' Edith said, 'do you good, Gary – you work ever
so hard.'

'I can't think,' Diana said, 'why you don't get a car of your
own.'

'I will when I've qualified.'

'Surely Di,' Edith said, 'you don't mind giving him a lift.
After all, you're both goin' to the same place. I'm sure it'll be
very nice ...'

'Oh leave it, mum, for Gawd's sake,' Diana said, 'who says I
don't want to give him a lift? If only you'd mind your own
business sometimes.'

'I'm sorry I'm sure,' Edith said huffily, 'I only ...' But
Diana had swung out of the room.

Gary smiled apologetically at his landlady and spread out his
hands helplessly as he followed Diana out.

Outside he said, 'Need you be so brutal to your mum?'

'She gets on my nerves. Dad does too with his silly bigoted
politics.'

'Mine used to,' Gary said. 'My dad and I almost came to
blows several times, but I think I've grown more tolerant since
I've been away from home.'

'Fat chance *I've* got of ever getting away from here,' Diana said moodily.

He went round to hold the door for her when she got in behind the wheel. When he was seated beside her, he said: 'You'll get away all right when you marry.'

She turned and looked at him with stony eyes.

'Who says I'm gettin' married?'

'I thought you and Jimbo Edwards . . .'

She took him up sharply.

'Jimbo Edwards and I were never like that.'

'Sorry.'

'I never asked him to come after me in the first place,' she said, 'he bored me to tears.'

'Yes, I should think he would, from what I've seen of him. I'd say he wasn't your type at all.'

'Because he doesn't wear a collar and tie for work? Because he earns his living mendin' pipes, instead of poncing about in an office showing people how to get divorced or getting them off when you know they're guilty?'

Surprised at this sudden attack, he said mildly:

'O.K. Sorry I spoke.'

Sulkily she said: 'I get so sick with people lately. Mum, dad with his red flag bull.' She slumped down over the steering wheel. 'And you,' she said, her voice muffled, 'you're so bloody smug and patronizing about my home and my parents, and I know damn well why. Because you know that any time you lift a finger, Miss Gaynor Scarlett will come along and take you right out of the miserable rut.'

'I don't need a woman to get me out,' he said. But ignoring him she went on:

'In the meantime, you're quite enjoying slumming with the peasants, you can even pretend to be one of them.'

He was really angry now.

'None of that is true and you damn well know it. I'm just the same as you. My home and parents are identical with yours.'

'But your *friends* are different. You don't pick them from your own kind, do you?'

'You don't pick friends. They just happen. Gaynor Scarlett and I were friends years ago.'

'But you preferred her to a kid from your own street?'

'Rot. We met when we were both at school. We had things in common. It had nothing to do with homes and parents. Anyway, she hated the big ridiculous house she lived in and hadn't much time for her snobbish parents. I hadn't much time for *my* parents, either, so it was a bond in common.'

'If my parents had money I wouldn't despise them,' Diana said, 'I'd feel they'd achieved something instead of how they are now, always griping and never having the brains or guts to do something about it.'

'Money wouldn't change them,' Gary said.

'It would if they'd earned it.'

'Gay's father earned most of his, but she still didn't have much time for him.'

Diana smiled thinly.

'I still say money helps.'

'I agree, but it doesn't alter people basically.'

'Don't be silly, it sets them apart.'

She switched on the engine, put the car in gear and drove slowly away from the house. They made the short trip in silence.

As they walked into the pub he said stiffly, 'Would you like a drink?'

'No thanks, I'll go straight up to the clubroom.'

He shrugged. 'O.K. I can't win, can I? You hate me and that's that. I'm sorry, Di, if I get under your skin. Perhaps you'd rather I found other digs.'

He turned away, but she stood still at the foot of the stairs leading to the clubroom.

'Gary.'

He turned back and looked at her.

'I wouldn't,' she said, 'I mean, mum would hate for you to leave. I'm sorry I was rude just now, but I was so fed up.'

The hostility had gone from her eyes and voice. She seemed almost pleading.

'But we never make it, do we?' he said, 'you and I? Five minutes' conversation and it's obvious I get on your nerves. O.K. That's that. It happens that way sometimes, you just instinctively dislike someone and there's nothing you can do about it.'

'I don't dislike you,' she said in a low, troubled voice.

He laughed curtly. 'You could've fooled me, then.'

They stood staring at each other, the fair-headed boy in sweater and jeans, the dark-haired girl, slightly shorter than him, her small breasts outlined provocatively through the tightness of her skimpy mini dress. The boy's thick, dark eyebrows stood out in startling contrast to his fair hair. Distinguished looking, he is, the girl thought unhappily, no wonder the Scarlett girl wants him. Any girl would find him attractive.

As for the boy, he had a sudden urge, and it wasn't the first time he'd had such a feeling, to seize this girl and kiss her sulky mouth, to shake some feeling into her stupid little working class brain. He'd never had such a feeling for Gaynor Scarlett and it worried him. With Gay he was comfortable and happy, but in Diana's presence he was never comfortable or happy, there was always a feeling of challenge, a desire to beat down the hostility he thought she felt for him. Now that hostility seemed suddenly to be disappearing and he was surprised at the excitement riding him. But over all that was the depression which had clamped him down all day, ever since he'd had the letter from Gaynor.

'That drink,' Diana said with ususual meekness, 'do you think we've got time?'

He continued to stare at her for a second longer, then he said quietly, 'Sure we've got time. I wouldn't have suggested it otherwise.'

He pushed the bar door open and followed her in.

' 'Lo, Di, 'lo, Gary,' the landlord greeted them, 'you're early tonight.'

'Yes,' Diana said. 'Mum was getting on my nerves, yakking away like Old Moore's Almanack. I had to get out to preserve my sanity.'

The landlord shook his head. 'I dunno, you kids. You forget you'll be like it yourselves one o' these days.'

'God forbid!' Diana said.

'And don't forget,' the landlord grinned, 'you know what they say,' he winked at Gary, 'look at a girl's mum and there you see the girl herself in a few years' time.'

'Never,' Diana said. 'I'd end it now if I thought I was gonna finish up like mum.'

'What'll you drink, Di?' the boy asked her.

'Half of bitter, please.'

'You should've stung him fer a gin,' the landlord said, 'there's plenty of money in the law, y'know. All them fancy conveyancing fees and the like.'

'Conveyancing fees don't find their way into *my* pocket yet,' Gary said.

'Never mind, laddie, one of these days.'

Depression swamped Diana again. Yes, one of these days Gary would be a partner. He'd be married to Gaynor Scarlett and living in one of the posh houses in the Brambles district where all the professional people lived, or maybe he'd go away altogether to another branch office somewhere. In any event, he'd got it made. And I shall still be here, she thought despondently, slogging away in the Town Hall cash desk or married to some no account like Jimbo Edwards.

'Cheers.' He smiled at her.

She thought how he'd changed since he'd taken lodgings in her home. In the beginning he'd worn the deadpan look that was the thing with young boys these days, never giving his good features a chance. Then, as he progressed in his mixing with older professional types in his work he'd developed a steady confidence. He ceased to be stilted in his speech and allowed himself to relax. He talked easily to her parents. Now Jimbo Edwards, whilst chatty enough with his own age group, dried up when with older people and went immediately on the defensive. Since Gary had been around she'd noticed all these things to Jimbo's disadvantage. She suddenly saw Jimbo as clumsy and ignorant. If Gary hadn't crowded her thoughts so much, she supposed Jimbo would have been O.K. Now, beside Gary Thompson, he was a peasant. Gary had that extra quality, Diana thought, that gets you out of the potato patch.

The bar began to fill up round them.

'What say we sit at a table,' Gary suggested, 'Otherwise we stand a fair chance of getting our drinks spilled.' He picked up her glass and his own and steered her across to a table in the corner. He held the chair for her while she sat down.

'When you qualify,' she said, 'I suppose you'll move away?'

'Probably. I have hopes of a partnership later on, if I make the grade.'

'You've done well.'

His eyes grew sombre. 'Not really. I've been lucky. You know about the scandal in my home town? David Lloyd who shot himself in Gaynor's father's cottage by the river?'

'Yes.'

'He fixed up my career for me, Luther Bale, the senior partner in my firm is a cousin of Lloyd's. He made Lloyd a promise that if I turned out all right he would take me into the firm eventually.'

Diana smiled thinly. 'It's *who* you know, all right, not *what* you know, even if who you know is a bad lot.'

'I could never really think of David as bad,' the boy said thoughtfully, 'he could charm the birds off the trees, the bad side of him was so hard to understand.'

'Mum said it was a horrible case,' Diana said, 'that man procured girls for rich men and ran a real vice ring. I shouldn't think there's any doubt that he was bad.'

Gary's mouth set in an obstinate line.

'You couldn't understand. You didn't know him.'

'I'm glad I didn't.'

'It's no use. You'd never understand without having known him.'

'I'd have thought you'd have hated him for what he did to your sister,' Diana said.

'I tried, but I couldn't for long. Greer was all set for that kind of life, anyway. If *he* hadn't helped her, someone else would have.' Gary smiled faintly. 'Like you, she hated her working-class surroundings.'

'There's no high class pimp to lure *me* away,' the girl said coldly.

He turned slightly away from her. It hurt to hear David described like that.

'I'm sorry,' she said. 'I've upset you. But he *did* kill that woman, didn't he, his wife who he pretended was his sister? Didn't he kill her in that old boathouse?'

'It was never proved. Katheryn Scarlett's evidence saved

him. She heard him leave before Harriet was killed.'

'Mum said it was obvious he did it.'

'He couldn't have if he left when Katheryn said he did. Anyhow, he's dead now, so it's best forgotten.'

Gary finished his beer and looked around him. He looked glum and worried. He'd looked fed up earlier when he'd announced he wasn't going to swot tonight. Also he'd said he hadn't slept last night. Maybe Miss Gaynor Scarlett wasn't coming up to scratch. Diana finished her beer and looked at her watch.

'Better go up. You know how they hate you arriving after the speaker. Betty and Les and Connie have just gone up. I saw them go past the window.'

She made to get up, but Gary put out a hand to detain her.

'Couldn't we have another drink? It's nice here on our own.' The gloom had gone from his face, he smiled at her. 'You know what the talks on, don't you, a trek over the Sahara and the speaker's a dried up old bird of over seventy.'

She giggled. 'Our names won't half be mud. The others saw us in here.'

'So what? I don't care if you don't.'

She was still smiling. He thought how very pretty she was when she laughed and she laughed so seldom in his presence.

'I don't care either,' she said, 'but let me buy the next drink.'

'Certainly not. This is an occasion, you agreeing to have a drink with me. Something I thought would never happen.'

'You'll give me a swelled head,' she said, 'nothing special in having a drink with *me*.'

He smiled down at her.

'That's what *you* think.'

She watched him appraisingly as he threaded his way confidently through the throng with the two empty tankards to the bar. When he returned with the drinks he sat back in his chair and heaved a great sigh.

'Why the sigh? Guilty conscience because you're not swotting?'

'I ought to be swotting, but I felt unsettled tonight, couldn't put my mind to it.'

'What's wrong then? You look fed up tonight.'

46

'Nothing really.'

She leaned forward. 'You can tell Auntie Di. I don't blab.'

He lifted his tankard as if to drink, but put it down again on the table.

'It's Gay,' he said.

'Oh. She's got another feller?'

Her elation was killed by his next words.

'No. She wants us to get married straight away.'

'Oh.'

She picked up her tankard, her eyes bleak.

'Cheers then. Here's to both of you. I hope you'll be very happy.'

He stared at her moodily.

'I don't want to get married, not yet.'

'That what kept you awake last night?'

He nodded. 'I owe her so much, you see. When Greer died I almost gave up, got on my high horse, all holy, and said I wasn't going to accept favours from a man like Lloyd. I'd give up all idea of going in for the law, to hell with him and his introductions, I'd go into a shop, but she talked to me and made me see reason. She said it would be stupid to foul up my life because of Greer.'

'Sounds a callous way of looking at it if you ask me,' Diana said sullenly.

'Not callous, sensible. What good could I have done Greer?' He smiled thinly. 'I remember it was raining that night, hard, and we walked around in it, Gay and I, two desperately unhappy kids. I remember she was crying because of David. She was very fond of him. I remember she said, "You don't stop loving someone just because they're bad," and then she said to me, "I'd still love *you* if you'd killed someone." '

'She was in love with you even then?'

The boy shrugged.

'Not really. Just kid stuff. She was fond of me, I suppose, like I was of her.'

'She must still love you if she wants to marry you.'

'We've sort of drifted into it, I suppose. We've just gone on from childhood. She's never been out with anyone else.'

'But *you* have?'

47

He smiled wryly. 'Once or twice, no powerful stuff, just making up a foursome for a chap I work with.'

'She wouldn't like it if she could see you here now with me.'

'I don't know. Probably not.'

Diana got up. 'I'll go then. I'd hate to come between an engaged couple.'

He shot up too.

'We're not engaged. Don't go, Di, please. Sit down.'

He took her arm and drew her back down on to her chair.

'Have you given her a ring?'

'No, of course not. I thought it would be years . . .' he paused, then he said. 'You see, her parents never knew about us, they were terrible snobs. They didn't even like her sister marrying Paul Earnshaw, and he had money and lived in the right end of town.'

They were silent a moment, then she said softly, 'So what are you going to do?'

He ran a hand distractedly through his thick blond hair.

'I honestly don't know.'

'You must've thought you'd marry her one day.'

'Yes, I suppose so. Once I thought she was the whole meaning of my life.'

'And now?'

'Now I've grown up.'

'And she's not what you said – the whole scene?'

Their eyes clung desperately, then he looked away.

'No she's not. She's been an important part of my life, I admit, but I'm on my own feet now. I suppose I always was only I didn't realize it. I sound like an ungrateful pig, I know, but it's true. The things that were so important once, suddenly don't matter. I didn't get on too well with my parents and there seemed to be only Gay who understood me. I got into a fight once at school because of her.'

'But now you don't want to marry her?'

He shook his head. 'It's come too soon, it's a shock.'

'But you must love her.'

'Not in the way I feel . . .' he stopped. Her hand gripped the edge of the table. He put his hand over hers.

48

Through dry lips she prompted him. 'Not in the way you feel . . .?'

'Not in the way I feel about *you*.'

It was out. He had said it. All those past weeks of sharing meals with her, of meeting her on the tiny landing in delicious intimacy, her hair in rollers, her slim body encased in a half open dressing-gown, catching the perfume from her as she passed with a cool casual greeting, hearing the muted sounds of her record player from her bedroom in the evenings and longing to go in to her, put his arms round her and share the music with her. It was almost like being married to her, this sharing of her home, married to her without touching her. Now miraculously he was touching her. His fevered dreams could be reality. Their hands locked on the table.

'You were always so hostile,' he said.

'I love you, Gary. God help me, I love you.'

'I love you, too, Di.'

'Will you tell her?'

'If I do it will be terrible for her. She's built her life all round me all these years.'

Her eyes clouded, her mouth was no longer softly sweet as it had been in her declaration of love.

'That's *your* fault,' she said coldly. 'Why did you let it be that way if you didn't love her?' She withdrew her hand from his clasp.

'It didn't seem to matter,' he said, 'until now. Now that I've met *you*.'

'And now?'

'Oh God, I don't know!'

Diana stood up, her eyes miserable, her mouth set in the old defensive line he had known so well. There was no softness in her now.

'I see,' she said icily, 'well, go and marry your little rich girl. I wish you both luck. It should be one hell of a marriage with no love and all her money.'

Tears stood in her eyes now, blinding her as she stumbled to the door. He stayed in the bar in lonely misery. He got another drink and sat over it, thinking, but no solution came. In his mind's eye he saw dear little Gaynor, tossing back her curly straw-coloured head in sheer happiness as she walked with him, her arm linked in his while she expounded her bright plans for their future. She always did most of the talking, but then she always had done, ever since the early days in their friendship. She had always been the leader. He remembered their first meeting, she on her way home from school, Miss Bateman's select private school for girls. She had got off her bike to walk up the hill when three bullies from Fletchley Senior school had lit into her. He'd run to her assistance, although she was already defending herself well, swinging her satchel round in powerful blows on her assailants. He remembered thinking how pretty she was as she'd thanked him and her voice had instantly charmed him. It still did. Di's voice was a shade common, and when *she* was confident, if anything her voice grew more careless and common. Yet Di affected him like Gaynor had never done. Di. Her perfume still lingered, stirring his senses. She was upstairs now, hostile again and miserable. He got up, all thoughts of Gaynor Scarlett pushed aside. He had to go to Di.

The dancing had started when he got upstairs. The lights were dim. At first he couldn't see her, then a couple passed under the lamp beside the record player and he saw them – Di and Jimbo Edwards – their cheeks pressed together. Her eyes were closed. Jimbo had a soppy smug expression on his sweating face. Without stopping to think, Gary stepped up to them and tapped Jimbo on the shoulder.

'My dance I think, mate.'

The couple stopped. Di's eyes opened and widened in surprise. Instinctively she started to move out of Jimbo's embrace, then, suddenly, her eyes hardened. She clung again to her partner.

'Get lost, no cutting in, get lost.'

'You heard what the lady said, ponce,' said Edwards, 'scarper, eh, before I fill in that pretty kisser o' yours.'

Gary's hatred rose. He put out a hand and spun Jimbo Edwards away from Diana. The leering, red face was close to his. He felt the same fury he'd felt years ago in school defending David Lloyd, his sister, Greer, and little Gaynor Scarlett, only, this time, the fury was greater because of the desire riding him for this girl. He wanted her and this lout had no right to touch her. He put up a fist, but before he could smash into that stupid red face, a hand came out from behind and caught him by the wrist.

'This,' a quiet voice said, 'is undignified and silly.'

Gary turned to see the grave face of the Reverend Willy Blick, leader of the club, a man well versed in all the sports and especially boxing.

'Tuesday is boxing night, Gary,' said the Rev. Willy, 'we've managed very well on club nights without cabaret and we don't intend to start that kind of entertainment now.'

Shame swamped the boy. He turned away with a muttered apology to the clergyman and pushed a path through the staring stationary dancers to the door. The Rev. Willy went back to his seat beside the record player. The dancers started moving again. Jimbo made to take Diana into his arms, but she pushed him away.

'Oh, go to hell,' she said, 'you make me bloody sick.'

She left him standing there, a bewildered expression on his bovine face, and stumbled through the dancers to the door.

She ran down the stairs and out into the yard to her car. From the doorway of the Gents' in the yard, Gary watched her. He waited until she had driven away, then he plunged his hands into the pockets of his coat and started walking. It was raining, the way it had rained that night when Gay had comforted him. He had only to make one move and Gay would be around to comfort him again, but now it was not Gay he wanted.

He heard the door handle turning. He had been half expecting, desperately hoping she would come. He had seen the light still on in her bedroom when he had come home at midnight after walking aimlessly through the streets. He had left his wet coat and shoes downstairs in the kitchen and, as he crept up the stairs in his socks, he had heard the snorting staccato snoring of Arthur Bridges, with the steadier even snoring of Edith in concert.

'You awake?'

'Of course.'

She came to the bedside, her perfume teasing his nostrils. In the darkness he reached for her hands and drew her down on the bed.

'I'm sorry, Di, showing you up like that.'

'I'm not. I wanted you to hit Jimbo. I wanted you to fight for me the way you said you fought for *her*.'

'Oh, Di!' He pulled her closer and their lips met and clung. He tasted the salt of her tears.

'I love you.'

'Love you.'

All the past weeks of desire for her swelled into a leaping crescendo.

'Come in with me for a minute.'

'Yes.'

He moved over and she was in beside him, the sweet warmth of her pressed against his fevered body. His hands eagerly fondled her.

'You're so lovely, Di.'

'I love you, Gary. I tried to hate you, but only because I thought you were in love with someone else. I never dreamed you cared about me this way.'

'I've cared for a long time now. Tonight when I saw you with Jimbo Edwards . . .'

'I hate Jimbo. I couldn't be like this with him, not with anyone but you.'

'Oh, darling!'

Slowly he lifted her flimsy nightie and stroked her little breasts. She shivered with delight and pressed closer to him. Her inexperienced hands faltered in their exploration of his body. He turned to make it easy for her.

'Hold me, darling, hold me.'

Their mouths clung again. Their bodies were together now, her arms had moved to his neck, as gently he thrust himself inside her. It was the first time for both of them. The boy had imagined it many times lately in the loneliness of his fevered dreams, and always the girl had been Diana. Now, when it happened, it was so natural, they had come together so easily. Both were bemused with wonder at such ease, then a singing ecstasy swung them both beyond the bounds of reason or care. For her there was a brief tearing pain, but it was all part of the ecstasy, without the pain there could have been no joy.

'Oh, Di,' he muttered when he was spent, 'I love you, oh God, I do love you.'

Gratitude for the release she had given him after the long weeks of waiting made him ardent without reason. At that moment he really thought he loved her.

She lay beside him, crying softly.

'I love you,' she sobbed.

'Oh darling, don't cry. Did I hurt you?'

She nuzzled against him.

'No, I loved it. I'm crying for joy.'

'I shouldn't have done it,' he said, 'but I couldn't stop to think. You were so lovely.'

'It was my fault,' she said. 'I shouldn't have come to your room.'

'I'm glad you did.'

'It was lovely, wasn't it?'

'Tremendous, my angel.' He stroked her gently. 'I dreamed of it so much with you, but the reality was much better than all the dreaming.'

'Gary,' she said softly, 'was it your first time?'

'Yes, love, it was.'

She snuggled again, closer.

'That makes me so happy. Darling, there's a stain on your sheet I think.'

'I'll wash it off in my basin after you're gone.'

'It'll be all wet for you to lie on.'

'I don't care, it'll remind me of you. I wouldn't sleep anyway.'

'Me neither.' She sighed and moved a little away from him. 'I s'pose I better go back now, in case they wake. I'd like to stay with you all night.'

'I wish you could.'

He held her and kissed her again before she left him.

'I love you,' he told her again.

When she had gone he got up, dragged off his under-sheet and put the stained portion in his wash-basin, rubbing it with his toilet soap. Then he rubbed it with his towel and put the sheet back on the bed.

Somehow, the sight of those little blobs of blood brought him to his senses, made him feel shamed and obscene. That which had been so joyous, now seemed sordid. He began to feel as he had felt long ago at the discovery of his sister, Greer's whoring. The whole damn business was rotten. Sex was filthy. He was rotten like Greer had been, bad blood. Poor Di. Poor darling little Gaynor.

He got between the covers, the dampness of the sheet seeping through his pyjama trousers. The enormity of what he had done held him sleepless until the early hours of the morning. He had taken, quite casually, a girl's virginity when he was as good as engaged to another. He had abused the hospitality and kindness of the girl's parents. He was a louse. He lay there, in Arthur Bridges' box-like semi-detached, steeped in shame and depression. The brief ecstasy he had shared with Diana was forgotten. Gaynor's blonde-capped little face smiled in blissful innocence all through his wakeful dreams.

He had, at last achieved his manhood and it had gone sour on him.

CHAPTER FIVE

THE Gunner-Cartwright house party to celebrate the silver wedding of Reggie and Lady Tabitha was getting off to a swinging start with a buffet party on Friday night. Saturday morning facilities would be available for those who wished to play golf at the nearby club or to ride, taking advantage of Reggie's splendid stables, or sporting in the fabulous swimming baths which Reggie had built on the site of the old coach house. There was a trellissed, heated, covered way from the house to this big building wherein lay a kidney shaped, gently warmed pool. Hothouse flowers adorned the walls and the white painted steps to the diving boards stood out in vivid contrast to the bright blue of the pool edging and lining. Four small changing cubicles were set unobtrusively in a corner, but not at all unobtrusive was the well stocked bar under a tropical palm tree. Everything that money could achieve for the enjoyment of the body was there in the elegance and luxury of the home of the Gunner-Cartwrights.

'He should have had a chapel as well,' one critic had remarked, 'then he could pander to our souls as well as our bodies.'

'You don't practice black magic in chapels,' was the reply of someone who knew Reggie well.

The guests would assemble for a light lunch on Saturday and, in the afternoon, would be free again to do as they wished. On Saturday night dinner would be followed by dancing in the great hall of River Grange, this spacious rambling mansion home of the Gunner-Cartwrights for four generations sprawled in well groomed grounds alongside the river. On Sunday, after morning cocktails and a buffet lunch, the house party would disperse.

There were around thirty guests, most of whom had eaten well from the astonishingly sumptuous buffet. Drinks were quickly and carelessly consumed because no one had to drive home afterwards. At 11 o'clock a cabaret was due to begin.

Paul Earnshaw, temporarily alone, stood in a corner of the great room studying the guests with jaundiced eyes. The ususal star-studded company cavorted before him. There was the famous ageing actress – Dame Elvira Hanson – who attended any party where the booze was free and plentiful. Then there was Aden Hickey, the pilot who did flying stunts for films. With Aden was Lesley Courage, wife of film producer – Hexley Courage – in a dress designed to quicken the male pulse and antagonize the women. Hexley was there, too, his thick lips curved in a perpetual smile; why shouldn't he smile when there was always a steady procession of little starlets trickling through his hands? The stagey voice of Jinny Jane rose in hysterical fervour as she talked to ex-ballet dancer, Constant Bedigo. Jinny Jane, one-time member of the infamous scandal set of David and Harriet Lloyd, now a notable television star, married to racing driver – Clement Barr. The way Barr was hitting the bottle lately, opinion was that Jinny would soon be a widow, *if* she stayed married to him, but the warning flag was up already. She and Clem had arrived separately and ignored each other ever since.

Paul's cynical survey moved on. They were all here, the queers, the lessies, the aristocrats, the nuts. Most of the guests he knew well. There was the usual gathering of chalk and cheese that Reggie found so amusing, the infamous underworld king and avaricious diamond merchant, Rudi Von Kramm, with his negress mistress, singer Bambi Collins, rubbing shoulders with the touch of top brass always flaunted by Reggie, a cabinet minister and his wife.

But this week-end there was another couple, completely different from all the others. They had arrived late and as Paul and Katheryn had been involved in a discussion with Hexley Courage, they had missed the introductions. Not that I need any introduction to *him*, Paul thought grimly. He turned to Tabitha Gunner-Cartwright as she drifted up to him.

'Darling,' she said, 'no drinkies? You look naked without a drink in your hand.'

She summoned a waiter who arrived with miraculous speed. Paul took a glass of scotch from the proffered tray.

'Don't scowl so, darling, at least *look* as if you're enjoying it. Reggie won't like it if you don't.'

'I wasn't scowling, Tabby.'

'Oh, but you were, darling. You had that "I am superior to these pillocks" look on your handsome mug. I broke away from the fascinating Von Kramm to come and talk to you and find out what's worrying you.'

'I'm flattered, Tabby, but you should know there are no diamonds up my sleeve.'

She touched his cheek with be-ringed fingers.

'Who wants diamonds? Why are you alone? Shall I fetch that terribly bad young actress, Noeleen Eden, to entertain you?' Tabitha glanced across at her husband who was talking intently to a startling blonde. 'Reggie mustn't monopolize her. His guests must come first. It's only manners.'

'No thanks, Tabby. I was just getting my breath back after Jinny. She's been telling me about a new head-shrinker she goes to.'

'Oh Christ!' said Tabitha softly, 'not another one. Most of this crowd are nutters anyway, aren't they?'

'It's a smashing party.'

She smiled at him brilliantly. 'Yes, it is, isn't it? Some people say house parties are old-fashioned, but I think it was a super idea of Reggie's. At least it's got all our bedrooms into use. You know, great-grandfather Gunner-Cartwright built this house apparently with the intention of having hordes of children to use all the rooms and grounds. Such a pity they all died off and it dwindled down to Reggie and me. The only patter of little feet we hear is the patter of footsteps sneaking back to their own rooms in the small hours.' She gave a mock sigh. 'No, I'm afraid we haven't done our duty to posterity.' Tabitha stopped. 'You're not listening, darling, are you? Why so much gloom tonight in one so young and lovely?'

He regarded her morosely, no answering smile.

'Tabby,' he said, 'don't *you* ever think of the past? I do, I can't get away from it.'

She looked at him steadily.

'No,' she said, 'I don't. I think about survival, atom bombs, pollution, fornication sometimes, and they all frighten me, but

I *never* think about the past, and I would advise you not to either, darling. The future is yours and, remember, Reggie doesn't like inquests and, after all, he pays the piper, he calls the tune. Get a little sloshed, darling, and you'll feel better. Some people get strength from prayer, but me, I've always got mine from a bottle. It's only because I'm scared of losing my looks that I know when to stop.'

Admiration flashed in his sombre eyes. 'You'll never lose your looks, Tabby.'

Tabitha laughed showing strong white teeth.

'You should have seen me when I married Reggie, darling, all fresh and starry-eyed. Can you believe that? It took me precisely three months to get the stars out of my eyes and then I had to make my choice – admit defeat and admit that the marriage of the year made in Heaven was a flop, or stay put with Reggie's peculiar little ways, and we all know about Reggie's peculiar little ways, don't we, darling?' She laughed again and it was a hard sour sound. 'I can imagine what my mother and father would have said if I'd gone running back to them, I'd have made them the laughing stock of Mayfair, oh no, there would have been no loving arms to welcome back dear disillusioned daughter.'

'I'm sorry Tabby,' Paul said. 'I always thought . . .'

'Oh, don't be sorry, darling.' She held up her hands, flashing with jewels, for his inspection, and smiled brilliantly. '*I've* got everything, too, so they all tell me.'

Paul studied her thoughtfully as she stood beside him, turning her head frequently to smile at other guests. She reminded him of a twisting, leaping flame.

'I do what I want,' she said, '*and* I have all this.'

As she talked, her lithe, restless body moved as if irritated by the confines of her tight black sheath dress. The diamond earrings quivering down below her sleek red hair, shimmered and shivered their pure sparkles as she turned her head. There was no repose in Tabitha Gunner-Cartwright, he thought, beauty yes, but no peace. He wondered what she was like as a lover, if she was expert and perverted as the lovely Harriet had been. Many men, it was said, had known Tabitha.

'Katheryn,' she said, 'is looking very lovely tonight.'

Paul looked at his wife who was talking, in her usual cool manner, to the cabinet minister and his wife. She has never once looked my way, he thought. She only sees me when I'm right under her nose.

'Katheryn,' he said, 'always looks the same, never a hair out of place.'

'That could be boring,' Tabitha said softly.

'Unfortunately for me,' Paul replied. 'I don't find it so.'

He knew that Tabitha Gunner-Cartwright had no love for Katheryn, although she was always correctly polite to her. She hadn't forgotten, either, how Katheryn Scarlett as she had been then, had ruthlessly flung everyone to the wolves in court, in a desperate attempt to save David Lloyd.

'How you can bring yourself to marry Katheryn Scarlett after what she said about you in court?' Paul's mother had said to him.

His gaze left his wife and came to rest on the other person in the room who affected him almost as deeply as Katheryn, in a different way.

'Tabby,' he said, 'whatever in Heaven's name possessed Reggie to ask Derren Rackstraw here?'

'I wondered,' she said, 'when you would ask me that.'

'Him, of all people.'

'Derren Rackstraw is the head of his Chambers. They won an important case for one of Reggie's companies recently.'

'I remember, the Grey-Coombes Development case.'

'Yes, Reggie was very impressed. He has great admiration for Derren Rackstraw, maintains he's the very king-pin of Q.C.'s.'

Inwardly Paul shivered. Would he ever forget that court room and that man's steely, uncompromising eyes, out for the kill, any kill? The man now was looking at Katheryn and the look in the man's eyes said that he hadn't forgotten either that cool little bitch who'd lied to him in court and cut him down to size.

'I swear that the evidence I shall give in this court shall be the truth, the whole truth and nothing but the truth.'

Only when Tabitha spoke did he realize he'd recited the words aloud.

'Don't be macabre, darling, you're getting as bad as Reggie. Y'know, asking that man here is probably Reggie's idea of fun. I've had the feeling lately that he's been manufacturing kicks automatically without any real enjoyment any more. Maybe it's because of that pain that's been bothering him recently.'

'What pain?'

'He clutches his stomach and goes rather pale for a few minutes.'

'Has he seen a doctor?'

'I wouldn't know, darling. When I mentioned it he said it was wind. I don't think it is, because he's got a lot thinner.'

Paul glanced across at Reggie, still talking to the young actress, and noticed that, in spite of impeccable tailoring, Reggie didn't look as massive and solid as usual. There was a drooping flabbiness about him that sat oddly on him.

'Don't you think you should insist on him seeing a doctor?'

Tabitha shrugged. 'Why should I? He's always managed his life very well without my help. He will, no doubt, manage his death in the same efficient manner when it comes.'

Paul was shocked.

'You think then it might be that serious?'

Tabitha smiled and shrugged again. 'I gave up thinking too much about Reggie long ago, darling. That way madness lies.'

Reggie had joined the barrister, Derren Rackstraw, and a woman who was, presumably, his wife, a faded insignificant creature, an odd mate for so magnificent a male.

Following Paul's gaze, Tabitha said,

'Remember what I said, don't brood on the past, Paul, look to the future like Reggie does. Remember that when one is on the board of eighty-nine companies, as Reggie is, a good Counsel's Opinion is necessary once in a while and Rackstraw's Chambers are good stables.'

'I'd have thought Rackstraw was the last barrister Reggie would want to engage.' Paul said.

Tabitha met his sombre eyes steadily.

'Reggie has a lot of nerve, darling, a hell of a lot, and he always wins. It pays to remember that.'

He knew she was warning him and he felt a little sick. Reggie used me because of a whim, instead of destroying me. I suppose

I shall never know why. The son he might have had? No, never cloying sentiment with Reggie. Paul shivered in his thoughts. I could have been found in an alley, knifed, like Gus Raymond, one of Reggie's accountants, or killed like that girl croupier who worked for one of Reggie's organizations. But Reggie hadn't even been in the country when Raymond had been stabbed by thugs, so who could associate him with that killing, and hadn't he been generosity itself to the widow? Yet the whispers still circulated, in clubs, over dinner tables.

'I really must mix around now, darling,' Tabitha said, glancing at her diamond and emerald wrist watch. 'I've monopolized you too long, the best looking man in the room, I should be so lucky.'

Katheryn's group had grown now and included the two queers, Marcus and James and still her eyes never searched for her husband.

A pretty hand was placed on Paul's arm, he turned to look down into the forget-me-not blue eyes of Noeleen Eden.

'Like to get me a drink, darling?'

'Delighted.'

He took her hand and led her across to the bar in the corner. They toasted each other, their glasses clinking. She pouted up at him.

'You were with Tabby Cartwright an awful long time. Do you sleep with her?'

He looked down at the pretty face, a slight smile twitching his lips.

'If I did, would I tell *you*?'

She sighed elaborately.

'No, I suppose not. Silly question.'

She rattled on and he nodded, hardly listening. Over there, so near and yet so far, was Katheryn, his wife, not strictly beautiful as Tabitha, Dorothy Trent and this Noeleen were beautiful, yet the set of her proud little face made his heart sick with longing. He noticed suddenly that the man, Rackstraw, was watching her again, the eyes fathomless now, giving no indication of the man's thoughts. The look gave Paul Earnshaw an even heavier feeling of dread than the man's earlier look had done.

'I'm bored, darling,' Noeleen Eden said, 'I'd like to go to the gaming room and try my luck. Will you come?'

Paul's eyes travelled back to Katheryn, hoping desperately for some signal from her, a questioning look, an acknowledgment, but none came. She was still deep in conversation with her companions.

'Why not?' he said to Noeleen, 'the night is ours. No one else wants it.'

CHAPTER SIX

KATHERYN EARNSHAW was the sort of girl who could pass unnoticed in a crowd and yet, at other times, look sensational. Sensational she was tonight in a white dress cunningly contrived to cover her small breasts before it merged into a series of lacings through which gleamed the creamy skin of her body. From the lacings the gown fell into a full, softly pleated skirt. The dress was fastened by a glittering strap of diamonte round her throat, leaving her back and shoulders exposed. The only jewellery she wore was her wedding ring, with the engagement ring above it. Her dark hair was swept up into a bunch of curls falling round her neck. Too tall, too thin, was the immediate assessment of the girl before one began to realize the fragile beauty of her, the melancholy repose of her eyes, the almost Victorian lack of animation on her pale face.

She had watched the cabaret seated between the two queers – James and Marcus – who treated her as if she were a precious child. She found their company undemanding and relaxing after the crude advances of men like Hexley Courage and the drink-sodden racing driver, Clement Barr.

'I haven't seen Paul around lately,' Marcus said, 'where is he?'

'Gambling I think,' Katheryn said, adding calmly, 'with the delightful Miss Eden.'

James pulled a face.

'No accounting for tastes. After you, darling, Noeleen must be like cider after champagne.'

Katheryn smiled. 'James, you're sweet. You say the nicest things.'

'And mean them, my dear.'

Other people were drifting up to them now.

'Yes, Reggie assures me there's a house detective dear,' Marcus was reassuring a female guest, 'Probably disguised as a housemaid.' He giggled. 'After all, with all these marvellous rocks and furs in the house, you never know, do you, there could be a raffles amongst us, could be you, or me, or James or even lovely Katheryn. Did I ever tell you, dears, about that gorgeous party James and I went to at Elsie-Jane Lanham's?'

Tabitha Gunner-Cartwright smiled as she watched them. Jinny Jane and Constant Bedigo waved to her from the wide staircase.

'Going for a little rest, darling,' Jinny called, 'be down later.'

Tabitha smiled her acknowledgment, her eyes straying involuntarily to the portrait of great-grandfather Gunner-Cartwright which hung near the foot of the great staircase, as if to apologize to him. This house, the prominent grey eyes of the picture seemed to say, this house was built for families, not for gambling and whore-mongering. She moved to the doorway of the gaming room and looked right in. Paul Earnshaw was seated at a table, playing cards, a drink beside him, and Noeleen Eden perched on a chair behind him, her hands possessively on his shoulders. Paul was weak. He could be a menace. If only he had a quarter of his wife's ruthlessness. Katheryn, that prime, confident, young bitch. Tabitha wandered back to rejoin the rest of her guests. She saw the Cabinet Minister talking to Katheryn Earnshaw, he had paid her quite a lot of attention tonight. The girl must have something for all her coldness. How different, Tabitha thought, was Katheryn now. God, she thought, I remember every detail of that night, even now, although I told Paul I never look back. That night, when David Lloyd, with his hellish appeal for women still blatant, even though he was tipsy and unhappy, stumbled into that dance room, his melancholy eyes flaring into sudden awareness as he saw the girl. And the girl, love had blazed across her face for all to see. Her heart and soul and body had yearned, that night, to the man, and David, that callous, ruthless sophisticate, lover of so many beautiful women, had taken her into his arms like a man answering a call. He had gathered her innocence against his heart as they danced, as if he would never let her go, he, steeped in a world of vice and corruption, he who took women as he took food and drink.

Ah David, Tabitha remembered, you and I had been to bed together so many times, yet never once did you look at me like that. What had that chit of a girl got that was so different, so precious for him? Was it love? Tabitha smiled twistedly. Could

64

a woman who had lived with Reggie ever recognize love?

She put her hand on Reggie's arm as he was about to walk past her.

'Was it a good idea to ask Derren Rackstraw here? He's done nothing but stare at Katheryn Earnshaw all evening.'

'Why shouldn't he?' Reggie's hooded eyes lifted to his wife's face, lit with pleasure. 'It'll be amusing.'

'Like the whip routine,' she said, 'how you do like to flog yourself.'

'He's no danger to *me*,' said Reggie. 'The case is closed, remember.' He laughed softly. 'Anyway, I always believe in attacking danger, not running away from it. You should know that, by now, my Tabby.'

'But the girl, Katheryn?'

Reggie laughed his throaty mirthless chuckle.

'She can look after herself, that one, hard as nails. I admire her.'

'And Paul?'

'What about Paul? He's happy enough, a rising executive, a fast car, fast women.'

Tabitha's mouth curled slightly.

'The grapevine says you've made over your Chinese woman to him.'

With a pudgy finger Reggie touched his wife's mouth.

'Your spies work well, don't they? Well, mine do too, so watch it, my sweet.'

He laughed again, coldly and passed on.

From another part of the room, the barrister, Derren Rackstraw, Q.C. stood with his wife, frowning as he looked around him.

His eyes were on Katheryn as she chatted and smiled in the midst of her little group. She's bored, he thought, her mind is miles away from that lot.

'I think,' Erica said, 'I'd like to go to bed.'

He turned then and regarded his wife with concern.

'Aren't you feeling well?'

'Yes, I'm all right, just so very tired. I'll feel better tomorrow if I don't stay up too late tonight.'

She seemed patently anxious now to get away, her hands

twisted together nervously. He knew the signs, knew she was yearning to get at the whisky bottle hidden in her suitcase. Erica wasn't a lush, oh no, she had her drinking strictly under control, only drank when her duty was done. So far, her drinking had never stopped her functioning correctly as a wife and hostess. She was, too, when occasion demanded, an intelligent conversationalist. A man can't have everything, he had often told himself. He was luckier than most, he had a satisfying, successful career, a suitable wife who had brought money into their partnership, money which enabled them to live up to a more than adequate standard.

Derren Rackstraw, since his marriage to Erica, had made love to many women, always with great discretion, women as sensual and, at the same time, as dispassionate as himself, women ripe for diversion of not too permanent a standing. Never, until now, had a woman got under his skin so much. As he stared at Katheryn Earnshaw he thought, relationships based on hate are always strong. Should a barrister hate a witness? Isn't that the one thing that should never happen? Shouldn't one be like a referee, completely detached? Did she hate *me*? Does she now? He knew that she had recognized him, as had her husband, when he and Erica had arrived. For one fleeting second Katheryn Earnshaw's eyes had stayed on him as she had glanced round the room, a flash of awareness had lit them for a second, then she had looked away quickly.

In Court, that time ago, he had thought at first that she was incapable of any real emotion and then she had looked at the man, the accused. After that, life had leapt into her thin little face. Yes, it had been hate she had felt then for her questioner, hate because I knew she lied, hate because I threatened her fancy man's life.

'That young actress, Noeleen Eden,' Erica was saying, 'is a very pretty little thing, isn't she?'

Derren Rackstraw followed his wife's gaze to where Paul Earnshaw lounged in the doorway, smoking a cigarette, the Eden girl beside him. Then, as they watched, Paul Earnshaw took the girl's arm and steered her through the throng so that they had to pass right close to his wife. Done deliberately, Rackstraw thought, but, for all the emotion on Katheryn

Earnshaw's face as the couple passed, she might not have known them.

With amazing clarity Derren Rackstraw remembered the words of Katheryn Scarlett as she spat from the witness box words denouncing he who was now her husband.

'He was Harriet Lloyd's boy friend, I believe. I do not converse with drunks,' and the boy, as he had been then, had looked back at her, not with hate as one would have expected, but with a kind of yearning despair. That boy was a man now, favoured of the tycoon and commerce king, Reggie Gunner-Cartwright, his face not so immature and mobile as it had been then. Even so, it was easy to read on that face a certain weakness and desperation.

'That Paul Earnshaw and his wife,' Erica said, 'I seem to remember . . .'

'Yes,' Derren interrupted her curtly, 'I was prosecuting for the Crown. She was a witness for the defence.'

'Ah yes, I remember,' Erica said, 'there were many witnesses, but little real evidence in that case.'

'There would have been,' he said sharply, 'but she lied.'

'Oh,' Erica said. She stared intently across at Katheryn Earnshaw for a few seconds, then looked back at her husband's lean, immobile face and cold eyes. She felt a little shiver run through her and longed for the warmth of her bed and a nice quiet drink.

'You come up when you're ready, dear,' she said, 'don't hurry, but I think I'll go to bed now.'

'I'll see you to the room,' Derren said, 'and explain to Lady Tabitha after.'

She was alone, staring out of the windows beside the big oak doors in the hall when he found her. He looked up over her head and saw the moon hanging low in the sky, its silvery radiance washing the shrubbery outside the windows with pale, unearthly light.

'It's like silver snow, isn't it?' he said. The girl turned then and regarded him without emotion or embarrassment. Sweet sentimental music drifted out to them from the big room off the hall.

'Would you like to dance, Mrs. Earnshaw?'

She shook her head. 'No thank you.'

No, of course not. Stupid to have asked her. As if she would want to dance with the man who'd tried to trick her into telling the truth. She had danced with *him*, though, that very night he was supposed to have murdered his wife. Was she remembering, now, that dance? How could she forget? For himself he knew he would always remember her proud little face, set in hostility, the lie coming so easily from her lips, so resolutely determined to save him who she loved, herself but a schoolgirl.

'We haven't been introduced,' he said, 'but I think perhaps you remember me. Derren Rackstraw.'

'Yes,' she said, 'I remember you.'

'Katheryn Scarlett you were then.'

'Yes.'

'Where are you living now?'

'Fairly near here. We have a house at Monk's Lee.'

'A lovely village. The house wouldn't be Monk's Folly?'

'Yes,' she said, 'it would. Do you know it?'

'A coincidence. We almost bought it once.'

'What made you decide not to?'

'My wife said it was too big. Also, she likes to be fairly near other houses.'

A faint smile curved Katheryn's mouth.

'The solitude of it is lovely.'

He liked the timbre of her voice. He wondered what it would be like raised in anger or lowered in love talk. Was she as hard as she looked, this girl, or was she just a walking dream, her thoughts miles away.

'So you live amidst noise?' she said.

'Not quite, a happy medium. We have a house in Maidenhead in a road with other houses. My wife's father bought it for us, in fact, he chose it.'

And you resent it, Katheryn thought, and hate that house in a road with other houses, because that doesn't suit your kind of arrogance.

'So you don't like the house,' she said with a flicker of interest.

'Oh yes, I like it. It's a nice house to come home to. While

68

I'm working I live in bachelor apartments in my chambers, very well appointed they are, too.'

Her mouth curved in a half smile.

'Bachelor apartments always are,'

Greatly daring he said, 'And have you seen so many?'

She shook her head.

'Not many. Mostly on films. My husband has a flat in town but I've never seen it. I shouldn't think it's like the bachelor flats you see on films. He's very untidy.'

'And you're neat?'

'Not particularly, but I'm not untidy. My sister . . .'

But he was not to be side-tracked to her sister.

'So it was a marriage of opposites,' he said.

She looked at him with a grave air of surprise.

'I don't think so.'

Greatly daring, he said, 'I must admit I was surprised to find you'd married Earnshaw. After all . . .'

Coolly she interrupted him.

'Are you still hounding people into saying what you want them to say?'

'I'm still accepting briefs. As for hounding . . .' his eyes held hers steadily, 'sometimes people lie and, in spite of hounding, as you call it, you can't shake them.'

'But you have the stronger weapons,' she said, 'familiarity with the awesome surroundings, all the impressive legal gear.'

'So you're on the side of the criminal, anti-law and order?'

She shrugged. 'I'm not on the side of anyone and I'm not anti anything.'

She turned from the window. Afraid that he would lose her, he said. 'You're not going to bed yet?'

'No. I'm going to get my car and go for a run in the moonlight. They'll be dancing and playing cards for ages yet, and I'm not tired.'

'You have an assignation in the moonlight perhaps?'

'Yes, with Winter Hill. The view is lovely.'

'You know the famous saying, solitude is only good when there's someone to share it with. Anyway, in these days, or nights rather, it's not terribly safe for a young woman to go driving alone and parking in lonely spots.'

'There will be no thugs at Winter Hill at this time of night.'

'Thugs can be anywhere at any time of the day or night,' he said 'or any*one*.'

Her smile was mocking.

'Of course, you know all about these things, don't you?' she said. 'Nasty people, it's your line of business.'

'My line of business, as you call it,' he said, 'can help people as well. There are two sides to it.'

'There are two sides to everything, I suppose.' The faint interest had left her voice. She was detached again. He had an insane desire to shake her into awareness of him.

'May I go with you to this Winter Hill?'

He was gratified by her sudden look of surprise, almost fear.

'Unless my company is repellent to you.'

Calmly she replied, 'Why should it be? Come if you wish. My husband and I arrived in separate cars, he had a call to make, so I've got my Porsche here. We'll take that.'

'We'll take *my* car,' he said.

'But I want to take mine,' she said obstinately, 'it's very fast.'

'I have a Mercedes, equally fast, but I don't propose to drive fast tonight.'

'I didn't ask you to come,' she said.

'No, I invited myself, but at least give me a chance to retain my male ego. Being driven by a woman is like a man pushing a pram.'

'And have you never pushed a pram?'

'I have no children,' he said abruptly. 'Now, are you going to get a wrap? You'll need one.'

For a second their eyes held, his compelling hers as if he were holding her fast in an iron grip, then, with a little shrug she left him and he wondered if he would see her again tonight, but, in a little while, she came back to him, swinging a mink jacket in her hand.

'Is your wife coming too?' she asked.

'My wife has gone to bed.' He paused, then he said, 'and are you bringing your husband?'

'My husband is gambling,' she said. 'He won't stop while there's still someone to play with.'

'We're free then,' the man said, 'both of us.'

At the top of Winter Hill the view stretched out before them.

70

Below, the river snaked through the trees in the moonlight.

'At the risk of sounding trite,' he said, 'do you come here often?'

'Yes.'

'It has associations for you perhaps?'

Calmly she answered him. 'No, none at all. I just like it here.'

Of course. Idiotic to think she would bring him to her secret places, the places she went to with *him*. Immediately, he scorned himself for this feverish dissection. The girl had lied, but it was over now. The guilty man had, himself, imposed his own punishment. The girl, you could say, was almost dull, no sparkle in her. Why this interest in her?

'My children like this hill,' she said, 'they love to run down it.'

'You look too young to have children.'

'I have twin girls,' she said, 'Lucy and Linda, three years old.'

'Sometimes I think,' he said, 'I would have liked to have had children. One's own yearnings channel into the lives of the children, they say.'

'No,' Katheryn said, 'I don't find it so. Everyone is a separate individual. I don't see my children as part of me.'

'You're a most unusual mother then.'

'I can't be intense about motherhood,' she said, as if trying to excuse herself. He wondered if she remembered how intense she'd been once.

'You don't have to be intense to be a good parent,' he said, 'my parents were very casual, but eminently satisfactory.'

She sounded amused. 'Yes, I'm sure they would be.'

'You think all barristers' lives and families are neat and well ordered?'

'Well, aren't they?'

'No more than those of other men in other walks of life.'

She asked him for a cigarette and, when he had lighted it for her, they sat in silence staring out into the valley below. Eventually she turned slightly from her contemplation of the view and, from her corner, studied him with dispassionate approval. He was very handsome with thick grey hair. If you'd been asked to guess his profession, she thought, you'd have replied, without hesitation, barrister or surgeon, or even a judge. He had that sureness, confidence in his own ability. Although his mouth was undeniably sensual, it yet held grimness that matched his uncompromising eyes. Once, it seemed long ago, in that courtroom she had been momentarily afraid of him, but the fear had quickly passed and she had known she was as strong as he. Then he had been the deadly enemy. Now they were sitting here together, talking amiably. She had a sudden desire to know more about him, like probing about a scorpion, perhaps, when you'd removed its sting.

'You must have a very high standard to live up to,' she said.

'Why? I'm not a judge, nor likely to be.'

'Why not?'

'I'm not ambitious. If I'd had children, I might have been driven to scale the heights.'

Directly she asked him, 'Did you want children?'

Equally he answered her. 'Once I did, but it was a phase that soon passed. I suppose if I'd been really keen, we could have adopted, but I always thought my wife might feel that as a reproach to her.' He hesitated, then he said, 'You see, my wife think there's madness in her family. One of her aunts was actually committed into an institution and Erica, my wife, has a sister who's harmlessly barmy.'

'How awful.'

'I was willing to take a chance on children. *She* wasn't.'

'I think she was right.'

'Don't *you* ever take risks then?'

Composedly she replied, 'No. I don't think I've had to.'

'Marriage is a risk.'

She shrugged.

'Unless,' he said softly, 'it isn't all that important to you.'

This was something he would never understand, her marriage to young Earnshaw when they had so obviously been on opposite sides of the fence at the trial.

'You and your husband came from the same town, didn't you?' he asked.

'Yes.'

'I believe your father's house is quite a show piece,' he continued, 'there on the river bank. I remember having the lawns pointed out to me once as I went by on a boat. Quite fantastic.'

'The house is being sold now,' said Katheryn. Then, almost with indifference, she added, 'My father is dead. He died a short while ago in a road accident. The house belongs now to my sister and me. My sister intends to get married, but she doesn't want the house, so we shall get rid of it.'

'I'm sorry,' Derren Rackstraw said, 'about your father, I didn't know. You'll feel it terribly, losing your father and giving up that lovely house.'

'The house I lost when I got married,' she said. 'I wouldn't want it now. I don't think I shall miss my father, we never really got on. I didn't miss my mother when she died either. I suppose I'm as bad a daughter as I am a mother.'

'Not necessarily,' he said, 'when one marries, one's new family is all-important, it makes for thowing off childhood dependencies.'

'I can't remember ever feeling dependent,' Katheryn said, 'we were always very separate people in our family.'

'Families tend to be more involved with each other when they're poor,' Rackstraw said, 'anxiety for survival creates dependence, one on the other.'

She shrugged. 'I wouldn't know.'

'Like Marie Antoinette,' he said softly, 'then give 'em cake.'

'I can't pretend to care about things when I don't,' she said coldly.

Ah, he thought, but truth wasn't always your game my lady. He wondered about the cottage in the grounds of her father's house where it had all happened. Would that go too? Wouldn't she care about that either?

'I shall buy a villa in Spain,' she was saying almost to herself as if the idea was absorbing her thoughts. 'I shall use some of the money my father left me, somewhere to take the children for sunshine.'

Rackstraw felt a fleeting sympathy for the unlamented deceased Hugh Scarlett. He remembered the simple expensive clothes this girl had worn in court, her confidence that was the hallmark of a prosperous background, all provided by the now un-mourned father whom she had never loved.

73

Katheryn, too, was silent, thinking of her father. She thought of his words after David's death. 'After all, Katheryn, they were just summer visitors, you hardly knew the man. Your feeling for him was no more than what you youngsters call a crush. *I* know.' He had smiled that bland stupid smile of his, 'I've even had crushes myself, you know.' Hateful, the memory of father, a white slug, slobbering against wicked, shimmering Harriet in the old boathouse. And, after that, father daring to say, 'The man's dead and the world's a better place for his death. I hope you won't brood, Katheryn.' Brood.

'What part of Spain will you buy your villa?' the man said beside her.

'I'm not sure yet,' she said, 'some are being built between Estepone and Marbella. I shall try for one of those.'

'I usually spend a little time in Spain each year,' he said, 'I go on there after visiting my brother in Tunis.'

'Doesn't your wife go with you?'

'No, my wife doesn't care for going abroad. The heat and the food upset her. We usually spend some time in Scotland together in the late autumn and when I go abroad she takes the opportunity of staying with her crazy sister. She feels she's doing her duty by letting another sister who looks after the crazy one off the hook for a while each year.'

'Your wife must be a very conscientious woman.'

He smiled slightly. No, he could have said, just a frightened, disillusioned woman who'd found that marriage wasn't as wonderful as she'd thought it would be, a woman who could relax in the company of her crazy sister and be the one on top for a change, instead of the second string in the partnership. Oh yes, he knew Erica very well. He knew that, subconsciously, she resented his career and hated him for knowing her weaknesses. With mad Ella she could dip into her Scotch as often as she liked and Ella would never notice it.

'Have you been to North Africa, Katheryn?'

'No, I haven't travelled abroad much. My father didn't approve of foreign holidays, we always went to Cornwall. I've been to Spain and Paris a lot since my marriage.'

'You'd like Tunisia. Africa is quite different from Spain, it has a rich, over-ripe vegetation scent and it seems to enfold you in its luxuriant atmosphere that's so essentially Africa.'

'What does your brother do in Tunis?'

'He's a merchant. He's half Moroccan, you see, we didn't have the same mother.'

'Oh.' She yawned and put her hand over her mouth. 'We should go now I think. We've had our breather.'

He took her hand as it dropped from her mouth.

'May I see you again Katheryn?'

She left her hand in his, limply.

'Is there any point?'

He took her other hand, unresisting, into his and drew her close. She closed her eyes, wondering if he would kiss her. But he didn't kiss her, just held her in a compelling grip. He was the first man since David, except Paul, her husband, who had held her thus, close to him. When David had held her in that immortal dance, the world had disappeared, there was only herself and David on their own planet. Now the world was still here and she was conscious of it, the way she was when Paul made love to her. Disappointment made her peevish.

'There's no point at all. I don't have affairs.'

'Did I suggest an affair?'

'Isn't that how they start?'

He released her hands and leaned forward on the wheel.

'You intrigue me greatly, Katheryn. You have all the poise of a young woman of the world and yet, I suspect, you know very little of it.'

'I know enough,' she said wearily, 'and now, may we go? I really am tired.'

'Katheryn,' he said, 'have you ever been to the ballet?'

She was surprised. 'Once, I think, in our local town hall.'

'The real ballet, Covent Garden?'

'No.'

'Will you come with me one day?'

'Why me? Why not your wife?'

'She doesn't care for that kind of entertainment.'

'Would she mind?'

'I don't know. I don't propose to ask her.'

Katheryn laughed. 'At least you're honest.'

'You forget, truth is my business.'

'Yet you would deceive your wife.'

'Taking you to the ballet is hardly deception.'

'I'm tired. May we go now?'

'May I ring you some time soon?'

'If you like.'

She leaned back, shading her eyes, as he started the car. As he looked down at her she seemed small and defenceless. He didn't see her now as that proud young woman who had coolly met his challenge in Court. The hardness was there though, in the heart of her. Inwardly he cursed the man who had taught this girl love and then disillusioned her so brutally. They drove back almost in silence to the big mansion where the lights still blazed and the guests still laughed, gambled, got drunk and made love. Love, he thought, what is love? There are so many different versions. He didn't love Erica, but he was fond of her. He didn't love this girl, yet he knew now that he wanted her. Why? To try to destroy another man's triumph? To try to cut her down to size for lying to him? He honestly didn't know.

'I shall see you again Katheryn,' he said when he let her out of the car.

'Of course,' she replied, 'tomorrow.'

'But after that, I mean,' he said, 'and after *that*.' She smiled vaguely. He would swear her thoughts had long since left him.

Derren Rackstraw, Q.C., felt again that same frustration as he'd felt in Court when he'd been prosecuting her lover. Katheryn Scarlett, he spoke her name silently. Her marriage to Paul Earnshaw he ignored. She was Katheryn Scarlett, young, without sparkle or expertise and she wasn't all that beautiful. She stood leaning against a pillar on the massive porch, her small piquant face looking upwards to the heavens as if yearning for something there. Then, conscious of his scrutiny, she dropped her gaze to him and smiled. Yes, he decided, she *was* beautiful. He parked his Mercedes between Clement Barr's gold coloured Mustang and Von Kram's Ferrari and walked back to the house. She hadn't waited for him. He was disappointed to find her gone.

CHAPTER SEVEN

'WHEN did you hear your mum wasn't well?' Diana asked suspiciously.

'Yesterday. I had a letter yesterday.'

Her shoulders hunched dejectedly.

'I had thought we might've gone down the disco with Bett and Dave tonight. It's Bett's birthday.'

'I know. I'm sorry, Di. I'd've liked that, but I must go home. I haven't been lately.'

She leaned forward and kissed him as he sat on the edge of the kitchen table.

'Careful, love,' he warned, 'your mum might come in.'

'What if she does?' She regarded him with affection. 'You're a long streak, young Gary. I don't reckon you'll ever put on much weight, and dark eyebrows with fair hair, kind of freakish isn't it?'

'Thanks.'

'Silly. Don't get the huff. It's nicely freakish. The whole effect's nice. I like it. In fact, I think I knew, deep inside me, the first time I saw you that you was the kind of feller I could really fall for.'

'You didn't show it.'

'No. Somehow, you always managed to get my rag out. Do you remember . . . .?'

He cut her short, looking at his watch. 'I'll miss my train, Di.'

'No you won't. I'll run you to the station.'

'There's no need. If I hurry I can make it.'

'You don't have to. I said I'd take you.'

'I hate not having my own car,' the boy said worriedly.

'Never mind. Just wait till you're qualified.'

'Yes, I reckon I'll have to.'

'In the meantime, love,' the girl said, 'what's mine is yours, in more ways than one, eh?'

In the car outside the station she held him, grasping both his hands.

'I'll miss you, Gary.'

'I'll miss *you*, Di.'

'No one to cuddle you in your bed tonight, I hope.'

'No.'

'Gary,' her eyes darkened as she asked him, 'You heard from her again, Gaynor Scarlett?'

'No.' The answer came glibly, but he was wretched, remembering Gay's phone call to him at the office yesterday, the pleasant, rapid voice that was so essentially Gaynor, as if she were always excited. 'Such a lot there seems to be to discuss, Gary, now I'm a relatively wealthy female. I'll come down to Harlow and pick you up.'

'No Gay, meet me in London. I'll come up by train.'

'But why, when I have the car? I have a new one now, an M.G.B.G.T. The solicitors have advanced me the money for the car on account of my legacy because it'll be ages and ages before the estate's settled.' Gaynor had giggled happily. 'Honestly, Gary, you'll love the car. She's dark blue. I call her "Bluey". Gary and Gaynor and Bluey. Stupid names, aren't they, but we're lumbered with them. Gosh, I'm so excited, Gary, at the prospect of seeing you again. Do let me come down and pick you up, then we can nip across country to Marbrook.'

'No, I'd rather come to London by train, Gay. I'll explain when I see you.'

So now he'd have to explain why he chose to travel to London by train instead of being picked up in the usual way by Gaynor in her car. What excuse could he make? Lies seemed to come easily to him these days. Had to go over some revision with a feller in the train. Yes, that had better be it.

'You won't be seeing her when you go home, will you?' Diana said.

'Who?'

'You know very well – Gaynor Scarlett.'

'Now that her father's dead the house has been shut up,' he said, 'she stays at her flat in London when she's not visiting her sister.'

'And you won't go to her flat?'

Truthfully he could answer that. 'No.'

'I don't want you to see her, Gary.'

Again the easy lie. 'I won't.'

'Have you told her yet?'

'Yes.'

Another lie. Well, hardly. He would have to tell her today.

'What did she say?'

'I haven't heard. I wrote.'

'Oh Gary, I'm so glad, love. The thought of her is torture to me.'

'I must go, Di, for that train.'

He made to take his hands from her grasp, but she tightened it.

'Love me?'

'You know I do.'

'Do I? I wonder sometimes.'

'What's that supposed to mean?'

She pouted. 'Often you seem preoccupied.'

'I'm supposed to be studying for exams, remember?'

'Well, you don't seem all that ardent this morning.'

'You wore me out last night.'

'So did you *me*, but I still love you this morning, and I want to shout and sing and tell everyone I love you.'

He leant forward and kissed her. Attempting lightness he didn't feel, he said,

'I'd rather you didn't. I'm not ready for my great public yet.'

She released his hands and sighed.

'I shall mope every minute of the week-end until tomorrow night. Shall I come to the station to meet you?'

'Better not. I don't know which train I'll be on. I might be late.'

'I don't mind. I'll meet each one.'

'What will your mum and dad say?'

'It's got nothing to do with them. Besides,' Diana laughed, 'I think mum's already twigged a bit. She said to me the other day, "You used to positively dislike Gary, what's made you change your mind?" ' She giggled. 'Poor old mum, if she only knew. She was trying to pump me. I clam up when I'm pumped, always have done even as a kid.'

The heaviness of his guilt stayed with Gary on the train journey. Life, a little while ago, had offered no problems save the passing of his exams. Now, it seemed, he was beset by complications. He acknowledged that the pleasure he took in

Di's body was important to him, but love, that was another question. She could inflame him with just a look and he was filled with anger at the mere mention of her going with another feller.

And Gaynor, dear, sensitive little Gay. He had known her so long he had never really stopped to analyse his feelings for her. They were crowding him, both of them, and he wasn't ready to be chained.

Gaynor was waiting, her eyes feverishly searching the crowds until she saw him, then they lit up with joy. She ran to him, folding her arms round him and kissing him on the mouth.

'Oh, Gary, it's been such a long, long time. How are you, darling?'

They walked, arm-in-arm, to the side street where she had parked her spanking new car.

'What a super car,' he said.

'I knew you'd like it. Like the telly advert says, I got it with you in mind. Anyway, from now on, it's going to be as much yours as mine.'

Like Di had said only a short while ago. All I have is yours. They were fencing him in, swamping him.

As they drove out of London Gaynor babbled away, forgetting to ask why he had elected to come by train, for which he was thankful. It spared him at least one lie.

'Must you really sleep at home tonight, Gary?'

'Yes, Gay, I ought to. My mother's not been too well. She's had high blood pressure again. She's never been right really since Greer died and dad gets very worried about her. A visit from me might cheer her up.'

Gaynor sighed. 'Poor thing! Yes, I suppose you must go home. I had thought we might've camped out at the Manor House. I've got sleeping bags in the car. It would have been fun. The light's still connected and the water.'

'Yes it would have been, but I'd better go home. What will *you* do?'

'Oh, I can run over to Katie's to sleep,' she said, 'Katie and Paul are away at the Gunner-Cartwrights' house party this week-end, but there's always a bed in the guest room where I can kip for the night.'

He looked at her smiling face as she drove along. Dear Gay. It seemed that there had always been Gay in his life. How could he hurt her?

'The cottage,' she was saying, 'David's lovely cottage. Katie just refuses to talk about it. She says she doesn't give a damn about it, but I'm not going to sell it, Gary, I just am not. I'm going to keep it in repair and I'm going to leave it in my will to Katie's daughters in the hope that they'll love it like their mother used to. Katie makes me feel so unhappy sometimes. If only I could get through to her, but she's as dead as a door nail, she just won't give an inch. And for her to say she doesn't care what happens to the cottage. When she was a little girl she was always there, it was her secret life and, for all that she was so young when it happened and she hadn't known David long, I think,' Gay's lips trembled, 'I think it broke her heart.'

'Here,' Gary said, 'don't get so emotional, little one.' He looked at her with affection. 'You're just the same now as when you were a kid, you get so worked up and involved.'

'I am involved, so is the cottage and I don't intend to sell it whatever Katie says.'

'It ought to be lived in,' Gary said, 'or it will get cold and damp.'

'Yes, I suppose so,' she conceded grudgingly, 'but it would have to be the right tenant. I couldn't bear to think of just anyone in *his* cottage.'

'David only lived in it for a short time,' Gary said practically.

'It was still his and he put his mark on it for ever,' Gay said obstinately, 'Katie said once it was as if the cottage had been waiting for David. I know he's still there. I feel it when I go inside.'

'I don't believe a practical girl like you could believe in ghosts,' he teased her gently.

'I don't really, but it's as if David's watching. I had thought you and I might have lived in the cottage when we're married, but it's too far from the beaten track to be realistic. Besides, now I've got money we can afford the kind of house we intend to stay in, one where we can rear a family, one . . .'

'Gay,' he interrupted her, 'I don't ever intend to marry until

81

I've qualified,' his voice dropped to an almost sulky tone, 'and I'd hate to have to use a woman's money to buy my home.'

She drew the car into the kerbside and stopped, staring at him in sheer dismay.

'You can't mean it. Why, ever since I knew about father's will, I've been planning.'

'I'm sorry, Gay.'

She stared at him, shocked and puzzled. Then, through dry lips, she said quietly,

'All of a sudden you sound like a stranger, Gary.'

'I am a stranger, to all this money. I want to have to strive. If I don't I might as well be a robot or a gigolo.'

Distress stood stark in her eyes.

'Are you saying you . . .?'

Not meeting her eyes, he muttered, 'I couldn't take your money, Gay, not now or ever.'

'But we love each other, we always have done, money doesn't matter.'

'It does to me.'

She was almost in tears now.

'But I thought we could marry straight away. I mean, I wouldn't even mind giving up University and living in Harlow until you've qualified if that's what you want. I could always take up my studies again later if I wanted to, if we didn't start a family.'

'Gay,' he said gently, 'we're parked on a double yellow line. What say we drive on down to the Nag's head at Spinney, we can get some sandwiches there. Then we can talk. We can't talk here.'

One or two tears were trickling down her cheeks now.

'I can't drive. I'm too upset.'

'Yes you can. It's not the end of the world.'

'It's the end of *my* world.'

'Nonsense. Not you, not my india-rubber, irrepressible Gay.'

She looked at him bleakly.

'After all these years, you don't really know me, do you?'

'After all these years, do *you* know *me*?'

Her voice was a miserable whimper. Her bleak eyes accused him. 'It seems I don't.'

He indicated a traffic warden bearing down on them.

'Look, here comes a wasp to give you a ticket.'

'I don't care.'

'Gay, don't be silly, dear. Let's move on to a better place.'

Wearily she obeyed him, started the car and drove off before the traffic warden could reach them.

He ordered beers and sandwiches at the Nag's Head at Spinney but she only nibbled at her sandwich and pushed the plate away. He made trivial, casual conversation and she answered him distractedly.

'Shall we go then?' he asked her when they'd finished their beer.

She nodded and walked quickly in front of him to the car. They spoke not at all as she drove the car slowly through the Manor House woods to the cottage.

'Let's sit on the balcony,' Gary said, 'where you say Royalty used to sit and have tea on Ascot Sunday in the old days of steam launches.'

She shrugged listlessly, but climbed with him up the wooden stairs. He drew forward chairs to the railing so that they could look out over the river shining in the spring sunshine.

'I used to love the spring,' she said, 'but this one I hate.'

'Yes, I suppose it's hardly the weather for sitting outside.'

'Not because of the weather, because of *you*, Gary.' She turned to look at him accusingly, her hair fair in the sunlight forming a halo round her face. Her legs encased in jeans were stretched out in front of her. Involuntarily he compared them with Diana's. Gay's legs were short and inclined to plumpness. Beside the sinewy grace of Diana, Gay would look ordinary. He thrust away the thought. He didn't want to think of Diana Bridges now. Which girl did he want? Did he really want either, yet? He looked across the silent river as if to find the answer there.

'Because of *you*, Gary,' Gaynor was saying, 'you're so different today.' Her voice rose almost to hysteria, but it was still cultured, so different from Di's. 'Something's happened to change you. Is it my father's money? If it is, I hate it.'

'If you were a man,' Gary said, 'would *you* want to live on a woman's money?'

'It depends if I loved her. If I really loved her, I wouldn't mind anything to make her happy.'

'What about pride?'

'There'd be heaps of time for you to retrieve that. Once qualified you can go on and on and pay all my money back if you like. I shall simply put it all in trust for our children. Oh, Gary, don't you remember how we used to build our castles when we were kids? How excited we were when David got you your chance, how we planned . . .'

'Yes, but we were kids then.'

'What's different now? Each time we've met, until now, it's always been all right. You like being with me, don't you?'

'You know I do.'

'And I'd rather be with you than anyone else in the world, even Katie.' Her voice trembled. 'You *are* my world, Gary. I can't imagine being without you.'

He loved her in that moment, the dear, loyal companion of his childhood. He wished desperately that he could put back the clock to when they were linked together in the problems of their youth. As if reading his thoughts, she said:

'I even wish we were back to those first days of our friendship. I was happy then, and so were you.'

'We have to grow up, Gay.'

She spread out her hands helplessly.

'So we're grown up. Where do we go from here?'

'We just go on.'

'Until you're qualified and have money in the bank.'

'I meant what I said, sweet. I don't intend to marry until I've qualified, got a car and enough money to put down on a house. All that I must have and I must do it on my own.'

She spoke bleakly and positively. 'And I'm not part of that plan.'

Now was the moment when he should tell her, but he knew he couldn't, not now while she was still so unhappy.

Without waiting for his answer, she went on: 'I'd always thought we were part of each other's plans. Maybe I took too much for granted. You should have stopped me earlier. All the light's gone out of the day,' she ended pathetically.

'It needn't, Gay. We're both very young and I'm still here,

aren't I? You're dramatizing again. Nothing is different.'

He condemned himself for a coward. He'd had his chance and lost it, but why should I stop seeing Gay just because of Di? Di needn't know.

'I had so many lovely plans,' Gaynor said despairingly.

'Plans for yourself. You didn't think that I might want to plan.'

'I thought *only* of you.'

'Gay, please try to understand.'

She shivered and got up.

'I'm cold. It's not warm enough for sitting on the balcony. Let's go please.'

'All right, and leave the cottage to its ghosts.'

He stood up and held out his hands. Ignoring them she walked to the rail of the balcony.

'Poor sad cottage. It's not lucky for us, Katie and me.'

'It's just a cottage, Gay.'

She stared at him miserably.

'Yes, to you, it's just a cottage. All right,' she turned away, 'let's go then.'

He took hold of her shoulders and made her face him.

'Better now?'

Her lips trembled. She broke away.

'I'll run you to your parents.'

'But you're coming with me, surely? I've told mum and dad you're coming. You know how pleased they are to see you.'

The day stretched before her, bleak, lonely. She shrugged.

'All right, for a little while.'

As they drove he talked cheerfully, trying to provoke response from her, but got little success.

'Dad hasn't got much since he finished with the Council. I know he likes talking to you, Gay. Funny, really, because you remember, once upon a time, he used to sneer like mad at my friendship with you.'

Friendship, thought Gaynor, despondently. Is that all it ever was, just friendship?

When they arrived at the little house on the Fletchley estate, Freda Thompson insisted on taking the tea into the sitting-room.

'Why not the kitchen, mum?' protested Gary, 'it's cosy.'

'The kitchen's not for guests,' Freda said firmly.

'I'm not really a guest,' Gaynor said with a wan smile.

'Of course you're a guest, dear, and a very welcome one. Dad'll be in soon, he's gone down the allotment. I sometimes think he's all the better for leaving that snobby Council. He's got hisself one or two very nice interests and he sells a lot of stuff off his allotments. Very sensible, he's bin, dad, I always think, considering everything.'

'And how are *you*, mum?' Gary asked, motioning Gaynor to the settee and sinking into an armchair covered in bright orange mohair with black edgings. He remembered how his sister, Greer, had sneered about these armchairs and settee. 'Mum's got no taste,' she had complained, 'you could only have these things in a really modern apartment.' Poor Greer. She'd wanted something different and she'd got it.

'I'd be fine if it wasn't fer me blood pressure,' Freda sighed. 'I has to take things easy, but we don't want to talk about ailments, do we? What about you, Gaynor, are your father's affairs settled yet?'

'They won't be finalized for a long time yet,' Gay said, 'although I think it's all straightforward. Father was very methodical.'

Freda looked at her anxiously.

'You look pale, love. Bin doing too much studying?' Without waiting for a reply, she turned on her son. 'You, too, our Gary. You look as if you'd lost a shilling and found sixpence. Too much of this swottin' e'nt good for you, you know. I hope that Mrs. Bridges feeds you proper.'

'She's very good,' Gary said, 'treats me like one of her own, really spoils me, she does.'

Freda didn't look too pleased at this.

'Got no son of her own, has she?'

'No.'

'Only a daughter,' Freda went on, 'well, maybe she wanted a son, p'raps that's why she's so good to you. Landladies are usually mean and penny-pinchin', e'nt they Gaynor?'

But Gay was not listening. Freda's words taunted her 'only a daughter'. Funny, Gary had never mentioned that daughter.

'How old is she?' Gaynor said, her voice sharp.

Gary looked at her, startled.

'How old is the daughter?'

'Diana? I don't know, about twenty I think.'

'Has she a boy friend?'

He hoped his face wouldn't betray him. Why did mum have to mention the daughter? Trying to keep his voice casual, he replied, 'She did have, someone called Jimbo.'

'What do you mean, did have?'

'Well, I haven't seen him around lately, but then I've been out a lot, back to the office. Two or three of us are using the office to study in, it's less distracting, no noises of television or people.'

'Very wise I'd say,' his mother said. 'Well, I'll just go and refill the pot.'

Anxious to divert Gaynor from thoughts of Diana, he said, 'How do you think mum looks?'

'She's lost weight.'

'Yes, she has. Mum's always been great on the respectability front. Greer's affair took it out of her. I know she still frets inwardly.'

'No wonder,' Gaynor said. She patted the settee which was upholstered in the same garish material as the chair. 'I like this room,' she said listlessly.

'You can't do,' he said, 'it's ghastly. Those two china birds on top of the telly are the most hideous things I've ever seen.'

'Not to your parents, obviously.'

'Dad doesn't care one way or the other. He uses them to hold all the household bills.'

Papers were tucked in the beaks of both birds, giving them a strangely jaunty look.

Gaynor looked around her. 'It must be fun choosing a home and furnishing it, however small.'

'The sort of fun,' Gary said, 'that *you'd* soon tire of, after the spacious rooms of Marbrook Manor.'

'I always hated the Manor,' Gaynor said, feeling in her voice at last. 'The girls at school used to laugh at me because I lived there, they used to make silly remarks about the coachmen, footmen and butlers. I was glad to get into my small flat. The

Manor's a horrible house and it was hardly ever warm.' She sighed. 'Katie liked it, though, she used to imagine herself living there in olden times, tripping down the staircase with her fan to waltz with be-whiskered gents or be driven out in her carriage. I'm not fanciful like Katie. The house was always cold and old-fashioned to me. I want something warm and smaller.' She leaned forward to him, her eyes pleading again, 'Gary, I always planned . . .'

But, to Gary's relief, before she could continue, the door opened and Ned Thompson came in. He had gone very grey since the tragic death of his daughter and his consequent resignation from the local Council. The fire had gone out of him, he was a man subdued suddenly in his prime.

'Hello, Dad,' Gary got up to greet his Father. 'How goes it?'

'Not so bad,' Gary sat down again as Ned turned to the girl. 'Hello there, Gaynor, hows yourself then?'

'O.K. Mr. Thompson, thanks.'

'Just down fer the week-end, then?'

'Just one night. I'm sleeping at my sister's.'

'Ah.' Ned Thompson sank down in an armchair corresponding to Gary's. 'Yeah, I hear your sister's father-in-law e'nt takin' too kindly to local government reorganization. It's made Major Piddlin' Earnshaw a little fish in a big pond, instead of what he used to be in the old days of the Council, a bloody great shark in a goldfish pond. Him and his daft monocle!'

Even, subdued as he was now, Ned Thompson still couldn't resist a jab at his one time Council enemy – Major Desmond Earnshaw. He shook his head. 'No, they tells me things is very different down Town Hall now. Too big fer personalities and the old pals' act. Maybe it's a good thing, means the town e'nt run by a bunch of shysters featherin' their own nests. Not that they got away with much when *I* was on the Council. I watched 'em every step of the way, I did. Yes sir, I served the town well all the time I was on. No one can say diff'rent.'

Anxious to get his father off his favourite subject, Gary said, 'How's things at the factory, dad?'

'Much the same, son. Had a week's strike since you come

88

down last. I didn't reely hold with it this time, but o' course, I had to come out along with the others.'

Usually Gaynor discussed politics with Ned Thompson when she visited with Gary and Ned looked to her as if expecting some stimulating conversation about strikes. He had to admit he liked this kid, she was totally unlike that pompous capitalist ass, her father Hugh Bloody Scarlett, another one-time enemy of his on the Council. But today Gaynor didn't come up to the bait. For the whole of her visit she spoke little and, just after six, she drove off to her sister's house.

'Thought you and Gay would've gone to the pictures or done somethin' tonight,' Freda said to her son, as she flopped down in front of the television.

'No, she was tired.'

'Well, she could've stayed here, you know, and had a rest. We've got . . .' Freda stopped just for a second, lips trembling, then resolutely she went on, 'I could've made up the bed in our Greer's room, but I never had a chance to tell her, she went off so sudden.'

'She'll be back in the morning, mum, we're going over to the safari park for the day.'

Freda sat looking doubtfully at her son.

'Well, seems to me you've wasted a perfectly good evening. I know when I was courtin' yer dad, we could never have enough time together.'

'We're not exactly courting, Mum,' the boy said stiffly.

'Let the boy alone, Mother,' Ned said, 'He's bin workin' hard and maybe he feels he just wants to relax with his family fer a change.'

'That's it, Dad,' Gary said gratefully, 'I'd like to watch the telly. I hardly ever do that.'

'You could've watched it with Gaynor here too,' Freda persisted.

Ned got up, went over to his wife, took her hands and pulled her up from the settee.

'Most women would jump at the chance to have their son all to themselves, Mother,' he said, turning her towards the door. 'Now, how about goin' and puttin' on that new percolator I bought you from the allotments profit and make us all a nice cup of coffee, eh?'

When she had gone, Ned turned to his son.

'Everything all right then, Gary?'

'Yes thanks, Dad.'

'Gaynor was very quiet I thought.'

'Was she? I didn't notice.'

Ned eyed his son keenly. Of course you bloody noticed, he thought, you could cut the air between 'em with a knife, must have had a tiff.

'Not frettin' about her dad's death, is she?'

'I don't think so. They never got on.'

'No,' Ned said, 'no one ever really got on with Hugh Scarlett. God, that's who he thought he was, God. Still, I got to admit he made a very good speech when I resigned from the Council. Said some quite nice things about me. Shook me rigid it did, I can tell yer.'

Gary smiled thinly.

'Perhaps it was relief at getting rid of you, Dad. After all, you were always needling him and Desmond Earnshaw, weren't you?'

'Pah!' Ned exclaimed. 'Earnshaw, that bloody toe-rag. He'd never say nothin' good about anyone, least of all me.'

Anxious to divert the usual tirade, Gary said, 'How's mum really?'

Ned Thompson shook his head.

'Gets very depressed. She cheers up when she sees you and Gaynor, of course. She's really taken to that girl. I must say I have, too.' Prompted by the sudden shut look on Gary's face, Ned added, 'Things O.K. between you two?'

'Of course, Dad, why shouldn't they be?'

'That's O.K. then. Well, I must settle some bills now I've got some money in. I'm makin' quite a tidy bit selling stuff off me allotments.'

'That's good, Dad,' the boy said absently.

He watched his father take some bills from the beak of one of the birds and go with them to a small desk that stood in a corner of the room. He tried to imagine himself and Di, or himself and Gay, in a house like this. He knew he'd hate it. He, like Greer had done, wanted something better. Well, with Gay's money you could have something better, but not yet, he rebelled, not yet. I don't want to be hooked yet, not by Di or Gay, perhaps I don't want to be hooked ever. I need Di. I love Gay. Why can't it go on like that? Why do women have to catalogue emotions and fence you in? If Di hadn't come along I'd probably have gone on with Gay and we'd have got married one day. Perhaps we still will, one day. This thing with Di may wear itself out.

His mood of depression lasted all next day. Gaynor came over and they went to Windsor and thence on to the safari park, but it wasn't a success. Conversation was strained and Gay's look of misery increased Gary's feeling of guilt.

They went back to his parents to tea and then she drove him to the station. He was thankful that she didn't offer to drive him all the way home.

On the platform he held her hand.

'I'll write Gay, tomorrow.'

She nodded.

'Will *you* write to *me*?'

'If you want me to.'

'Of course I do, and Gay . . .'

'Yes?' her voice lightened with hope, but all he said was, 'Write to my office. I'll get it quicker that way.'

The expectancy died on her face.

'I usually write to your digs.'

'I know, but then I don't get it till the evening and often Mrs. Bridges puts letters on the sideboard and they get covered up. I'm always afraid they'll get lost.'

'All right.'

'Good luck with the new car.'

She looked at him unhappily.

'There's no fun in it any more.'

'Then there ought to be. Gosh, I know if it was mine I'd be over the moon.'

'It could have been,' she said bleakly.

'Now, Gay,' he said, his voice hardening slightly. 'I told you before, if you want a gigolo, don't look at *me*.'

'I want *you*,' she said.

He bent and kissed her on the mouth.

'I better get in now love, they're shutting the doors.'

He got into the train and let down the window.

'Write.'

She nodded dejectedly and turned away. He watched her walk slowly along the platform until she was swallowed up in the crowd.

As she went to her car Gaynor could think of only two things. There was a girl in Gary's digs. Letters couldn't be sent there any more.

She unlocked the door of her spanking new car and got in. She stared around. The newness of the car seemed cold and impersonal suddenly. She felt lonely and terribly rejected. Katie has Paul and the twins. I used to have Gary, we'd always been so close, knowing each other's thoughts. Faint hope struggled through the misery. Gary had said nothing had changed. Maybe the girl and the letters had no significance. Maybe it was just jealousy, seeing things out of proportion. He was in the train now, on his way back to her, she who once had a boy friend called Jimbo.

Trying still to hope, Gaynor Scarlett drove slowly away.

'Love me?' Diana asked as he got into her old car, so different from Gay's, outside the station.

He kissed her. 'Course.'

'Missed me?'

He nodded.

'I missed *you*, terribly. Gary, don't let's go straight home.'

This suggestion he welcomed. At least tonight the loving would have been done before they got back to her parents' home. There wouldn't be the awful fear and guilt that he suffered when she came to him in secret to his bedroom. Already his body was aflame for her. Her lightest touch set him trembling, yet, while they made love, it was another girl's face he saw in his mind – Gay whom he had hurt – the look of misery as she turned and walked away from the train.

'I love you Gary,' Diana was saying as she stroked his cheek. 'I'll never, never let you go.'

CHAPTER EIGHT

JINNY JANE shook her hair free of the petalled bathing cap as she sank down beside Katheryn Earnshaw on the edge of the pool.

'Some pool this. Reggie didn't get this for Green Shield stamps.' Jinny gazed about her thoughtfully. 'Do you know, when I was a kid I used to go to the town swimming baths with all the other snotty-nosed kids from my school. I used to share a cubicle with another sour smelling kid like myself, and then we used to learn to swim in a belt held by some beefy leering attendant who used to make any excuse to maul the fleshiest of us when the teacher wasn't looking. Me,' she patted her flat stomach, 'me I never had much flesh or looks either then. No one wanted to maul *me*.'

'Too bad,' Katheryn replied, dabbling her toes in the water.

'You don't like me, do you?' Jinny said.

'I've never really thought about it.'

Jinny Jane grinned. 'Oh yes you have. I was at that fête, wasn't I? I opened it, darling, remember, at *his* invitation? Some invitation, it merely cancelled out a little obligation I had to dear David. I got no fee for it, just my arm twisted and, boy, could that one twist. I saw the way you looked at him that day, and then you were with him one day after that in the Island Hotel and I saw the way *he* looked at *you* then, the way he give me the brush-off,' as Jinny became more vehement, so her grammar lapsed, 'Oh, I knew what he was up to, tried not to see me so he could keep you all to himself. Me, Jinny, the gal whose virginity he sold to Reggie Gunner-Cartwright when I was only sixteen. I bet that shakes you, kid.'

Jinny stopped and peered intently at Katheryn, but Katheryn's face was expressionless.

'God!' Jinny exploded, 'you're like one of those bloody statues in Reggie's grounds. I don't know what David Lloyd ever saw in you, Katheryn Earnshaw.'

'What do you want me to do,' Katheryn asked coolly,

'clasp my bosom, tear my hair, or just kick you in the teeth?'

Hugging her knees, Jinny laughed.

'I asked for that. Christ! Look at those two lessies.'

She pointed with her foot to the pool where the magazine woman, Agatha Morton, was tenderly coaxing her fluffy friend into the water.

'Don't you reckon it'd be great to be a lessie,' Jinny said, 'all soft and gentle and loving? I mean, fellers couldn't hurt you then, could they? I mean, no woman could be such a mean bastard as a man.'

Katheryn's face registered now a faint expression of distaste.

'Oh hell!' Jinny said, 'I've shocked you at last. Ah well, I couldn't expect you to like me, could I? I mean, even apart from *him*, we'd never speak the same language, I *breathe*.'

She hoisted herself up and stood looking down at the graceful girl sitting on the edge of the pool, dabbling her toes. I'd like to shove her in, she thought, her and her precious snottiness. Yet there was something about Katheryn Earnshaw that fascinated Jinny. There was a kind of loneliness about her that made you sorry for her even when she was being her snootiest. David Lloyd, you were a bastard, Jinny said silently.

'Jinny angel!' Constant Bedigo said, drifting up to them trailing a deep purple towel over his shoulder. 'Haven't I been looking everywhere for you, pet, in the flower pots, in the ovens, in the dungeons . . .?'

'Down the loo,' Jinny supplemented, laughing, 'and here I am, all the time, darling, just having a nice little gossip with Katheryn about old friends. So long, Katheryn darling, we must resume our little chat some other time. Come on, Beddy darling, let's go get a bit of the action.'

Katheryn sat very still when they had gone. She saw not this blue pool with the bathers sporting in it, but the dark green river by the Island Hotel and the two swans on the weir steps picking at the weeds. 'Lucky, the ones who cross your path,' he had said that day. Well, he had crossed it and gone. She remembered the text of the vicar's sermon in church the first miserable Sunday after David's death. 'How art thou fallen from Heaven, oh Lucifer, son of the morning.' And father had nodded his head, crossed his legs and smiled complacently at mother, and the church had smelled of decay, the way the old boathouse smelled where Harriet had died.

'Good morning, Katheryn.'

She looked up from her dreams to see Derren Rackstraw standing over her, his hands thrust into the pockets of a towelled jacket. She thought, with detachment, how handsome and distinguished he looked.

He sank down beside her, thinking how vulnerable her little face looked under the gold bathing cap, bereft of the adornment of hair.

'I noticed you being honoured by the famous Jinny. I believe she's a little raw when she's away from the cameras.'

'Ineffective,' Katheryn replied.

But effective enough to upset you, he thought.

'Are you anticipating before you dive in?' he asked her.

'Yes, I seldom jump in straightaway. I used to when I was young.'

'Today's funny,' he said, 'when you were young.'

'Sometimes I feel quite old.'

He touched her arm briefly, 'But not today. Today is good.'

'Yes.'

As his steely compelling eyes assessed her, she felt a little shiver of excitement. His love-making, she thought, would be hard and satisfying and not sentimental. Sentiment had no place in this thing between them. She knew that he knew that.

'And are you a good swimmer, Katheryn?'

She remembered the day by the river when she had streaked across the water with Paul just to show Harriet and impress David. The man beside her now was thinking, too, of course it all happened by the river.

'I used to be able to beat my husband,' she said, 'but I don't know if I could now. We used to race when we were young, my sister and Paul and I.'

'Was he still up when you got back last night?'

'Yes, he was gambling for hours.' She smiled at him. 'Was your wife asleep?'

'Yes, very soundly so.' He could have added, and drenched with perfume to try to hide the smell of the Scotch.

95

Katheryn hugged her knees. It was as if they were conspirators together.

'Shall we swim?' Derren Rackstraw asked her, 'and then take advantage of Reggie's excellent bar.'

'Aren't you going to wait for your wife?'

'She doesn't swim. She's resting upstairs until after lunch. She has a slight headache. What about your husband? Do you want to wait for him?'

She looked around her briefly.

'I left him sleeping. I'm not waiting for him.'

She stood up lithe and dainty, in her gold bikini. She had the perfect figure for a bikini he thought, but she was not dazzlingly lovely like Jinny Jane or silly Noeleen Eden, neither was she a scintillating coversationalist. Where then lay her attraction for him?

With an exultant laugh, she dived in. Her sudden animation was lovely, he thought, like a lamp suddenly coming alight. He shrugged off his jacket and dived in after her. They swam round the pool several times, exchanging spluttering breathless pleasantries with other swimmers, then, with mutual accord, they clambered out. She shook her hair free of the gold cap.

'I enjoyed that. I'll go and dry off now and then I'll be ready for that drink.'

They stood a second smiling into each other's eyes, exhilarated by their swim, then, 'I'll see you in a minute at the bar,' she said, and she whirled away from him.

When he arrived at the bar, having donned blue jeans and a silver grey shirt, she was already seated on a stool sipping a bacardi and coke. Her long legs were encased in black jeans and she wore a daffodil yellow shirt blouse. Yellow sandals clung to her feet by a single strap. He had just ordered a scotch and soda where there was a scream behind them. They turned in time to see Jinny Jane, still clutching her petalled bathing cap, pushed lightly in the chest by Reggie Gunner-Cartwright and sent backwards into the pool.

'That should cool her off for you Con,' Reggie said, placing an arm around the shoulders of Constant Bedigo.

'But sweetie,' Constant protested, clasping the pillar with

both arms like a lover, 'I don't know that I wanted her cooled off, not yet.'

Derren Rackstraw raised scornful eyebrows at Katheryn.

'The idle rich at play.'

She smiled and they turned their backs with one accord on the noisy merriment beside the pool, but just as he started to talk to her, Paul Earnshaw jostled his way past the funmakers at the water's edge, fetching up beside his wife.

She turned from Derren Rackstraw and greeted him.

'Good morning.'

'Why didn't you wait for me?'

He moved round and insinuated himself between Katheryn's stool and Derren Rackstraw. She took a long swig of her drink then, not looking at him, she replied coolly, 'When I left you were snoring.'

'I went up from the gaming room around midnight last night and you weren't in bed, so I went back down again. Where were you?'

'I went for a drive.'

'What on earth for?'

'Because I felt like it,' she said flatly. 'Did you win last night?'

'I broke even,' he answered sullenly.

She smiled and her eyes slewed quickly towards Noeleen Eden who was now one of the noisy group beside the pool.

'Bad luck. I thought you usually won.'

She turned and leant in front of Paul to Derren Rackstraw.

'By the way,' she said, 'I don't think you've been introduced. Derren Rackstraw, Mr. Rackstraw, my husband – Paul.'

She bent down to her drink and, over her head, the eyes of the two men met. Derren Rackstraw's eyes were steady, even friendly, but Paul merely nodded and looked quickly away.

'Hi.'

He was obliged to move away from between Katheryn and Rackstraw then because Noeleen Eden came up, demanding a stool.

'Don't scowl so, Paul,' she said. 'Mercy me, I must sit down. I ache from all that swimming, and my tongue's hanging out. Get me a drink do, there's a pet.'

Katheryn, he noticed, had quickly taken the opportunity to resume her conversation with the barrister, shutting him out. Annoyed and jealous he loudly ordered two vodkas for himself and Noeleen Eden.

'You do look cross this morning, darling.'

He took a swallow of the drink which had been quickly served to him.

'I've been swimming round and round that blasted pool like a goldfish waiting for you,' Noeleen said pettishly.

'I've been to morning prayers.'

She laughed softly.

'Funny man. Well,' she lowered her voice, 'what about all those lovely things you said to me last night?'

'Last night I was stoned,' he said. Stoned because my bloody wife wasn't in her room. He stared morosely at the silly pretty girl beside him and the piquant face of Dorothy, his secretary, floated into his mind. He wondered what Dorothy would be doing now. Would she, for all her protestations to the contrary, be offering that expert pussy of hers to some other guy? He found himself hoping not. He was relying on Dorothy Trent to help him live with the torment that was Katheryn.

'The dance tonight,' Noeleen was saying, 'I'm so looking forward to it. Reggie does everything so well.' She smiled archly. 'Although, of course, I don't know about *every-thing*, I don't know him all that well, but he seems so sort of dynamic.'

'Reggie could sell sand to the Arabs,' Paul said shortly, 'and, the next minute, be burying them under it.'

'You don't like him?'

'Would I be here if I didn't?'

The little mouth pursed into a shrewd smile.

'Oh yes, I think so,' she said softly, 'lots are here, but few are here because they *like* Reggie, or even dear Tabitha for that matter.'

Paul was just about to order another drink when he saw Katheryn slide down from her stool. Derren Rackstraw was walking away from her towards the end of the bar.

Paul leaned over and caught his wife's arm.

'Where are you going, Katheryn?'

She smiled slightly and spoke with faint annoyance as a mother might to the tiresome questioning of a child.

'Home for lunch.'

'Why?'

'Well, you may remember, it's Mabel's week-end off. She wants to leave at twelve-thirty, her boy-friend's picking her up then, so I'm going to stay with the twins for lunch until Mrs. Hopkins comes to take over at 3 o'clock.'

'I'll come with you.'

'There's no need. I'll be back as soon as I can.'

She twisted away and ran swiftly along the edge of the pool.

'She's dumped you,' Noeleen said.

'Like hell she has!'

He ran after Katheryn, catching up with her as she was about to get into her car.

'Katheryn.'

She paused, holding the door open.

'I told you there was no need for you to come, Paul. It's rude for us both to leave.'

'No one will notice whether we're in for lunch or not, as long as we're back for the ball.'

He opened the passenger door for her, but she stayed where she was on the driver's side of the car.

'You know I hate other people driving my car,' she said.

'I'm not other people. I'm your husband, remember? Come on, get in; I refuse to be driven by a woman when I'm sober.'

With a hunch of resignation she walked slowly round the car and got in the passenger seat. As he settled himself behind the wheel he said:

'We might go for a run in the country this afternoon before we go back.'

'What on earth for?'

He turned on her angrily.

'For the same reason that you go buggering off alone on these jaunts.'

'I go because I want to be alone.'

'Thanks.'

He sat there glaring sullenly ahead.

'I don't understand you.'

'I've always liked being alone,' she said, 'I can't change, I'm afraid.'

'It's unnatural.'

'Please start the car, Paul,' she said. 'I told you I don't want to be late.'

He raced the car down the drive, skidding to a halt as he reached the big gateway opening on to the road.

'But last night,' he said, 'going off alone like that, so late, away from a party. It's risky for a woman driving round lonely countryside at night.'

'Actually I wasn't alone last night,' she said. 'Derren Rackstraw came with me.'

Paul's foot came off the accelerator, the car rolled on, slowing down.

'Rackstraw? Christ! You told me you went alone.'

'No I didn't. I merely said I went for a drive.'

'Why didn't you mention it before?'

'I didn't think it necessary. Do *you* give *me* a catalogue of the people you lunch with, gamble with?'

'I would if you were interested.'

She smiled, and her smile infuriated him.

'I'd find a day-to-day account rather juvenile.'

'Katheryn, bloody hell! Why did that man go with you?'

'Because he asked me if I was going to bed. I said, no, I was going for a drive and he said he felt like a drive, too, so we went together. I didn't know I had to get a permit first.'

Paul glanced sideways at his wife's composed little face as she stared ahead at the road. He had an urge to reach over and slap it, slap some feeling into her.

'If you needed company, why didn't you ask *me*?'

Katheryn smiled slowly.

'And have deprived you of your gambling and the company of the celebrated Miss Eden?'

'Noel Eden means nothing to me,' Paul said.

'Oh,' Katheryn said amiably, 'I thought you seemed on very good terms.'

'I lunched her once or twice, with her photographers, when they were doing that commercial for the company – all in the line of duty.'

'Naturally.'

He glanced at her and she was smiling slightly. Too much to hope that she might be jealous.

'I just can't understand it,' he said, 'you being matey with that arrogant Rackstraw.'

'Being civil could hardly be called matey.'

'Even civil,' he said. 'I'd have thought the very presence of the bloke at the party would have thrown you; it did *me*.'

'Why should it? He was only doing a job.'

'Do you discuss the trial with him?'

'Of course not.'

'What do you talk about then?'

'The twins, cars, driving, his wife's mad sister.'

'Christ!' Paul said, 'when I saw him at Reggie's, it made me cold.' He gave a harsh little laugh. 'I must say Reggie certainly likes playing with danger.'

She looked at him sharply.

'Why should Reggie be in danger from Derren Rackstraw?'

'I didn't mean that exactly. It was bad form of Reggie inviting the bloke and even worse for him to accept.'

Katheryn shrugged and gazed out at the landscape. They drove on in silence, then he said:

'This Rackstraw . . .'

'Yes?'

'You like him?'

She answered quickly and easily:

'I haven't really thought about it.'

He sighed and put his foot down hard. The little sports car shot forward with a roar.

No, he quite believed it. She hadn't really thought about it. Who *do* you think about, my Katheryn? He knew the answer. As always it left him with a sick feeling in his heart.

CHAPTER NINE

REGGIE GUNNER-CARTWIGHT's free hand stroked the telephone as he spoke softly into it.

'I thought I told you never to ring me here. This is the second time, darling. It's got to stop.'

'Today is different. It's your silver wedding anniversary, isn't it? Surely I'm allowed to congratulate you.'

'As if you'd want to.'

Dorothy Trent gave a short miserable laugh.

'Yes, as if I'd want to. I just needed an excuse to speak to you.'

'I'm just about to sit down to dine with my guests. They're all waiting.'

'Today's another anniversary, Reggie, or had you forgotten?'

'I can think of nothing,' he replied coldly.

'Three years since that wonderful Saturday night in Oslo.'

For a moment the big man's mouth curved sensually, then silkily he murmured into the telephone, 'I suggest you try making a few anniversaries with your current lover. I don't think you're doing a very good job on him. He's been walking about with a sour look on his handsome face all week-end and he's drinking far too much. You're not the girl you used to be, Dorothy, evidently.'

'He's nothing to me compared with you, Reggie, nothing.'

'Lots of girls would give their eyes to have a young man like Paul Earnshaw to lay them. Now, I really must go.'

'When will I see you, Reggie?' she pleaded desperately, 'It's been so long. You promised we could start again.'

'I told you it was difficult, it still is. I'll come to you as soon as I can. That is, if you liven yourself up a bit. Show me that our mutual friend is being well entertained and it might arouse my interest to the point of indiscretion.'

'You used to be indiscreet. You said you didn't care.'

'I was younger then, darling.'

'Men like you never grow too old.'

'You flatter me, darling. Now, it's really good-bye and if you want to get back to what we had before, never ring me here again. You know the rules, Dorothy.'

He replaced the receiver and stood frowning down at it. Blast the girl! She was like a leech. He'd have thought that finding her a young stallion like Paul Earnshaw would have kept her satisfied, but no, she had to bleat about love. She had been sweet in the beginning, though, he would always remember that. He pressed a hand to his stomach and bent over in agony. If only this damned pain wouldn't flare up so sharply when he thought about women. In a moment or so it receded into the dull ache that he was seldom without these days.

He wished suddenly that David Lloyd were still alive. Strange how you still missed the feller. David had been able to provide everything, stimulants for the jaded and, by Christ, I'm jaded now, Reggie thought, kicks for the perverted, even the best quacks when anyone was ill. Remarkable chap, David, Reggie mused, wicked as hell, but a bit of the Christ in him too – a wonderful shoulder to cry on. Hell, who wants to cry? He straightened up. Stroking the lapels of his faultlessly cut dinner jacket, Reggie Gunner-Cartwright strode into the big dining-room where waiters were ushering guests to their places. Tabitha blew him a kiss as he came in. She had been a good invest-ment, he thought; dear Tabby, even if she did get hot pants sometimes. Anyway, she was entitled to her fun so long as she didn't step out of line. The cabinet minister was on Tabby's right and Derren Rackstraw the other side of her. It had been Reggie's idea to place the barrister next to Tabitha, give the bloke a signal honour. It was really rather funny when you came to think about it.

The sumptuous meal progressed with much laughter and gay, surface conversation. Waiters glided in and out, glasses chinked, diamonds glittered, the silver sparkled on the long banquetting table.

The cabinet minister was telling Tabitha how splendid it was to find a marriage that had endured for twenty-five years in such permissive times. Tabitha smiled her acknowledgment. She glanced down the table at the rest of her guests, all ex-pensively clothed – the women flashing with jewels – the men impeccably suited. Her eyes appreciated the lovely panelled dining-room with its valuable original paintings, the cunningly carved ceiling, the glittering chandeliers. All this is my world; my position is secure. I have all the comforts and luxuries any woman could wish for. Is then the love and fidelity of one man so important? She looked round Rackstraw at the girl who was sitting the other side of him. Katheryn looked quite striking tonight, her long brown hair falling loose from a pearl tiara, her throat encased in a swathe of silver and white tulle which seemed to be the only link holding the scant white dress over her small pointed breasts. Katheryn, Tabitha thought, was no fool in her choice of white. Yes, even if she wasn't crazy about him, marriage to Paul Earnshaw had certainly given her poise and know-how. Tabitha found herself wondering how David Lloyd would have felt for the girl had he been alive to see her now. Would he still have wanted her, or had her youth and immaturity been her only charm for him? Tabitha sighed for her secret bitter thoughts.

She found it odd the way Derren Rackstraw seemed to be drawn to this young girl when he had plainly shown his contempt for her in their brief dramatic battle in court.

'Katheryn,' Derren Rackstraw was saying, 'what's your opinion?'

Ah, so they're on Christian name terms, Tabitha thought. This won't stay platonic for long, not with a man like Rackstraw.

Katheryn was unusually animated tonight. She had drunk more than usual and her inhibitions loosened. She looked down the table and saw Noeleen Eden place her hand possessively on Paul's arm. She was filled suddenly with a strange desire to slap that pretty face. The urge lasted only a second. She turned back to her dinner companions.

When coffee and liqueurs were served, Marcus got up to propose a toast.

'As one of the oldest friends of Reggie and Tabby,' he announced, glass in one hand, French cigarette in the other, 'I would ask you, ladies and gentlemen, to drink to our excellent host and hostess and to wish them another twenty-five years of undiluted happiness like the first twenty-five they've endured together.'

'Crap!' said Clement Barr audibly.

Ignoring the interruption, Marcus turned to smile at another more polite interruption.

'"Endure" is an unfortunate word, Marcus,' said someone, 'you make it sound like a road test.'

Smiling, Marcus bowed.

'I apologize. Instead of "endure" I substitute "enjoy". Now, to resume, ladies and gentlemen: they say that married men live longer. Reggie assures me this isn't true – it just *seems* longer.' He paused, looked round expectantly and received a mild ripple of applause. 'Anyway, they tell me you never know what happiness is until you're married, and then it's too late, but then I know, and you know, that's not the case with Reggie and Tabby. Ladies and gentlemen, raise your glasses with me and drink to Reggie and Tabby.'

As voices and glasses rose, Reggie and Tabitha sat, he smiling, bland, she eyes downcast, her fingers twisting round the stem of her glass.

'Speech, Reggie,' someone called, but Reggie got up, shaking his head.

'No speech. This is a party, not a board meeting. So now, when you're ready, go out into the hall and dance. There's gallons of grog out there so I want everyone to be happy.'

Can we be happy, any of us, Tabitha thought. Strange, Reggie not wanting to make a speech. Usually he loved it. She stared at him thoughtfully. The quantity of new suits he'd acquired lately, in a smaller size, dieting he had said when she questioned him, but she was sure he was not on a diet. He looked, she thought, like a man in a skin one size too big for him. His colour wasn't good, either, that faint tinge of yellow. She thought dispassionately, would I mind if Reggie died? My life would be nothing for a long time, he's dominated my body and soul for so long. The cabinet minister turned to her saying, 'I expect you'll have the first dance with your husband, Lady Tabitha, may I escort you to him?'

Katheryn was standing uncertainly between Tabitha and Derren Rackstraw when Paul strode swiftly round to them. She smiled a welcome and prepared to let him claim her to dance, but he ignored her completely and went to Tabitha.

'Will you dance, Tabby?'

His eyes were dangerously bright, the set of his handsome mouth ugly.

'Well, I should have the first dance with Reggie,' Tabitha said doubtfully, 'and you with Katheryn.'

'Katheryn,' he said loudly, deliberately keeping his back to his wife, 'hasn't even seen that I'm here.'

Tabitha, anxious to avoid a scene, quickly held out her hands to him.

'By all means Paul,' she said, 'let's dance.'

As Paul led her swiftly into the hall, she glanced with apology at Reggie, but he hadn't even seen her. He was talking to Jinny Jane, still at the dinner table. Reggie was holding both Jinny's hands and seemed to be lecturing her. Tabitha felt a little sick as she looked. Reggie with that poor girl was like a sleek cat with a wretched scrawny mouse.

'You were terribly rude to Katheryn, Paul,' she said as they circled the dance floor.

'Good. I meant to be. She makes me puke sometimes with her cold, bitchy ways.'

'*You* married her. Anyway, it was bad to wash your dirty linen in public.'

'Let her fancy man console her.'

'Don't be silly. You know he isn't that.'

'He soon will be, the way they're behaving.'

'Like you and Noeleen Eden?' she said slyly, 'or,' she paused, 'Chinese Dorothy?'

'Oh Christ!' he said, 'what a circus.'

Curiously Tabitha asked him. 'Does Katheryn have affairs?'

He put back his head and stared at her stormily.

'Sometimes I think she does, but then I know she doesn't. No, I don't know. Do you ever know about people?'

'Well, if she does,' Tabitha said softly, 'it's hardly for you to complain, is it? You couldn't exactly claim a medal for fidelity.'

'But *him*, Paul said.

She laughed quietly. 'Stop treating him as your enemy, Paul. You know who *your* enemy is, don't you? Yourself.'

He looked at her with unhappy eyes.

'My enemy is dead,' he said, 'but he won't bloody lie down.'

Left alone together, Derren Rackstraw said to Katheryn.

'I'm sorry.'

She hunched her shoulders and smiled faintly.

'Paul is a very spoilt young man I'm afraid. His mother spoils him and other women spoil him because of his good looks.'

'He's lucky to have such a loyal wife.'

'Is he? I doubt if he'd agree with you. See,' she said, 'your wife seems to be looking for you. You'd better go to her.'

'And you?'

'I'm going upstairs to change my shoes. They hurt.'

'When you come back, may I dance with you?'

'If you're free.'

'I shall be,' he said, 'and you?'

'The original wallflower,' she said smiling, and left him.

CHAPTER TEN

'YOU sound drunk to me,' Dorothy said.

'I *am* drunk, but I'll have sobered up by the time we meet.'

'But Paul, you can't just walk out on a party.'

'Why not? I'm crazy about you and I must see you, or have you got some other bastard in that pad of yours?'

'Of course not, but I shouldn't really have been here. I was going away for the week-end to my aunt's. It was only when I discovered that my father and stepmother were going to be there too that I opted out and stayed home.'

'I'm glad you did, darling. Get in your car and come down the motorway and turn off at Creely Hatch. You can meet me at Joe's place in half an hour, it's about half-way. I'm leaving here now.'

'Driving when you're drunk?'

'I drive better drunk.'

'Joe's place at Creely, isn't that a club?'

'Yes, it's run by a bookie I know. We can dance and drink and have our own party. By the way, have you eaten?'

'Yes.'

'Well then we'll just drink and dance.'

'You're crazy, Paul.' She paused, then she said, 'What will Reggie Gunner-Cartwright say?'

'I doubt if he'll miss me.' Paul snickered. 'He's too busy trying to lift the songbird spade off Von Kram.'

Her voice tight, she asked.

'What spade?'

'You know, Bambi Collins.'

'I'm leaving now,' Dorothy said, 'see you at Joe's.'

She replaced the receiver and stood staring into space. Reggie, the dirty bastard, how could he? She shivered, remembering his soft teasing hands, his tender obscene endearments. How well he'd known the sensuality that lay hidden in a young girl, how skilfully he'd used it until she could see no other man but him. Yet, when he was not with her, her body clamoured for other men. He knew that, that was why, at Reggie's command, she was now the mistress of Paul Earnshaw.

Paul arrived at Joe's before her.

The lights were low, but she saw him instantly, sitting hunched over his drink. As she sat down at the table beside him, he made to rise, but sank back in his seat. She could see that he was very tight.

'You look good, honey.'

His wavering glance appraised her naked shoulders in the black dress looped round her neck and draped over her breasts. She really was a looker, his Dorothy. Katheryn couldn't hold a candle to her for looks.

'What will your wife think of your skipping off like this?'

He smiled sourly. 'She should care! She skipped out on it herself last night. Anyhow, by now, my wife will probably be in the arms of the law.'

She was startled. 'Arrested?'

He laughed tipsily.

'Not exactly. A certain Derren Rackstraw has his beady eye on her. He had it on her once before, but she wasn't so keen on it then.'

The waiter came for the order.

'Two vodkas,' Paul said, 'big ones.'

'A small one for me,' Dorothy said. 'I have to drive home.'

'Why? We can stay here.'

She shrugged. 'All right. What have I got to lose?'

Face impassive, the waiter said, 'Two vodkas, big ones.'

They drank and danced, but Paul was unsteady on his feet.

'I think,' he said, 'it would be better if we found our room before I get too kalied to perform.'

Dorothy shrugged. 'As you put it so delightfully.'

She wondered who or what had upset him to make him leave a swinging party, obviously that bitch of a wife of his who stayed so much in the background.

'I didn't know it was residential,' she said, as they went up the stairs, Paul gripping the bannister tightly.

'It isn't exactly, but they cater, if you know what I mean.' He stopped, turned and winked at her. 'They cater, like when one is too tight to drive, see?'

'Yes, I see,' Dorothy said. At one time, she thought, I'd have felt cheap, now I don't even feel that any more.

He made love to her with feverish urgency as if trying to punish her for something.

'Well,' she said afterwards, 'if I were not a woman of the world, I'd say you needed that, that you hadn't had a woman for a long time, but I know that can't be true.'

He telephoned down for more drinks and, while they were drinking, she said:

'What was that you were saying about your wife and Derren Rackstraw? Isn't he a Q.C.?'

'Yeah, Queen's bloody Counsel.'

'What is he doing with your wife?'

Paul turned, smiling owlishly and tickled her cheek with his finger.

'I talk a lot of cock.'

'Paul,' Dorothy said, 'would you say your marriage was a success?'

He stopped smiling. 'It's no worse than any other.'

'No worse? That surely isn't the way to describe a happy marriage?'

'Who said it was happy?'

'It surely must have been, once.'

'If it was, I can't remember it.'

'Yet you're in love with your wife.'

'Am I?'

He poured another drink.

'Paul,' she said, 'should you? You'll be paralytic and you really ought to get back to that party some time.'

'Why should I? Bloody Reggie and his perverted sense of humour.'

The girl tensed.

'What do you mean? What's Reggie done now?'

'Invited that feller to his party, didn't he? Playing with danger, that's the bastard's sense of humour.'

Paul's words were very slurred now. He laughed foolishly.

'And now, tell me, where were *you* the night the woman was murdered, eh? Well, *I* know where Reggie was, don' I? Makes me feel real powerful sometimes, powerful like that barrister bastard, and powerful like Katheryn was in Court when she told him to get stuffed – him and his law degrees. Oh yes, she told him all right, and he couldn't shake her, could he, although he knew it was a bloody lie she was tellin', a lie that could've dropped any one of us in it, but it didn't drop Reggie in it, did it, he's always bin a lucky bastard, clever too, but to invite that bloke to his party! Derren Bloody Rackstraw, Q.C., I mean, oh Christ, sometimes I wish I'd never met Reggie, I, oh hell, I'm a bleedin' flop for all my chrome office and name on the letter heads.'

Quietly Dorothy said:

'You said you knew where Reggie was the night of the murder, what murder? Was it that Lloyd woman who had the cottage belonging to your father-in-law, is that it, the big murder scandal that rocked society?'

'No,' said Paul, 'there wasn't any murder. I made it up. I told you, I talk a lot of cock.'

Although drunk, he realized he'd said too much.

'What had Reggie Gunner-Cartwright to do with it?' Dorothy was asking.

More than a little alarmed now, Paul said:

'Nothing, nothing at all. No murder, jus' makin' it up to amuse you, doll.'

'That woman who was murdered at your wife's home, Reggie knew her, didn't he?'

'Lots of people knew her.'

Dorothy was silent, her mind working furiously. Then she said:

'And that barrister was the one . . .?'

'Forget it, Lotus, it's bin a long time dead.' He snickered. 'Told you, load of cock, should've bin a writer – a great imagination. Come on, baby, love me, put your arms round me and coax me, we can't waste this lovely bed.'

Automatically Dorothy put her arms round him whilst her mind still raced feverishly. It all fell into place, the strange advancement of this young man by Reggie, a young man who had been nothing at all to him, not even in the same social strata at one time. What had Paul Earnshaw seen that night that had set him up for life? He groaned in her arms as she stroked his hot forehead.

'I get pretty damned miserable at times, Dot.'

Pity stirred in her at his surprising shortening of her name, like a brother would call a sister.

'You've got *me*, darling,' she soothed him. 'Try and sleep a little now, love, and then you must go back to your party.'

'Lotus,' he muttered, 'you're bloody lovely, do y' know that? The loveliest looking girl I've ever seen, you'd knock spots off those scrubbers at that fancy party.'

But she's got nothing for me, his miserable heart told him with stark truth amidst his drunkenness. All I want is Katheryn, she's all I ever wanted, long before those others came to Marbrook and bitched it all up.

'I'm glad you think I'm lovely,' Dorothy said gently.

After he slept, she lay wakeful beside him. I know now, Reggie, and when I tell you what I know, you won't be able to leave me again because you'll be afraid. Yes, you Reggie, you'll be afraid to leave *me*. Dorothy lay very still beside Paul, dreaming of the day not too far distant now, when she would have her lover back, and not any bitch, black or white, should ever take him away from her again. If he had killed that Harriet Lloyd, she'd probably asked for it. That was over now. In future there would only be Reggie and Dorothy. Reggie liked a girl with spirit, well, he should have one. He had always done all the manipulating, now it would be her turn. Reggie, she was sure, when he got over the shock, would laugh and admire her for it, and they would be back together again like it was before.

Paul was sleeping soundly now, and snoring gently. She moved out of his embrace to the other side of the bed, and lay back on her pillow.

Some miles away Katheryn lay awake, her arms across the empty pillow beside her. Where was Paul? Out drinking somewhere probably, but not with Noeleen Eden because she had spent most of the evening with Hugo Oliver of London's night world. Katheryn's thoughts veered from Paul to Derren Rackstraw. Although tonight they had only danced, she knew that easily they could become lovers. His mouth had brushed her cheek as they danced and she had wanted so badly to turn her mouth to meet his. Was it loyalty to Paul, who had made such a bad bargain in his marriage to her, that had stopped her? She tried to tell herself it was. Paul deserved some consideration. She thought again of the man and remembered how her body had thrilled in his embrace. It could so easily happen some day, she knew that, in spite of loyalty to Paul. Where then was the magic? Where then was David?

Katheryn Earnshaw flung herself down on the empty pillow and wept.

CHAPTER ELEVEN

In a fury Paul drove home from the party and cursed when he saw his parents' Daimler in the drive. He'd had one hell of a hangover this morning. He'd crept into the Gunner-Cartwright house when all the guests were still abed and only the servants stirred. He'd sat in a lounge, dozing until the others came down and he could mingle unnoticed. Katheryn, Paul had seen only briefly at the farewell buffet luncheon. She had studiously ignored him. The sight of her looking about sixteen with her hair brushed up into a casual topknot had increased his disgust with himself even more. She looked so fresh and young in a crisp white blouse and yellow pleated skirt, the way he remembered her when he had first known her, and so remote.

When the time came for good-byes he had looked for her and was told by an amused Reggie that she had already said her thanks and had gone.

He raced his car to the garage and found her garage next door, empty. Where was the bitch? Off on another of her crazy jaunts, or with *him*? Damn Gunner-Cartwright, he'd intended this to happen. Reggie's purring voice stirred the jealousy in him. 'Katheryn and Rackstraw danced last night like a dream. I'm glad to say she didn't seem to be missing you, Paul.'

As Paul mooched back from his garage his mother opened the front door, the twins beside her.

'Hello, darling. We've let Mrs. Hopkins go, said we'd hold the fort till you and Katheryn got home.' Grace Earnshaw peered towards the garages. 'Oh, where *is* Katheryn then?'

'She's got her own car.'

'Oh,' Grace's face fell slightly. Then brightly she said, 'And did you have a lovely time?'

'Not bad.'

Paul bent down and kissed his daughters.

'Lots of exciting people, I expect, as usual,' Grace Earnshaw said.

'Exciting flops.'

Grace sighed. Nothing, it seemed, these days, pleased Paul, even though he mingled with the greats and was such a success himself. It must be young Katheryn Scarlett giving him hell. Funny, Grace could never think of that young madam as Katheryn Earnshaw. Still, I did warn him against marrying her. 'That girl has no love for you,' I told him, time and time again, 'secondhand goods after that horrible Lloyd man,' but Paul had blazed at her. 'Katheryn is not secondhand goods and I should know, shouldn't I?' Grace sighed. Yes, Paul had always been antagonistic, never the friendly, mother-adoring son she'd always desired. 'Because you've always spoiled him,' Desmond would tell her. Thank goodness Desmond seemed to have settled down now. At one time I thought I was losing him too.

Major Desmond Earnshaw got up from reading the paper to greet his son. He had put on weight, but was still a handsome man. Looking at him, one could see the same stamp of good looks as in the son.

The little ones left their granny and clambered up on to the settee beside their grandfather as he sat down again.

'Let me wear your eyeglass again, granad,' demanded Linda.

'No, it's my turn, granad,' pleaded Lucy, edging in beside her sister.

'Now children,' Paul commanded. 'Granad's monocle isn't a plaything.'

'No,' said Grace, 'come on, dears, into the kitchen with granny and help me do the tea. Granad,' she used the children's word for their grandfather, 'Granad wants to talk to daddy.'

'We were on a drive round and thought we'd call in on the way back.' Desmond told his son. 'Your mother wanted to hear all about the party. Usual crowd there?'

'Yes, all of Sodom and Gomorrah.' Paul said gloomily, flopping down into a rocking chair opposite his father.

Desmond regarded his son critically. Paul was looking unusually dissipated. Rumour had it that he wasn't exactly a model husband, too fond of the high life and women. Well, rumour often exaggerated and, Desmond thought indulgently, there was a time myself when I looked for fun beyond dear old Grace. That kid, Greer Thompson, for instance, nice mess she could have got me into if I hadn't been lucky and played it cool.

On the whole, it doesn't pay to play around, but it wouldn't be any good me telling Paul that, he's got to learn for himself. After all, he's done pretty well so far, a rising young rubber executive, entrée into the racy smart set and a wife with both beauty and money.

'Where's Katheryn?' Desmond asked. 'Didn't she come back with you?'

'No. She's got her own car. She may have given someone a lift. I didn't see her leave. I was talking and the champagne was flowing. God, I've got a mouth like a birdcage.'

'Your mother's making some tea,' Desmond said, 'that should put you right. Mid-day drinking is a foul habit I always think, spoils the rest of the day for you, never could stand it meself. Jinny Jane amongst the guests, was she?'

Paul stretched back and began rocking the chair slowly.

'Yes, and Clem, but Clem'll be all washed up soon if he goes on hitting the bottle.'

'Pity,' Desmond said, 'been a fine driver in his time.' He smiled reminiscently. 'I remember when Jinny Jane came to Marbrook to open that fête. How impressed they all were that I managed to get her there. I was a bit staggered myself, I seem to remember. Now, it seems, my son rubs shoulders with celebrities as a matter or course.'

'And that's a doubtful privilege,' Paul said sourly. He sat up suddenly in his chair as he heard Katheryn's car go past the house towards the garage.

His mother called from the kitchen. 'Here's Katheryn.' Paul went to the front door, the twins ran to join him. Katheryn came from the garage towards them, carrying her suitcase. He went forward and took it from her.

'Thanks,' she said, 'it isn't very heavy.' Then she bent down and kissed her daughters in turn.

'Mummy, I was sick last night.'

'No, she wasn't, just pretending. *I* cried. I wanted *you*.'

'Well, I'm back now,' Katheryn said placidly, 'and I don't want anyone being sick or any more tears, right?'

She hoisted her handbag up on to her shoulder and gave a hand to each child, walking towards the front door. Behind her Paul called: 'Katheryn, wait.'

She halted. 'Yes?'

'Where have you been? You left ages before me, apparently.'

For a second he thought she was not going to answer him, then she said:

'I ran Jinny Jane to Windsor.'

'But she had Con and Clem to look after her.'

Katheryn shrugged.

'She didn't seem to want to ride with either of them, and she had no car there.' Katheryn paused, then she added, 'She wanted to visit her son who lives with her sister in Windsor.'

'Mummy, come on.' The twins were pulling at her. She took a step forward.

'Her son?' Paul said, 'I didn't know she had a son.'

You didn't know, either, what a poor lost creature she is, Katheryn thought. Jinny Jane, that scintillating TV personality who weeps in her heart and lives for visits to her bastard son.

'A son?' Paul was saying, 'who's the father then?'

Katheryn's laugh was like the fall of pebbles.

'How would I know? One doesn't ask such questions.'

'But why did she ask *you*?' Paul persisted, 'you're not even civil to her usually.'

'I just happened to be there, I suppose, when she asked if someone could run her to Windsor.'

Katheryn, herself, was still surprised at the impulse which had made her offer Jinny a lift. Jinny hadn't seemed surprised, though, she'd just grinned and said, 'I'm glad I'm going with you. I could do with some class.'

Katheryn walked on into the house with the children, Paul following with her suitcase.

Grace was waiting in the hall to greet her daughter-in-law. The twins rushed past her to their grandfather shouting 'Mummy's home.' Katheryn shrugged out of her short leather coat, then, dutifully, she leant forward for Grace to peck her cheek, the coat over her arm.

'Why Katheryn, at last.'

'Hello, Mrs. Earnshaw.'

Grace had never invited Katheryn to call her 'mother' be-cause she was sure Katheryn wouldn't. Anyhow, she was cer-tain she wouldn't want to be a mother to this haughty young creature. Grace Earnshaw was a woman who wanted desperately to stay young and girlish with her son. Now her figure was thickening and any attempts at matiness with Paul were still met with rebuffs. Therefore, the sight of this young girl in her youth and freshness, who held Paul in the palm of her hand, was a constant pain to Grace.

'Did you enjoy the party, Katheryn?' she asked politely.

'Yes, thank you.'

'I've taken the liberty of letting Mrs. Hopkins go and making some tea. Paul says he's got a mouth like parchment.'

Paul took Katheryn's coat from her.

'Thanks,' she said.

She treats him like a porter, Grace thought angrily, and me like a skivvy.

'I'll do the tea,' Katheryn said.

'I've started it,' said Grace. 'I've got the kettle on and the tray laid.'

Katheryn gave in gracefully, with a brief smile.

'Thanks then, if you're sure you don't mind.'

Grace looked affectionately at her son.

'It won't be the first time I've made tea for Paul, will it, son?'

'Obviously not. What a stupid remark, mother.' Paul scowled his irritation.

'Sorry, dear,' Grace said huffily, 'I'm not a clever conversationalist, I'm afraid, like your smart friends.' She turned back to Katheryn. 'You go on in and I'll bring the tea in.'

'No tea for me, thanks,' Katheryn said, 'I've not long ago had a cup of coffee.'

From the foot of the stairs Paul said, 'You had coffee with Jinny Jane?'

'Yes, and her sister.'

'Oh really,' Grace said, forgetting her resentment, 'where was all this, then?'

'I ran Jinny to her sister's at Windsor,' Katheryn replied, 'she had no car. They insisted on giving me coffee.'

'Fancy,' Grace said, 'Jinny Jane. Such a lovely face she has.'

Katheryn was silent, remembering Jinny's face as they entered the tiny house in a back street of Windsor.

'Listen, kid,' Jinny had said, her face suddenly alight,' 'I've had more abortions than you've had hot dinners, but this is one abortion I'm bloody glad I didn't have.' And she clasped a small boy to her in a frenzy of adoration, laughing and crying at the same time. 'Hey, kid, it's yer mum.' As she had watched, Katheryn had wondered why *she* was unable to show such emotion over *her* children. Jinny's sister, an older homely woman, had reproved Jinny for swearing in front of the child.

'Oh, this is Susan, my big sister,' Jinny said, 'quite different from me, she's glad to say, and if you're wondering why she lives in a rabbit hutch while I'm loaded, it's because she and her old man are too bloody stiff-necked to take help.'

Susan sighed and looked helplessly at Katheryn.

'There are some things our Jinny can never understand,' she said.

Katheryn detached herself from thoughts of Jinny Jane to find Grace staring at her disapprovingly, and Paul suspiciously.

She smiled at them both.

'I'll take your case up,' Paul said.

Katheryn went into the sitting-room where her daughters were climbing all over their grandfather. Desmond put them aside and stood up to kiss his daughter-in-law. Unlike his wife, he was quite pleased to have Katheryn Scarlett as his son's wife, even though he had, for many years on Marbrook Council, been at loggerheads with her pompous ass of a father. This girl had money, too, a not unimportant factor to a man like Desmond Earnshaw who, prosperous himself, loved money and what it could buy.

'Katheryn, my dear, you look very lovely today.'

'Thank you.'

Katheryn had never called Desmond Earnshaw 'father' but she did sometimes use the name the twins had fastened on to him when they first started to talk – 'Granad'. She said now to the children:

'Don't worry Granad, let him have his tea in peace.'

Sinking down again, Desmond smiled.

'They don't worry me, bless 'em, two little beauties like their mother.'

'Lucy is like Paul,' Katheryn said, sitting down opposite her father-in-law, 'and some say Linda is like Gaynor. Gaynor was so podgy as a child, I hope Linda won't be.'

Coming in with the tea, Grace Earnshaw said:

'Oh, I nearly forgot to tell you, Katheryn. Mrs. Hopkins said your sister stayed last night here and went off early this morning.'

Katheryn was surprised. 'Gay did? I wonder why? She knew we'd be away.'

'Perhaps she came to see young Thompson,' Paul suggested.

'He works away now, I think,' Katheryn said.

'He was possibly home for the week-end.'

'And what does Gaynor intend to do now?' asked Grace.

'She's still at University,' said Katheryn.

'Yes, well, I mean, she doesn't have to be, does she? She'll have money now from your father's estate.'

'I think she intends to marry,' said Katheryn.

'Not the Thompson boy? Oh dear,' Grace shook her head. 'Yes, I've heard she's been seen with him. Freda Thompson boasts about it I believe. "My son and Gaynor Scarlett from the Manor House. Such a pity and if he grows up anything like his ignorant blustering father." I mean, with Gaynor's money now, she could have anyone.'

'For Chrissake, mother!' said Paul, 'who in hell is anyone? What's wrong with young Thompson anyway?'

Before Grace could answer this attack, Desmond said mildly, 'I did hear in Council at one time that the boy was articled to a firm of solicitors somewhere, doing quite well.'

Linda and Lucy were delving into a tin of biscuits and fighting over the contents. Quickly Katheryn bent down and picked up the tin, giving a light slap to each contestant.

'You've both had enough, you'll be sick. Now sit quietly or you'll go to bed.'

Cold with the children, too, she is, Grace thought, not a bit motherly. Having been away from her kids all week-end, you'd think she'd be extra loving now. I know I used to be after I'd left Paul. Whatever possessed my son to marry her? She said as much to Desmond as they drove home after tea. Having heard it all many times before, Desmond replied automatically, 'It was always one-sided, Grace, you can never accuse Katheryn of leading him on. I quite like the girl myself, in spite of her parents.'

'She was crazy for that man, Lloyd,' Grace said. 'Disgusting, only a kid she was then.'

'Just a schoolgirl crush,' Desmond said. 'She was young and susceptible and that feller certainly had more than his share of charm.'

'Paul should have had more pride than to take another man's leavings,' Grace said.

'Oh come now,' Desmond protested. 'Hardly leavings, Grace; you said yourself she was only a kid. Lloyd went for more experienced women than the little Katheryn Scarlett.'

As he drove along he mused, my little Greer, for instance, the voluptuous Maggie Petch, Jinny Jane and a hundred more. Desmond sighed as he turned into the driveway of his home. He knew not whether he sighed with envy of the deceased David Lloyd, or relief at the reprieve David Lloyd had given *him* in that Courtroom what seemed now a long, long time ago.

'Paul and Katheryn will make it, you see,' Desmond assured his wife, 'once they've settled down.'

'It's a loveless marriage on her part,' Grace said, 'and sometimes it frightens me.'

Katheryn came into the bedroom and closed the door. Paul was lying on the outside of the bed in his pyjamas smoking a cigarette.

'Where the hell have you been?'

Katheryn picked up her nightdress and walked with it to the far end of the room where she started to undress.

'With Mabel, she's been crying. I've given her some brandy and two aspirins to make her sleep.'

'What's wrong with Mabel?'

'Her boy-friend's broken the engagement. He's found another girl.'

'Good,' said Paul, 'now she won't leave. We'd never get another Mabel. The kids adore her, too.'

Katheryn wriggled her frothy nightgown over her body.

'Rather a selfish attitude, isn't it?'

'I thought you disliked sentiment.'

'One can still show a little pity,' she said.

He got up off the bed and stubbed out his cigarette in an ashtray beside the bed.

'Katheryn.'

'Yes?'

'Don't you want to know where I went to last night?'

'If you want to tell me.'

'Damn you, you couldn't ask, could you?'

She made no reply, just picked up a brush and started brushing her hair.

'You like to keep your pretty little head buried in the sand, don't you, all the dirt nicely swept under the carpet.'

She put down the brush.

'I like to think there isn't any dirt,' she said evenly. She turned to go through to their bathroom, but he strode across the room and grabbed her.

'You're a hard bitch.' Then his tone changed to pleading. 'Love me, Katheryn, just a little.'

She gave a little laugh and slipped out of his grasp.

'Paul, not now. I want to clean my teeth.'

She turned from him but savagely he twisted her round again.

'Are you denying me my rights?'

'You sound like a bad film.'

'Are you?'

'No.' She looked at him squarely. 'Is there any reason why I should?'

He let go of her and turned away.

'Get your teeth cleaned then, and come to bed.'

When she came to him the scent of her perfume mingled with the spicy fresh smell of toothpaste. As always when he took her slim young body in his arms, he found himself trembling. It was like taking a virgin schoolgirl.

'I love you, Katheryn, I love you.'

He waited for her answering cry 'I love *you*.' It never came, just the usual sigh and ecstatic shudder as he thrust himself into her. Oh yes, she enjoyed that all right. He knew he was adequate for her in that way. For a moment he forgot and soared into ecstasy with her; then, as passion died, the old depression rode him.

If only she would fondle him afterwards and murmur tender endearments the way lovers did after the act, but she never had, she never would, he thought in despair.

He called her 'Katie, Katie.'

Immediately she stiffened and moved away from him.

'Don't call me that. My name's Katheryn.'

'Gay calls you "Katie". You used to let *him* call you "Katie".'

She lay silent. He persisted. 'That bloody Lloyd called you "Katie".'

'Then I was a child,' she said coldly. 'Now I'm a woman. Nicknames are absurd.'

'You've never seen any other man but him, have you? Not even bloody Rackstraw for all his big man charm.'

Her body went taut as it always did when subjected to these brutal attacks, like when Gaynor had said almost the same thing. 'You never even really see your lovely children.'

'Have you?' Paul demanded.

She yawned again, relaxed now.

'I don't know what you mean.'

'Oh Christ!' said Paul. 'If I didn't feel like crying, I could laugh, it's so bloody ironical. I got what you wanted so much to give to him – your precious virginity.'

'You had it because I chose to give it to you,' Katheryn replied steadily. 'And now please may we go to sleep?'

He reached up and put out the light.

'Good night,' he said and turned away from her.

In her bed miles away, Dorothy Trent lay thinking happily of the future and how soon she could contact Reggie. But her plans were doomed to be deferred. After the party Reggie went into a nursing home for a few days and, immediately he came out, he left with Lady Tabitha for two months holiday in Jamaica.

Dorothy went with Paul Earnshaw, still in her capacity as secretary-mistress, to Stockholm the day Reggie left with Tabitha for Jamaica, and later to Amsterdam and Rome.

During her husband's absence, Katheryn went out many times with Derren Rackstraw. She enjoyed the pleasures he found for her – opera, ballet, concerts, theatres. He played on her sensitive mind with the fine skill of a lover playing with her body and she found great physical excitement in his arms when she danced with him after an intimate dinner. She knew that he wanted her. She wanted him, too, but it pleased her to keep him at bay. Also, Katheryn had an ingrained respect for the marriage vows that made her despise those who indulged in affairs.

As for Rackstraw, he knew he would enjoy teaching her about sex when the time came as, he suspected, young Earnshaw had never been allowed to do, and the other man had not *lived* to do. How her marriage to Paul Earnshaw had come about, Derren Rackstraw just could not understand. True they had apparently been teenage sweethearts, but the advent of David Lloyd had put an end to all that. What then had sent Katheryn back to Paul Earnshaw and why did *he* take *her* when she so obviously made him miserable? Derren Rackstraw pondered on these things, and on his own involvement with Katheryn. He knew with certainty now that they would have an affair and he wondered if he would be able to forget her when the affair ended and she had gone.

CHAPTER TWELVE

THEY sat, side by side, in the front seats of her old Austin on the fringe of the woods. It had been raining and the trees still dripped fresh spring tears on to the fragrant grass. The odd thing was, he felt no leaping excitement now at being with her alone, in fact, the excitment in their relationship had died completely in the past few weeks as their fears grew and now it was an awful certainty. She'd been to the doctor today in the next town. It was the first time, he thought, that spring held no enchantment for him.

'We'll have to tell mum now,' Diana said bleakly.

He ran his fingers distractedly through his hair.

'If only I could raise the money . . .'

Her voice was razor sharp. 'What for?'

'You know what for. Gin and hot baths didn't work, did they?'

'I don't want to get rid of it now, Gary. I love you. I want your baby.'

'For God's sake, Di, not this way.'

'Why not, if we're married?'

His voice grew shrill with shock.

'Married? How could I get married and keep a woman and child?'

Tears in her voice now, she said: 'I'm not a woman – I'm darling Di who you're supposed to love.'

Tears ran down her cheeks.

Automatically almost he took her in his arms.

'I know, love, I know. It was lovely, but I never thought of this. I always assumed that you . . .'

She drew slightly away from him.

'That I what?'

'Well, you know . . .'

'I know what *you* think, Gary,' she gulped noisily. 'I'll never forget how you were when I first told you I was late. You were suddenly like a stranger, downright cruel the way you spoke to me then.'

'Well, love, I naturally thought that you'd know what to do.'

'Like a common tart?'

'Don't be silly, Di, but I thought that girls these days are supposed to know how to look after themselves, what with the pill and all that.'

'Why should I be on the pill? I was a virgin, wasn't I?'

'I know, love. I suppose we should have discussed it. To think how we went on and never mentioned that side of it.'

Her voice hard, she said:

'I trusted you. Besides, it would have spoilt it to talk about sordid things like that. It would have destroyed all the romance, if you know what I mean.'

Common she is, he thought; she sounds and talks commonly. She moved closer to him.

'I trusted you, Gary,' she said again. 'I never thought . . .' She turned and one of her small breasts came warm against his hands. Pity for her choked him suddenly.

'Oh, Di.'

He drew her against him and put his cheek against hers.

'What are we going to do? We can't marry for ages and ages – I've got nothing. Where would we live?'

She lifted her head. There was no trace of tears in her voice now.

'With mum,' she said promptly and practically, 'until you're qualified, that is, and we can start to save. After the baby's born I can leave it with mum and go out to work so we can put some money away. Mum wouldn't charge us much for our keep and she adores babies. She'd be in her element, after she gets over the first shock, of course, and she's ever so fond of you, Gary. We'll have to marry, darling, for the sake of the baby.'

This time he was the one to draw away.

'You've got it all worked out haven't you?'

'Someone had to. We couldn't just drift on hoping for a miracle.'

Oh God, how was he going to tell Gaynor? The past weeks had been bad enough, phoning her secretly, writing and receiving letters at the office, even getting time off to sneak up to meet her for an hour or two in the afternoons. How unsatisfactory those meetings had been, though, and how puzzled and unhappy Gay was at the change in him.

'A miracle,' he said bleakly. 'Yes, that's what we do want – a bloody miracle. God, I hate the idea of bumming for charity.'

Coldly she answered him:

'You mean you hate the idea of living with my mum and dad.'

Did he? Yes, he did. They were all right as landlords, but could he live with them as one of the family, having to endure the corny jokes, Arthur Bridges belching and Edith saying archly, 'Come in Vicar. Really Dad!' and Edith's drivelling conversations: 'And they've got colour telly, I mean, I don't know how they do it, I says to dad only last week, I says, that man's bin out of work more than he's in it and they've got colour telly.' Oh Christ!

'A little while ago,' Diana said, 'you were tickin' me off for being a snob and telling me how marvellous my parents were.'

'It's not that,' he said. 'I wanted to get a home of my own when I was ready. I'm not ready.' He groaned. 'Oh hell, I had such high hopes of making it big. Now it seems I'm just like my poor bloody father. He was always going to make the big time one day and where is he now – bloody nowhere – he's pathetic. Christ! What a family – dad and Greer and now me – all bleeding failures.'

She turned his face gently to hers. There were tears of his own on his cheeks. Anxiously she said:

'If you really love me, Gary, we *could* make it one day, when you're qualified. It might be a bit hard at first, but if I work too ... but you've got to love me, darling; you've got to love me.' Her voice broke, she started to sob noisily. 'Oh Christ, sometimes I wish you'd never come to Harlow, Gary.'

He stroked her hair and murmured sympathetic noises to her. After a while her sobs died down. She lay against him, her body still shuddering from the weeping. When she was calm he put her gently away from him.

'Come on then,' he said, 'we'd better go and tell your mum.'

She stroked his face.

'It's bad for you, Gary, I know,' she said, 'but it's worse for me, you see, in the mornings I feel so sick I want to die.'

Her simple plaintive statement stirred him to pity.

'My poor little Di,' he said.

'I don't mind if you love me, Gary, honestly.'

'I love you, Di,' he said. His heart was heavy in him, like lead.

Edith Bridges swung the saucepan with an angry flourish, as if she were emptying boiling water over a victim instead of draining potatoes into the sink.

'An' it was bloomin' ages before she even offered us a cup o' tea, wasn't it, Dad?'

Arthur Bridges, from behind the Sunday paper, agreed. 'Yeh, Mother, no one could say they hung the bloomin' flags out fer us, eh?'

Edith tipped the potatoes back into the saucepan and put it back on the stove.

'Don't know who they think they are, their house isn't even as big as this one *and* most of the houses on their estate is Council houses, and look it, eh Arthur?'

Arthur grunted agreement. He wanted to read the paper. Sunday wasn't Sunday if you couldn't get stuck into the *Sunday Mirror*. This Sunday Edith had made him wash and change into his best suit, instead of going down the pub for a Sunday pint in his casual clothes, and she'd yanked him off on this trip across country to Gary's people. She might have known they wouldn't exactly put out the red carpet. Now that they were home again, he wanted some peace.

'I said to her, I said,' Edith went on, 'I said my daughter was a nice respectable girl till your son came along and, do you know what she said?'

'I don't want to know, Mum,' Diana said unhappily, looking up from her baby knitting. 'You sound like a bloody cheap novel. I told you not to go, didn't I? I mean, they weren't exactly marvellous to *me* when Gary took me there. Polite, oh yes, but my God, you could see what they were thinking – he's lumbered himself with this when he could've had Miss Gaynor Scarlett from the Manor House. Oh yes,' she added bitterly, 'it stuck out a bloomin' mile, even Gary couldn't deny it.'

'Where *is* Gary?' Edith asked.

'Upstairs swotting,' Diana replied wearily, 'where he's bin

most of the bloomin' day. You could've left me alone in the house with a eunuch and I'd have had more fun.'

'Now then, Di,' Edith said, 'let's have none of that dirty talk.' Resuming her grievance on the Thompsons she went on: 'When I tried to tell her how sorry I was about her great sorrow, you know, that daughter of hers, Greer, dying like that, she shut me up as if she was Lady Muck.'

'Oh no!' Diana cried, 'you didn't mention *that*. My God! What tact!'

'Why not?' said Edith huffily, going through her aggressive motions now with the sprouts. 'We're all gonna be the same family, aren't we, and I thought, one mother to another, you know, knowin' how it feels . . .'

'Oh Jeeze,' Diana said wearily, 'you're like a bloomin' steam roller, mum.'

Edith swung round.

'Oh, am I? And where would you be now, Miss, I'd like to know, without me and yer dad?'

Arthur looked round the paper.

'Now, Mother, Di, it's no use gettin' at each other. I know you're both upset, but the thing's done and we can't do owt about it, as they say in Coronation Street. At least, the Thompsons said they'd come to the wedding.'

Diana shook her head despairingly.

'They can please themselves,' she said listlessly, 'I don't bloody care either way.'

'And swearin',' Edith said, as she swung the sprouts saucepan back on the stove, 'that's somethin' you never used to do, our Di.'

'Before and after,' Diana said with a thin smile, 'and this is after.'

'I'll call Gary down,' Arthur said. He got up, folded his paper neatly and put it on the chair.

Upstairs Gary lay on the bed, his books beside him. He had tried to swot, but his mind just wouldn't work. His thoughts veered miserably from the prospect of his coming confrontation with Gay to the talk he'd had with his parents last week-end when he'd taken Di home to meet them. Freda had waited until Diana had gone up to bed, and then she had started. Dad, surprisingly, had said very little. It seemed it was mum Gary had let down most. She'd had such high hopes of him after her sorrow over Greer.

'The girl's common, Gary, ever so workin' class.'

'Hell, mum, so are we.'

'I know,' Freda had said wistfully, 'but I always thought *you*'d get out of it with young Gaynor now. Such a nice refined girl, that, real class and not a bit of a snob. Yer dad and me got real fond of Gaynor and now . . .'

'I didn't love her mum, – not enough.'

'No?' Freda had said sharply, 'then you gave a bloomin' good imitation of it at one time, before you went into them wretched digs in Harlow. I wish to God you'd never gone there, you was all right before that, before *she* got her hooks into you.'

Freda had nodded angrily towards the door where poor Diana had gone through half an hour before to her lonely bed.

'They're not sleepin' together in *my* house,' Freda had said to her husband, 'not till they're married. It wouldn't be right. I know what dirty things they've done, but I'm not condonin' it.'

'Poor little Gaynor,' Freda said to Gary. 'Does she know yet?'

'No. I'm seeing her soon.'

'She'll take it ever so hard.'

'She's not our kind, Mum.'

'She's *your* kind, Gary, you were meant for a better life, like what our poor Greer wanted. With Gaynor you'd have got it, known the right people. With this one you'll drop right back.'

Gary had listened wearily to his mother's recriminations which, after all, were but an echo of his own thoughts, but his father's words at parting had cut him most of all.

'Reception in the Scouts' hut, son, bit diff'rent from the Island Hotel, yer mother would've loved that. Always thought the Island Hotel was Mecca, yer mother did. Times she's said to me: "Bound to go there when our Gary weds Gaynor". Ah well, the way things've turned out, I'm glad I'm not on the Council now. At least down the allotments I'm on me own – the only ones there who can mock me are the birds.'

'More pie, Gary?' Edith Bridges asked.

'No thank you. It was very nice.'

'You haven't asked how yer parents were, Gary,' Edith said, as she shovelled more plum and apple tart on to her husband's plate.

Gary lifted his head.

'Oh no. How were they?'

'Not exactly overjoyed at seein' us.'

'Oh, I'm sorry. Mum is always shy at first with strangers. I remember she . . .'

He stopped. He had almost told them how she was shy at first with Gaynor. He mustn't think now of Gaynor.

'I'd hardly call it shyness,' said Edith coldly.

'Mum,' Diana said, 'give it a rest, eh? You shouldn't have gone uninvited. If anyone came to my place uninvited, I know how I'd feel.'

Unable to stop himself Gary said:

'Only you haven't got a place, Di.'

Diana put down her spoon and fork and stared at him with startled accusation. Before she could answer, Edith put in soothingly:

'Now then, Gary, that's daft. Of course she's got a place, and so have you. This is your home as long as you want it. It's lovely havin' you here, en't it Dad? I mean, I always thought of you as one of the family right from the start and we got no-one else, Dad an' me. It'll be ever so lonely when you *do* go.'

Diana's eyes had filled with easy tears. Unashamedly Gary took her hand.

'I'm sorry, love.'

Edith regarded them fondly.

'There. It'll work out all right in the end, you see. I'm not gonna pretend it'll be easy.' She laughed complacently. 'I mean, I'm gonna have to stop meself spoilin' that baby when it comes, aren't I? I mean, with madam here and her Dr. Spock notions. As long as it don't cry during Sale of the Century, eh Dad?'

Gary smiled with the rest, but his mind had veered back to Gay. Tomorrow he would see her. It couldn't, it mustn't be for the last time.

'I was never in your class, Gay,' he said. 'You should never have taken up with me in the first place, then I wouldn't be so bloody miserable now at losing you.'

They sat together on a settee in the tiny lounge of the cottage on Marbrook Manor estate by the river.

'You were my world,' Gaynor said. She said it simply, with no drama or accusation in her voice, just despair.

'No Gay, your world is very different from mine.' Self pity made his voice tremble. 'My destiny is to marry and rear snivelling kids in some two by four box – kids who I shall come to regard as marvels – and I shall make stupid family jokes like Diana's father does and sink comfortably into my little niche in a horrible machine.'

'It doesn't have to be like that,' Gaynor said tonelessly, her eyes dead. 'You and she are young . . .' She stopped. My God, she thought, in spite of it all, here am I actually consoling him the way I've always done. That must be the only way he's ever seen me, a shoulder to cry on.

'You and I wouldn't have been like that,' he said. 'Together we had vision, we could . . . Oh God, what chance do I have without *you*?'

She turned on him then, her voice suddenly suffused with anger. Life leapt into her dull eyes.

'I, I, I. All this is how *you* feel, Gary, what you're missing. What about *me*? Have you stopped to consider how I feel in all this – what you've done to *me*?'

He groaned and tried to hold her, but she moved away from him.

'Oh Christ! You're right, oh Gay darling, I'm a selfish pig.'

'Gary,' she said, her voice hard and tight, 'you wanted this girl so much that you had to have her. You didn't care about me then. Why all the devotion now?'

'Haven't *you* ever had a moment of madness?'

She looked back at him steadily.

'No. I've loved you since we were children. That has kept me warm all through the good and the bad times – that and the thought that you loved me too. Now I've got to start all over again. I don't know how I'm going to do it.'

Her voice was controlled again. Only her eyes betrayed her misery.

'I can't lose you altogether, Gay. Don't go right out of my life, please.'

She gave a bitter little laugh.

'How can I stay?'

'We could see each other sometimes. I must still see you, Gay.'

She laughed again, loud and harsh.

'Rub salt into my wounds, is that what you want to do? And I used to think you were so fine, so idealistic. Now you want to make me into a tramp, a bit on the side, away from your wife. Oh, Gary,' the harshness left her voice, her lips trembled. 'I wonder if I ever really knew you, the real you. Did I see someone who never existed?'

'You should've stayed in your own class, shouldn't you?' he said, his voice ugly and sullen. 'We're poles apart, we always have been really. You could never have gone native with *me* and I could never have come up to the Manor House with *you*. I know I knew it all the time, but you never faced reality.'

'With love,' Gaynor said unhappily, 'the comparison would never arise. There was no difference between us before *she* came along and took you so easily from me.'

'Not easily, darling. You were always in my mind?'

'Even in *her* bed?'

'It's possible to love two people at the same time.'

'But unfortunately you can't have both.'

'You are my real love, Gay. Don't leave me.'

'I'm not,' she said, '*you're* leaving *me*. You came here to tell me so.'

'But you mustn't go right out of my life. Perhaps one day . . .'

'Perhaps one day you'll tire of her and come back to me. Oh no, Gary, I may have been blind. Leave me a little pride, please.'

'I love you, Gay.'

She stood up.

'So much so that now you come to tell me you're fathering another girl's child. Somehow, I can't think of that as love. I'm trying to wish you well, but part of me is hating you both.

Living with her parents won't be easy for you. The kitchen's never been built that's big enough for two women to share. I shall find myself hoping that some of the misery rubs off on you. I'm not noble, Gary, just human, and now, if you don't mind, you'd better go. I've let the cottage to a student friend of mine and he's due here soon to take some measurements.'

Reluctantly Gary rose too and held his hands out to her in one last plea.

'Not the end, Gay, after all we've been to each other.'

'The end came,' she said coldly, 'when you first set eyes on *her*. Good-bye.'

Paul said: 'I heard the car on the road before you turned into the drive. I knew it was an M.G.B.G.T. They have a distinctive sound like . . .'

Gaynor smiled forlornly and flung her coat on to a chair.

'Like a pot bubbling.'

'Yes, a kind of gobbling noise.'

Listlessly she asked him: 'Where's Katie?'

'Gone to fetch the twins back from a party. Have you come to stay?'

'Just for the night, if you'll have me.'

He smiled at her. 'We shan't chuck you out. I'll just yell through and tell Mabel there'll be one extra for dinner.'

'Don't worry. I'm not all that hungry.'

He looked at her sharply before he went to the door.

'Mabel, make it one more tonight. Miss World's come to dinner.'

Paul indicated his half empty glass.

'I was just having a pre-dinner snifter. Want one?'

'Yes please.'

'What would you like?'

'A good strong Scotch.'

His eyebrows arched in surprise. Usually Gaynor didn't drink anything stronger than a sherry before dinner. Watching her covertly, he said:

'Hangover? Hair of the dog? Students' revels, protest marches, chained to railings . . .?'

She smiled wanly and shook her head.

'Just fed up.'

He sloshed Scotch into a glass for her and refilled his own.

'So you're fed up.'

'To my bloody teeth.'

He hunched his shoulders. 'Me too, most of the time. Life's a bloody circus.'

She took a good swig of her drink and shuddered. Tears came into her eyes.

'Too strong?'

'No I . . .' She sank down into a chair and put the glass on a table beside the chair. Then suddenly she began to cry. Instantly Paul was on his knees beside her.

'Baby, don't. What's the matter?'

She put her arms round his neck like a child seeking comfort.

'Oh Paul!'

'Tell me, baby. What is it?'

At first her words tumbled out, punctuated by sobs, in such a jumble that he couldn't understand, then more coherently she cried:

'I'd planned such a lovely wedding, and then the furniture, and children and . . .'

He held her against him whilst the frenzy of her grief lasted, then, as she quietened, he laid her gently back in her chair. He picked up the glass and held it to her lips.

'Take a good long drink. It'll do you good.'

She took a gulp of the whisky and pushed the glass back at him.

'Young Thompson?'

'He's got a girl into trouble, his landlady's daughter.'

Paul was silent a moment, then he said gently:

'I didn't think that sort of thing happened any more.'

She stared at him accusingly.

'Would it have been different if she hadn't been in trouble? I mean, if he really loved me, he couldn't have done that with her.'

'And that,' Paul said, still on his knees beside her, 'is where you're wrong, baby. He *could* love you and do that with her. It happens all the time.'

Gaynor sniffed. He handed her his hanky and she blew her nose.

'Not in *my* code.'

'Not many of us live by such a high code, love.'

'Gary did, once.'

'Maybe you only thought he did. Childish ideals are apt to be blown sky-high when the subjects grow up. You're so young, Gay, you'll meet someone else, someone more mature and then you'll wonder what all the fuss was about.'

'*You* didn't,' she said, 'you always wanted Katie, no one else, and you were lucky, you got her.'

Was I, he thought? Katie. If only she *was* 'Katie' to me.

'Must he marry her, couldn't she get an abortion?'

Affronted she said:

'Do you think I'd let him do *that*?'

'If he loves you, and you love him.'

'He can't love me,' she said woodenly. 'If he'd loved me, he wouldn't have touched *her*. Not Gary. He must love her and now they'll have their baby and I . . . I'm out in the cold all alone.'

'Hush, baby. You're not alone. You've got us and, very soon, you'll find someone else.'

'No, I never will. Oh, Paul, I'd planned such a lovely wedding – I'd planned that you would give me away and Katie would be my matron of honour.'

'Why me?'

'Well,' she gulped back a fresh spate of tears, 'well, you and Katie are all the family I've got.' She smiled miserably. 'Your wedding was such a beautiful, shining affair. It was lovely.'

He grimaced.

'With your parents looking down their toffee noses at mine, and *my* parents patronizing as hell; oh yes, a lovely wedding.'

'It didn't matter about the parents,' Gaynor said, 'it was you and Katie who mattered. She was such a lovely bride, too. I know I couldn't have looked as good, but . . .' – her voice shook, – 'Gary always said I was pretty. He . . .' Sobs shook her again – long, deep shuddering sobs – that wracked her whole frame. Paul gathered her against him again. She clung to him, her cheek wet against his – he thought – like one of the twins. He'd never realized before just how fond he was of his sister-in-law.

She was so vulnerable, not intact like Katheryn.

'He always seemed to love me so much till that beastly girl came along.'

'I know. It happens, love, all the time.'

'I never thought it would to us. We had so much.'

'Were you lovers?'

'Not in *that* way. We didn't have to be.'

'Maybe if you had been, this wouldn't have happened.'

'No, not Gary and me, we belonged without that, we knew that would come later, but now . . .'

She seemed in danger of collapsing again. He shook her gently.

'Now, Gay darling, don't . . .'

She gave a long, shuddering sigh and sat up.

'I'm sorry Paul.'

She dried his cheek with his hanky.

'I've made you all wet.'

'I don't mind. The twins frequently use my face as blotting paper.'

'I was cheap,' Gaynor said. 'I said spiteful, bitchy things about him living with *her* parents. Now I wish I hadn't. It was stupid and cheap and unnecessary.'

'Forget it, love,' Paul said. 'I'm surprised you didn't kick his teeth in.' He lifted his head. 'I hear Katheryn's car and the chatter of the young. I'm afraid they're back. Would you rather go upstairs?'

She smiled wanly and shook her head.

'No. I'm all right now, Paul, and thanks.'

He took her hands and pulled her to her feet.

'I'll be giving you away to some lucky chap, yet, you see.'

'No, it's too late. I don't want anyone else.'

The twins flung themselves on her in tumultuous welcome. She bent down to kiss their sweet, shining faces and fought back her tears.

That night, in the double bed she shared with her husband, Katheryn Earnshaw lay awake, her arms embracing her pillow.

'I'd like to shoot the careless young bastard,' Paul said. 'Thoughtless idiot.'

'He's typical of his class.'

'Rot. He's a human being. Class doesn't exist any more.'

'Breed will out,' Katheryn said. 'I find it humiliating, our family being stood up by people like the Thompsons.'

Paul laughed and put a hand caressingly on her thigh.

'Sometimes you're awfully like your mother, a right prim little snob.'

'Thanks.'

She moved so that his stroking hand fell away from her leg. Once, long ago, David had teasingly accused her of being a snob.

'Well, go to sleep now,' Paul said, 'there's nothing we can do for poor old Gay. Only time can help. At the moment she swears it's first love, last love, but you never know. You die of many things, but seldom, they say, die of love, which is one blessing for the less fortunate of us.'

He turned away and was soon asleep. Katheryn remembered David's voice that time in the woods. 'The first love always hurts the most, though it's seldom the last.' But you were wrong there, my David, for me it was the last. For Gaynor it's the last, too. David seemed very close tonight – David.

CHAPTER THIRTEEN

'I'VE never 'phoned him before when he's been abroad.' Katheryn said doubtfully.

'Would you rather I went home and rang him, then?' Desmond offered, 'but I was on my way back from Santon's place and, being so close to here, thought I'd call in and give you a chance of a word with Paul. I can easily do it from home though if you'd rather.'

'No, no, of course not.'

One hand hovered near the telephone, with the other hand Katheryn gently massaged her brow, as if to try to iron out her doubt.

'You see,' Desmond explained, 'when Grace told me Paul was in Amsterdam again, I thought, what a bit of luck, he could save me a journey. It won't take him long to do my errand.'

'I'm sure Paul wouldn't mind,' Katheryn said.

'Well, that's the hotel number,' Desmond said, indicating a piece of paper beside the telephone. 'I thought if you rang him first you could have a little chat with him. Be nice for you, him being away.'

'He's only been gone two days.' Katheryn said. She lifted the telephone. Desmond sighed. Perhaps Grace was right. Katheryn *was* cold. Most girls would have jumped at the chance of a word with an absent husband. Desmond wondered if the young women of Katheryn and Paul's set, with whom she frequently played golf and bridge, ever got close to her. He thought not. He had never heard of one particular woman in that set who was Katheryn's special friend.

He watched his daughter-in-law now as she booked the call. Lovely she looked in her yellow blouse and black velvet jeans, the picture of an elegant young wife of a prosperous man, fitting easily into the gracious setting the man had provided for her.

'Would you like a drink?' Katheryn asked him.

'Yes if you'll join me.'

'Why not?'

They went into the sitting room together.

'Shall I mix them?' Desmond offered.

'Yes please. Choose yours. I'll have a Vodka-Martini please.'

As Desmond dispensed the drinks he said:

'I suppose the twins are asleep?'

Katheryn grimaced.

'Upstairs, but not, I fear, asleep. They chat for ages, and often fight. I threatened them with dire punishment if they fight or swop beds tonight.'

'Little monkeys.' Desmond smiled indulgently. 'You're lucky, you and Paul, you have two lovely girls. Cheers.' He took a sip of his drink and looked at her covertly. 'They only need a brother now to make it quite perfect.'

'Little boys scare me,' Katheryn said, 'I can find nothing to say to them.' She looked at her watch. 'Do you think this is a good time to catch Paul in?'

'I should think so. It's dinner time. A man's got to eat even if he is on a high-powered business drive.'

In the hall the telephone rang. Katheryn put down her drink.

'That should be it.'

'You start off,' Desmond said, 'have a word or two with him first, then call me and I'll come out.'

She got up and went out to answer the telephone.

A gutteral voice announced in bored tones the names of the hotel.

'May I speak, please, to a Mr. Paul Earnshaw who's staying there?'

There was a clink then, after a few seconds, an English speaking female voice announced the room number with crisp efficiency as if she were speaking on an office telephone.

'Mr. Earnshaw, please.'

'He's out. Who wants him?'

Quickly, feeling a little sick, Katheryn reacted.

'Mrs. Earnshaw, there is a call from England.'

The crisp voice replied a trifle impatiently.

'All right, put it through.'

Her voice calm and cold, Katheryn said clearly:

'Mrs. Earnshaw, this *is* the call from England.'

There was, what seemed to her an eternity of silence, then the voice spoke again, not confident this time, but halting, unsure.

'Is there a message?'

'Yes, there is,' Katheryn replied sharply. 'Tell him to call his father's home in England as soon as possible. That's all.'

She replaced the receiver with a trembling hand. The trembling sensation was in her legs and stomach now, too. With a great effort she turned to her father-in-law who had come into the hall.

'Paul's out. I left a message for him to ring you when he comes in.'

'Oh good.' Desmond said. 'I'd better finish my drink and get home then in case he rings. Of course, he may be out somewhere dining with a contact or the meeting may still be going on.'

'Probably.' Katheryn said.

'These foreign business trips are not all beer and skittles,' Desmond laughed, 'although most of the wives seem to think they are. Never can make Grace believe that. I expect Paul finds the same with you.'

'Paul works hard.' Katheryn said woodenly.

Desmond sighed. Yes, sometimes Katheryn could be heavy going. He wondered how Paul managed to break the ice. Perhaps it was Katheryn's fault that Paul was wild the way it was rumoured he was.

'Yes, well,' Desmond said. He drained his drink. 'Better be on my way in case Paul rings. Perhaps you'll ring Grace when I've left and tell her what to say in case Paul's call comes through to her before I get home.'

He gave Katheryn the message for Amsterdam and left.

In the morning at half past nine, for the first time since her marrage, she telephoned Paul's office.

'I'd like to speak,' she said, 'to Mr. Earnshaw's secretary.'

'I'm sorry,' came the reply, 'but Miss Trent is in Amsterdam with Mr. Earnshaw on business. Would Miss Flack be able to help you?'

'Thank you, no.' Katheryn said calmly, and hung up.

Little facts slotted sickeningly into place. Gunner-Cart-wright's sly insinuations about Paul's lovely secretary, Paul's strange absences, his irritable weariness after late business sessions.

The maid, Mabel, stood in the kitchen doorway.

'The twins are ready, ma'am.'

'Oh yes, my mother-in-law's collecting them at 10 o'clock isn't she?'

'That's right.' A hesitant smile crept over the girl's sad face. She seldom smiled now since her lover had jilted her. 'Mrs. Earnshaw's taking 'em back via Windsor so they can see the soldiers march up to the castle for the guard change.'

'That'll be nice,' Katheryn said. 'Well, I shan't be home for lunch so why don't you take an hour or so off, go into town or to the hairdressers or do something to cheer yourself up.'

The little smile died. 'No thank you, ma'am, I'd just as soon stay here. I've no heart for goin' out these days.'

'Well, have a rest then,' Katheryn said. She went into the kitchen and said good-bye to her daughters.

'Be good with Granny,' she warned them.

Katheryn kissed them again and stood looking down at them for a moment. Once Gay and I were small and uncaring like this. Mr. and Mrs. Earnshaw in Amsterdam. How odd it had sounded to hear that woman taking the name Mrs. Earnshaw, like finding yourself suddenly written out of the lead part.

'Well come on then,' Mabel was saying to the children, 'let's go and play quietly upstairs until Granny comes, and let Mummy get away.'

Katheryn drove fast as if she had an appointment and was late. At the edge of the woods she slowed down and cruised along until she came to the wide gateway of her old home. It was the first time she'd been here since her father's death. Someone – Gaynor probably – had made changes. Once inside the gateway, a new fence divided the wide driveway into two, so that now there was a separate roadway leading down through the woods to the cottage and the river. Katheryn took the lane to the cottage, glancing briefly at the big manor house as she passed. There were signs that the Research Institute which acquired it had started using it. Three or four cars stood in front of the house and there was a builders' lorry parked at the side.

A feeling of suffocation enveloped Katheryn as she drove slowly down through the woods. Before the cottage came into view she got out of her car and started to walk. It was May and a sunny warm day, but in here the woods were cold and very dark. She had never noticed before how dark they were. Once they had been so beautiful, now they were sinister and lonely. She turned the bend and caught her breath. There it stood, the cottage, the river a silent, silver ribbon strung along behind it. She stood motionless for a second and then, like one mesmerized, started to walk towards it, her legs leaden, her heart beating wildly. Everything was just the same. Carved in the wall above the porch was the date 1857 with the two ornate stone scrolls around it. Hesitantly her gaze rose to the wooden balcony above as if afraid of what she might see there, but there was nothing save two empty wooden chairs, with protecting canvas half blown off them. There were voices everywhere, but they were only in her heart, the woods were empty and silent. There was the vibrant voice of lovely, wicked Harriet, inviting, mocking; Gay's excited, spilling-over chatter as she waxed eloquent with an amused, attentive David; father's voice, pompous, hypocritical; and David's, deep and intimate as his eyes. 'Why did you come here today Katie Scarlett?' he was saying, 'Because your husband is unfaithful and you know it's your fault, so you come to wallow in self-pity to the place where your heart is chained? I told you you'd marry Paul Earnshaw, didn't I, that day in the woods? You didn't believe me then.' She ran her hands down her body, that treacherous body that made her break faith with her vows and give in to its desires. Oh David, why did you leave me?

She moved forward like one in a trance and pushed open the cottage door. Before she saw *him*, she saw first the marks on the wall where the picture had hung, the picture of the lady with the parasol getting into the steam launch on the river. Her gaze dropped from the wall to the man. He was stooping down examining an electric point. He straightened up to face her as she came slowly into the room. He was wearing the same light blue jeans and black sweater that he had worn when she had first seen him digging alongside the stone steps that led down to the river, that lovely April day so long ago. She saw his beloved face and the dark, tired eyes that looked as if they'd been put in with smudgy fingers. 'David.' She spoke his name with a sigh of thankfulness and then she fell forward, fainting, into his arms.

'My name's not David.'

She opened her eyes. His face blurred in front of her. He was looking at her anxiously.

'It's Hedley,' he said. 'It was my mother's maiden name, silly name really. How are you feeling? Better now?'

His face was in focus now. From the depths of the armchair where he had laid her she looked up at him with bleak eyes.

'Yes, thank you.'

How could she have thought he was David? He had dark eyes and was wearing light blue jeans and a black sweater and there the resemblance ended. His voice was quiet and young, not rich and deep like David's.

'I'm sorry,' she said, 'I went giddy suddenly.'

The dark eyes regarding her were compassionate.

'I reminded you of someone, someone called David?'

She struggled to sit up shaking her head. Through cold lips she said:

'No, no, not really.'

She handed back to him the glass of water he had brought her.

'Would you like something stronger? I have some brandy.'

'No thank you. I'm sorry to have intruded on you. I must go now. I was just passing . . .'

He had been kneeling beside her chair. He got up now.

'You're Katheryn, alias Katie, aren't you?'

'Yes. You must be Gaynor's tenant.'

'Yes, I'm Hedley Strong. I'm only here for a short time. I'm going into the priesthood, you see. My parents are against it and I'm not very welcome at home at the present time, so Gaynor suggested I took sanctuary here during the waiting time. You see, my brothers are conforming and going into the family business.' Again the slow, sweet smile. 'A Roman Catholic father in the family is something they feel ashamed of. You see, they're not Catholics, they're not anything really. My elder brother said, "Why, it's almost as if you were a queer." '

A flicker of interest flitted over the girl's pale face.

'A celibate,' she said, 'won't you mind?'

'I don't think so. I can't answer with complete truthfulness yet.'

He stood looking down at her. He was taller than David. There was no man–woman flash in his eyes as their glances held, yet there was a kind of intimacy, not sex, a special gentleness, something personal to her. She was amazed by it. She had never seen that look in a man's eyes before except when a man looked at children.

'That brandy,' he said, 'I think a little of it will do you good, *and* I have four sausage rolls. Join me before you go on your way.'

'But you were working when I intruded.'

'No, I wasn't, just fiddling with an electric point. Come through to the kitchen, it's cosy in there.'

He took her hands and pulled her up out of the armchair. She stood like a statue, looking neither to right nor left. As if reading the fear of memory in her, he said briskly:

'Gaynor's had the kitchen completely altered and re-decorated. You wouldn't know it now.'

He led the way and she walked with her eyes fixed on some vague point ahead. The tiny kitchen was papered in a bright design of lemons and oranges linked with red nasturtiums and vivid green leaves.

'Bright, isn't it?' Hedley said.

'Shudderingly so,' Katheryn replied.

'One of Gay's student friends did it. He came down one week-end to get rid of his repressions,' Hedley grinned. 'So he put them all on the wall.'

David would have hated it, but David was dead. It didn't matter any more what they did to the cottage. She sat at the kitchen table sipping brandy and munching a sausage roll.

'I shall miss the river when I leave,' Hedley said.

'Yes. It's lovely.'

'Gay tells me you used to swim in the river a lot in summer.'

'Yes, not very hygienic now, I'm afraid.'

'One doesn't care for hygiene when one is young, one sees only the beauty.'

Yes, the beauty and sadness of a summer long gone.

'We have a swimming pool at our house,' Katheryn said, 'very hygienic.'

Through the window she could see two men fishing on the opposite bank.

'An old ex-lock-keeper named Simon Pitman used to fish near the cottage,' she said. 'Gaynor used to swim over to him and he said she disturbed the fish with her chatter.'

'She chattered a lot when I first knew her,' Hedley said.

'But not now.'

'No, not now.'

'What will she do, I wonder?'

He glanced at her sharply.

'Hasn't she told you?'

Katheryn shook her head. 'She hasn't been to see us since . . . not lately. I rang her flat but she wasn't in.'

'She intends to get her degree and then go overseas to teach.'

'Where?'

'I don't think she knows yet. She's still making inquiries.'

Gay abroad. The last one link in the old chain, gone. Speaking her thoughts aloud, she said woodenly, 'There'll be no one left for me then.'

He seemed surprised.

'You'll still have your husband.'

Will I? Paul in Amsterdam with beautiful Dorothy Trent. Shall I offer him a divorce? No, I'm too tired to bother. He must ask me if he wants one. The children will miss him.

'Your husband and your children,' the young man was saying, 'Gay tells me your children are lovely.'

'Yes, I suppose they are. I'm a bad mother.'

He smiled that melancholy sympathetic smile.

'Why? Do you beat them or neglect them?'

'No. I try to feel, but I can't. I just can't feel.'

Oh God, she thought, those eyes of his have got me acting as if I'm in a confessional.

'Why can't I feel?' She asked the question of him desperately, almost angrily as if it were his fault. 'My husband's being unfaithful to me. I mind. I think I'm jealous, but I can't really feel. Why?'

His compassion washed over her like a warm wave.

'Because you're probably still in shock,' he said calmly.

'In shock?'

'In shock over something which may have happened to you, years ago maybe. Shock can last a long time. Another shock might put it right, or sometimes it just has to recede slowly.'

She looked at him with puzzled eyes.

'What about Gay? Is she in shock?'

'Yes, but she's strong.'

'You think she'll find someone else?'

Hedley Strong shook his head. 'No, I don't think so. This Gary appears to have been her whole life. I think now she will look for a different goal, but I don't think it will be another man.'

'You know her well.'

'Yes, I think so.'

'I don't,' Katheryn said, 'but then families seldom know each other do they?'

'Unfortunately, no,' he said, 'that's one of life's biggest tragedies.'

She stood up.

'Well,' she said, 'maybe you'll be in a strong position soon to put the world right. Thank you for sharing your loaves and fishes with me. I feel much better now.'

She held out her hand, he took it in a firm clasp, putting his other one over it.

'The good Samaritan,' she said, 'you've started off well.'

He smiled into her eyes.

'Have you far to drive? Sure you feel up to it?'

'Yes, I'm fine. I shall go up to town and do some shopping.'

He smiled. 'A woman's cure for all ills.'

She stepped back, her eyes feasting on him.

'Thank you again, priest.'

'I don't suppose we shall ever meet again,' he said, 'so Katheryn, good-bye and God go with you.'

'Thank you,' she said, 'and God go with you *too*, but then of course He will, won't He? What a silly thing to say. Good-bye.'

'Champagne,' Derren said, 'this is the first time you've visited my chambers, definitely champagne.'

'In Harrods this morning,' Katheryn said, 'I bought a toothbrush. I didn't think I'd need anything else.'

He paused, the champagne bottle hovering over the ice bucket. Then, his eyes lit with triumph, he carefully bedded the bottle into the ice.

'Now please,' Katheryn said, 'may I phone my maid.'

'Of course.'

She went out into the hall and dialled her home number. Mabel answered her call.

'I shan't be home until tomorrow morning, Mabel. I'm staying in London tonight.'

'Oh, but Madam,' Mabel said in her unnatural telephone voice, 'Mr. Earnshaw rang this morning just after you left to say he was coming back this evening instead of tomorrow night.'

'My plans are made,' Katheryn said, 'will you tell Mr. Earnshaw please that I expect to be home between ten and eleven tomorrow. There's plenty in the deep freeze for you and him if he should be home tonight in time for dinner.'

'Yes, Madam,' Mabel hesitated, then she said, 'May I tell him where you are, Madam, in case he wants to telephone you?'

'It would be no use,' Katheryn said. 'I shall be out with friends. There won't be anything so urgent that it can't wait until the morning.'

'Very good, Madam.'

Katheryn could detect disapproval in Mabel's voice.

'Kiss the twins good night for me. Good-bye.'

'Are you sure, Katheryn?' Derren Rackstraw asked when she went back.

She looked at him steadily.

'Yes, I'm sure. I've wanted to for a long time.'

'And you know *I* have.'

'Yes.'

'So now something has happened,' he said, 'that's made you come to me.'

'No.'

She looked squarely at him and he knew she was lying, the way she had lied to him in Court, without a qualm. Anger mingled with his desire for her.

'It won't be gentle loving.'

'I know. I don't want it to be gentle.'

'Have you had others?'

'Only my husband.'

'As I thought.'

A faint smile wooed her lips.

'You're very romantic. I feel like a criminal answering Counsel.'

'You are,' he said, 'and you're being sentenced.'

She closed her eyes as he came to her.

'Before dinner, sweetheart?' he whispered.

'Before and after.'

She would be passionate, he thought, the way outwardly cold women could be, and the satisfaction temporarily made him forget his anger.

It was the next morning, early, as she lay in his arms, that she told him she was going away.

'When?'

'As soon as possible. I saw the agent yesterday afternoon. There's a villa ready if I want it. I intend to take the children and go.'

He was silent pondering on what could have happened, but it was no use asking her, she would still lie in her pretty teeth.

'For how long?'

'Three weeks perhaps. The villa is in Estepone, complete with a daily maid.' She paused, then she said, 'if I like it, I can buy it. I probably shall.'

The picture of her in Court flashed back to him, proud, haughty little rich bitch. Hard to believe that he now had her against his heart, naked, her body to use as he wished.

'Why don't you come with us, Derren?'

He massaged her soft cheeks with the tips of his fingers.

'I can't get away now. Don't you think you're being very mean?'

'Mean, why?'

'To go now, just as we . . .'

She moved his hand from her face and put it on her leg.

'We can go on when I come back.' She laughed softly. 'Will you be faithful to me while I'm away, Derren?'

'I'm not a stud animal.'

Her hand caressed his leg, moving upwards.

'Aren't you?'

'Bitch.'

She moved so that her light body straddled him. He was amazed at the passion of her loving, like a woman starved. When it was over he kissed her gently. He was always annoyed at the protective instinct she aroused in him.

'One day,' he said, 'we'll go to Spain together, and, for every star in the sky I'll make love to you.'

She tensed beside him.

'Not stars.'

He was silent a moment, then he said gently:

'Why not stars, Katheryn?'

'Stars make me sad.'

So many stars that night, teardrops in a black sky.

Was she vulnerable at last? He made to gather her back into his arms.

'Katheryn.'

She slid easily away from him.

'We must get up, Derren,' she said, 'I have to go home.'

'So I'm being punished,' Paul said.

'I don't understand. I'm taking the children to Spain for a few weeks. I assumed you'd have no objection.'

She stood facing him in the dining-room, dressed in the new trouser suit of brown and white check that she'd bought yesterday at Harrods. He thought, she looks too immaculate to have been off all night with a man. God, I could strangle her, the bitch! I'd like to see those cold eyes bulge with fright if I put my hands round that little white neck.

Controlling his savage urges he said evenly:

'You know I can't get away yet. We can go to Spain later.'

'I'm going now,' Katheryn said.

'I see. This is your revenge.'

Her eyebrows shot up.

'Revenge?'

'For Amsterdam.'

She avoided his eyes, opening her handbag, extracting a pair of ultra-large trendy sunglasses and placing them on the sideboard.

'You know I wasn't alone in Amsterdam, don't you?'

For a second she was silent, then she said:

'Yes. Are you expecting me to do something about it?'

'Christ! Yes!' he shouted. 'Act like a human being, a deceived wife, for Chrissake.'

'Do you want a divorce?'

'You know I bloody don't, but I suppose you've got the evidence if you want to use it.'

'Why should I?'

He gave a muttered oath.

'Don't you care?'

She smiled thinly.

'I thought it was an occupational hazard for directors' wives, accommodating secretaries.'

'It depends on the wives.'

'Then perhaps you'd like to change yours. If you wish Miss Dorothy Trent to take over, please tell me.'

'Dorothy Trent means nothing to me except a shoulder to cry on and she's been a frantic bedmate just when I've needed one.'

A look of distaste crossed Katheryn's face.

'I disgust you, do I? Too bad. And where were *you* last night?'

'I stayed in London.'

'Who with?'

'Friends. No one you'd know.'

'I know all your friends.'

She took a hanky out of her bag, picked up the sunglasses and started to polish them.

'I think not.'

'You could be lying.'

Calmly she agreed with him. 'I could be. Have *you* any right to question me?'

He turned away with an exclamation of despair. 'You've got me with that, haven't you? Just what you've been waiting for. To think I rushed home early afraid you might be unhappy, might care about what I'd done. How big a bloody fool can you be?'

They were silent, he standing shading his eyes with one hand, Katheryn still gently polishing her glasses. Then he said dully:

'When will you be leaving?'

'As soon as a flight can be booked. It won't take me long to pack.'

'I see.'

He waited a second, then he said: 'Shall you be there alone except for the kids?'

'I thought I'd invite Gay to come and stay.'

'She won't. She's taking some important course.'

Katheryn was surprised and showed it.

'How do you know?'

'I rang her and we talked.'

'I rang, but couldn't get a reply.'

'Maybe you didn't try often enough.' He looked at her squarely. 'So you'll be alone out there?'

She shrugged.

'In the light of things is it your business?'

She put the glasses and hanky back in her bag and snapped it shut.

'I must see Mabel about food. Will you be in to lunch?'

'No. I might as well get back to the office and I won't be in to dinner tonight, either.'

She smiled slightly. Dining with Miss Trent to tell her how things stood. As if reading her thoughts, Paul said curtly:

'I'm dining with a client, male. It might interest you to know I'm off women, for the time being, anyway.'

She smiled again and started to walk away.

'For your sake and Miss Trent's I hope it's only temporary.'

For a second hope blazed within him. That was a remark like a jealous wife would make, but Katheryn was looking at him coolly.

'By the way, your father doesn't know, about Amsterdam I mean. I simply said you were out.'

'Thanks.'

'You're welcome,' she said. 'Good-bye.'

As she crossed the hall she thought, I had the chance to end my marriage then. I wonder why I didn't. She looked up and saw the twins sitting at the foot of the wide stairs, each clutching a little Dutch doll in chubby hands.

'Look what Daddy brought, Mummy, from Holland.'

She smiled and moved forward to examine the proffered dolls.

'We must give them names,' Katheryn said, 'Dutch names, now let's think . . .'

Picture of a happy family, Paul thought morosely. One of the twins looked up and saw him. Eagerly came the excited cry: 'Daddy!'

He moved forward to join them. A bloody happy family!

CHAPTER FOURTEEN

It was five days before the wedding when Diana had her miscarriage. She had a week off work to help mum turn what had been her bedroom into a bed-sitter for herself and Gary. Twice Edith had warned her daughter, 'Don't lift that Di. Be careful up them steps, Di, wait till yer dad or Gary gets home and let them do it.' But no, nothing would suffice but that the new curtains should be up and the easy chairs, small bureau and settee in place by the time Gary got home from the office.

'Those antique ornamental plates on the wall make it look like a sitting-room, don't they Mum?'

'Lovely dear. I like plates better'n pictures. You got nice taste, Di.'

Diana sighed.

'I hope Gary thinks so. If we had money, like some people I could name, I could really make a lovely home for him.' She glanced round critically. 'I want it to look nice by the time he gets in so he can see how cosy it's gonna be for us until we get a place of our own.'

'Yes, well,' Edith said doubtfully, '*he* should be the one thinking of the home providing, not *you*. After all, he got you into this mess.'

'It's not a mess, Mum. We love each other.'

Edith gave an impatient flick to a cushion on the settee.

'Yes, well, I'd like to see him pay you a little more attention, proper mopey he's bin lately. No one could say he's bin actin' like an eager bridegroom.' She sniffed. 'But then, I suppose when you jumps the gun like, there isn't a lot to look forward to. Can't be the same, can it, as havin' a virgin bride?'

'Thanks Mum,' Diana cried, 'that's all I bloody need.'

She flung herself down on to the settee and burst into tears. Instantly Edith was contrite. She got down on her knees beside the weeping girl.

'Oh love, I'm sorry. I am truly, pet. I get bitter, I'm afraid and can't stop meself. It's just that I always wanted the best fer you and I sometimes wonder, and I know yer dad does too, if Gary *is* the best.'

'It's that bloody girl,' Diana sobbed, 'that bitch, Gaynor Scarlett, she got her hooks into him when they were kids, and now he's upset because she's upset.'

Edith got up off the floor and straightened her apron.

'Well,' she said reassuringly, 'it'll be O.K. you see. When the dear little baby comes, he'll be all right, will Gary. Ecstatic, you see.'

'Yeah, ecstatic.'

Diana rose and stretched her arms wearily.

'Anyway, I'd rather he was O.K. because of me, not the dear little baby. God, I feel tired today and my stomach aches something awful, just as if I was havin' my periods.'

'You ought to rest up a bit,' Edith said anxiously. 'Stay up here and put yer feet up on the bed while I go down and make us some tea.'

'No. I'll come downstairs for tea,' Diana replied. She gathered up an armful of cretonne material. 'I want to iron these chair covers before I go to pick up Gary. I'll do 'em while I'm drinking me tea.'

'Can't they wait?' asked Edith.

'No, I want it all finished by the time he gets in. First impressions are so important.'

'O.K. then,' Edith sighed, 'you always was obstinate, Di, just like yer dad. I'll go and put the kettle on.'

Before following her mother from the room, Diana scooped up some clothing from the bed and placed it on top of the bundle of chair covers in her arms, packing it all down with her chin.

Edith was just going into the kitchen when she heard the fall. She turned in time to see Diana in a cumpled heap at the foot of the stairs, the materials scattered round her.

Edith screamed. 'Di!' She ran to the girl and put her arms round her. Diana was very pale and her mouth contorted with pain.

'My ankle, I think it's bust. Oh God, my stomach! Mum, quick, the doctor.'

Her face as white as the girl's, Edith laid her daughter gently back against the bottom stair and made a pillow for her back with the chair covers. Then she went to the telephone and called the doctor.

In the hospital Gary sat awkwardly, holding her hand, painfully conscious of the other staring patients.

'I caught my foot,' she said pathetically, 'the chair covers I was carrying slipped down and I tripped over them.'

'You shouldn't have been carrying them,' he said gently, 'why didn't you wait for someone to help you?'

'I wanted the room looking nice when you first saw it. I didn't want it to be half finished.'

'It wasn't that important.'

'To me it was, darling, very.'

The nurse came up to them then.

'You ought to sleep dear.'

Diana clung to Gary's hand.

'You'll come tomorrow, love?'

He bent and kissed her on the brow.

'Of course, Di. The minute I leave the office I'll be here.'

He kissed her again and drew his hand away. Her eyes beseeched him.

'Love me?'

The nurse was standing close, smiling impersonally. He was embarrassed. He nodded.

'Tomorrow then?'

'Tomorrow.'

Outside, Arthur Bridges was waiting to drive him home.

'How was she?'

'She'll be all right. She's going to have a good sleep.'

'Yeah,' Arthur said. 'She's lost the baby then.'

Gary was startled.

'Lost the baby? You mean . . .'

'Yeah, miscarriage. Coo, didn't you guess, boy? Don't think they'd keep her in hospital just fer a sprained ankle, do you?'

'I never thought, I didn't realize,' Gary spoke automatically. His thoughts were buzzing in his head like angry bees.

'Crumbs, didn't she tell you? Edie wonders whether she'd a

kep' it, anyways, says she was complainin' of pains in her stomach before she fell.'

'She's lost it.'

Gary spoke the words aloud, almost in triumph. The miracle he'd prayed for had happened. Vistas of wonderful freedom stretched before him as he rode along beside Arthur Bridges. Everything would be back to normal now and there was Gay again, dear sorrowing little Gay. How soon could he tell her she need grieve no more?

'Five days to go,' Arthur Bridges was saying, 'with a bit of luck she should be up and about again in time fer the weddin'. I remember Edie had a miss once, only laid up fer a couple of days, she was, and Di's a tough 'un, just like her mum.'

Gary stared at him. There didn't have to be a wedding now, didn't the idiot realize that? Something stopped him from mentioning it, though, and they drove the rest of the way home in silence.

The next morning he went early to the office and asked for a day's leave, scarcely coherent in his reasons. In the train to Town he couldn't settle, the journey seemed endless. What would she say when he told her? Of course, the process back would have to be gradual, one couldn't hand out a blow like he'd delivered to Gay and expect to be received back all at once with open arms. There was Di, too, she'd have to be let down gently and gradually. Surely she, too, would be relieved. She'd probably be grateful for her freedom eventually, a pretty girl like Di. Yes, they'd been foolish all right, but now they'd had a second chance handed out to them. Life was good after all.

The answer he received from one of the porters at the college was correct. At twelve o'clock precisely she came out, her books under her arm, to cross the yard to the canteen. He stood in the cloisters watching her. After Di she seemed short and rather plump, but very dear. As she drew closer he saw that she looked older, the usually alert eyes were dull. Her mouth was set in a hard line. He stepped out and called her name, waiting to see her face leap into life, but she froze in her tracks and there was no smile of greeting on her lips, no love in her eyes. Her voice, when it came, was stiff and unfriendly.

'Why are you here? What do you want?'

He tried to take her hands, but it was impossible with the books thrust tightly under her arm. At a loss, he stood there looking at her, his hands dangling down awkwardly.

'I have news, Gay,' he said, 'wonderful news for us both.'

Her face didn't change. She stood waiting.

'Di,' he said, 'has had a miscarriage. There needn't be a wedding now, we can go back, Gay, to the way we were before. Oh, I know how I've hurt you, but I shall spend the rest of my life making up to you for it. All the things you'd planned for us ... we ... later on, I mean, when we've both had time to look around, enjoy a little breathing space ... we don't have to rush into anything now, Gay. Honestly, I know now what a complete and utter fool I've been.'

Her voice cut him like a whiplash.

'Have you finished? Shouldn't you say after you've had time to look around for some other filly to amuse you, and then, after that, it'll be my turn.'

'No Gay honestly,' he pleaded. 'I didn't mean that at all. I mean we can wait now till I'm qualified, as long as ...'

'You bastard!' she said, 'you bloody, rotten bastard!'

'Gay!'

She was laughing now, high, horrible laughter.

'You really mean it,' she said. 'I think you really mean it.' The strange laughter stopped as suddenly as it had started. 'Get out of my sight,' she said. 'Go back to her and put your proposition to her, but, if she's any sense, I shouldn't think she'd want you now.'

She stepped smartly sideways to avoid his outstretched hands and marched off to the canteen building. The door slammed behind her. Other students were trickling across the yard now, some looked at him curiously, some not at all. Heart sick, he turned, and mooched slowly away.

He put the flowers by the bed and kissed her cheek. She kept her face turned from him.

'Not much choice of flowers I'm afraid,' he said, 'not in my price bracket.'

She turned then and looked at him.

'Did you buy them in London?'

He stared at her in surprise, repeating stupidly, 'London?'

'Yes.' She smiled miserably. 'They brought the mobile telephone in this morning. I was feeling so low so I rang your office, thinking to have a chat with you. They said you'd gone to London.'

'I had to go,' he said, 'there was, you see, for the office, a completion to do in London.'

'Don't lie, Gary,' she said wearily, 'you went there on leave, they told me so.' She massaged her forehead with her finger tips as if to ease her aching head. 'I know where you went. You went to see *her*, didn't you?'

'No, Di, you see, I . . .'

Relentlessly she repeated: 'You went to see her. I know it. You did, didn't you?'

Defeated, he nodded unhappily.

'Immediately you knew I'd lost it, you went dashing off to her. You couldn't wait.'

He sat silent, his eyes on the floor.

'And she turned you down.'

He looked up then, appealingly, 'Di.'

She laughed, dry, hateful laughter like Gay's had been, only more quiet.

'I take my hat off to her, she's got pride.' The laughter died. Diana's eyes filled with tears, her mouth twisted painfully. 'More than what I have, eh? I want you, Gary, at any price.'

He took her hand. 'Oh, Di.'

'Stay with me, Gary.'

'Yes, Di, of course.'

'When we're married it'll be lovely, you see. I cried for the baby, Gary. After all, he had been here inside me for a little while, but then I thought how good it'll be, us both working. We need only stay at mum's for a little while, we can save and save . . .'

'We could postpone the wedding,' he said, 'till we're better off and then have a decent one, instead of the Register Office.'

'No,' she cried. 'No.' The tears coursed down her cheeks now. She clung to his hand with both hers. 'No, Gary, if we put it off, we'll never get married, never. I know it. I don't trust you, God help me, I love you, but I don't trust you. If you let me down now, Gary, I'll die, I'll . . .'

'Hush.' He looked around him in embarrassment. Other patients and their visitors were staring curiously now. 'Hush, Di, don't get upset. Of course we'll go through with it if that's what you want.'

She gulped back her sobs and drew her hands away.

'Go through with it, like it was a bloody ordeal?'

'No, of course not. It's just that I thought if we'd waited we could have had a proper wedding, but we'll go on as arranged if you want it.'

She looked at him steadily.

'Yes, I want it, but you don't.'

'I'd rather have waited and done it properly.' His heart heavy as lead inside him, he added, 'But I want what you want Di. Will you be well enough, do you think?'

'Yes,' she said her voice bleak now. 'I'm going home tomorrow. Maybe I'll try and get a better job after the wedding and p'raps we can get a Council mortgage.'

'Yes, you never know.'

Yes, a Council mortgage on a property I despise, where I shall live, sleeping with a girl I don't love, and there, eventually, I shall rear my kids telling them what I'm going to do, one day. And if I'm lucky I'll get a junior partnership in the firm, but I'll never get very far in the social strata with a wife like Di. With Gay now . . .

'Gary,' Diana's voice cut into his bitter reverie. She was crying copiously now. 'Gary, I don't think I shall ever forget, as long as I live, that you went back to *her*.'

He took her hands and pressed them to his lips, regardless of the curious looks. Compassion for her and disgust at himself made him gentle.

'Oh love,' he whispered, 'I'm sorry. I'll make it up to you, you see.'

The scout hut was decorated for the occasion by Edith Bridges and the next door neighbour who had been invited to the wedding. Freda and Ned Thompson arrived late, looking as if it were a funeral they were attending, instead of a wedding.

'Christ!' Ned said to his son on the quiet, 'you're a bigger bloody fool than I thought, goin' through with this when there's no need now. You must be a perishin' maniac, asking fer punishment.'

'She loves me Dad,' Gary said, 'I couldn't let her down.'

'Huh,' Ned snorted, 'and Gaynor?'

'It's too late for Gaynor and me,' Gary said stonily, 'in fact, the truth is, Dad, I'm not really ready to marry either of them. I don't think I'd have started with Di in the first place if Gay hadn't been so eager to slip the harness on me. Trouble is, I shied, and shied right into another trap. Now that I'm in this trap, I tell myself it's Gay I wanted, but is it? Do I want anyone for keeps just yet?'

Ned faced his son with gloomy eyes.

'I suppose we'd all have liked to play the field,' he said, 'but trouble is, we haven't got the bloody nerve.'

'No,' Gary said, adding passionately, 'but we should have, Dad, we should have. We shouldn't let them tie us down like . . .'

He broke off and turned as his mother-in-law came up and tugged at his arm.

'Di's waitin' Gary,' she said, 'it's time you was cuttin' the cake.'

After the cutting of the cake, Ned and Freda Thompson left and the merriment waxed louder and unrestrained. Diana's uncle Jim whirled round one of the young protesting cousins in a boisterous, old-fashioned waltz, and crashed into a festoon of balloons which burst to the tipsy laughter and applause of the other guests.

'Uncle Jim's a real scream when he's kalied,' Diana said with an indulgent smile. She tugged at her bridegroom's arm. 'Look a bit happy, Gary, for Gawd's sake. Shall we dance?'

'Not to this 1914 vintage,' he said, 'can't we leave, Di?'

'What, leave now, while the fun's at its height?' Diana said. 'Seems stupid when we're only going up to London for one night. It'll be more fun here for a while yet.'

As he watched his bride applauding and encouraging her tipsy relations, Gary wondered where the other Di had gone, the girl who had confided to him her fears of becoming like her parents. She had yearned to get out, she had said, to make something of her life. Well, I know now, he acknowledged wearily, that was just her jealousy of Gaynor talking. Di's got her wedding ring and her little niche in this piddling corner of the universe and there she intends to stay put. His gaze roved contemptuously over the scouts' hut, made even more hideous by the pathetic attempts to deck it out for the occasion, and he thought of the Island Hotel in Marbrook with its soft lights, thick carpets and lovely floral arrangements, men and women laughing quietly in correct wedding clothes, sipping champagne, and Gaynor and himself moving amongst their guests, guests who were worth knowing. Diana's aunt Bee grabbed him by the arm, her red grinning face under the ludicrous wispy hat made him think of a beetroot hanging from a muslin bag.

'Come an' dance, love,' she urged him, pulling him into the throng, 'you won' get to know your new relations standin' there like a spare thing at a weddin'. She laughed coarsely as she fell up against him. Hiding his disgust, he put his arm gingerly round the fat sagging body. Sickness and frustration rose fiercely inside him and suddenly he wanted to cry.

'I've sausage rolls and brandy,' he said, smiling his melancholy smile, 'just like I gave your sister. It seems to be my staple diet, sausage rolls and brandy.'

Gaynor stopped in her restless pacing of the kitchen. 'Katheryn?'

'Yes,' Hedley Strong said. 'She came down here one morning. I had the feeling she was on a kind of pilgrimage to make a decision and wanted to be in this cottage when she made that decision. I may be wrong.'

'I'm surprised Katie came here,' Gaynor said, 'she pretends to hate the cottage now.'

'Actually she fainted on me,' Hedley said as he opened the fridge and took out a packet of Marks and Spencer sausage rolls. 'She didn't see me very clearly as she came in and she thought I was someone else.'

'David,' Gaynor said.

'Yes, David.'

'Did she speak to you of him?'

'No.'

A tiny smile curved Gaynor's sad mouth.

'No, she wouldn't. We used to have lovely walks in the woods by the river, Hedley, David and I, when I was a kid. He talked so wonderfully and he knew me so well. Some people are like that, aren't they, sympatico?'

Hedley nodded gravely.

'The gift of personality.'

'Yes, David certainly had that. I think I knew, even then, that he was in love with Katie, before he did himself probably, not just lusting after her as he did other women, but really loved her. I wish you'd known him, Hedley, you would have liked him. He'd have liked you.' She sighed. 'The priest and the sinner.'

'Often the same,' Hedley said.

Gaynor stopped pacing and sat down on a kitchen chair.

'My pride is my sin,' she said. 'I'm still choking with humiliation. His girl friend had a miscarriage so he came flying to me, Hedley, willing to ditch her and call off the wedding. "Don't let's do anything in a hurry, Gay," he says, "we can take our time now." ' She laughed bitterly. 'He was probably thinking of running us both while he looked around on the side.'

'And you sent him away?'

'Yes, I sent him away.'

Hedley poured two brandies and put one in front of her.

'It seems I never really knew him. I must have been so blind all these years to the real Gary Thompson.' She smiled a pathetic, wintry little smile. 'Like the song says – "Love is blind and I was too blind to see." '

She sat staring into her drink for a few seconds, then:

'Today is his wedding day,' she said.

'And you?' Hedley queried, raising his glass.

'Soon I shall be gone.'

She got up with her drink and went to the window. The sun was sparkling on the water, the willows dipped gently in the breeze. A small flock of birds, disturbed suddenly by some river noise, wheeled sharply up and went swirling swiftly and gracefully over the cottage and into the dark shelter of the woods behind.

'For Katie,' Gaynor said, 'as long as there's the cottage, it will never be the end. It got her when she was still a child, it seemed to have been waiting for her like she said it was waiting for David.' Gaynor gave a mammoth sigh, and turned from the window. 'As long as the cottage stands,' she said, 'for Katie it will never be the end.'

CHAPTER FIFTEEN

'YOU'VE got so thin, darling,' Dorothy said.

Reggie shrugged. 'I've been in a hot climate and I've been dieting.'

She put a hand up to his sagging cheek.

'I don't like to see you losing weight like this, it doesn't suit you.'

'I was always too fat,' he said, 'if I'd gone on as I was going I'd have soon lost sight of it, and,' he gave a little snickering laugh, 'and where I was putting it.'

Jealousy enraged her.

'Such as into that nig-nog who belongs to Rudi von Kram?'

The heavy-lidded eyes became alert.

'What was that?'

Dorothy laughed nervously and poured herself another drink.

'I know how you drool over her. Paul Earnshaw told me.'

'So that young puppy talks about me.' He laughed but she knew he was angry. At one time it had been hard to read his expression, but the face of this new queerly gaunt Reggie was easier to read.

'I make him talk about you, darling. It seems to bring you closer to me. Reggie, is it true, do you want Von Kram's spade?'

'If I did, would I be here?'

'I asked you to come.'

'I was coming anyway after I got back from Jamaica, but I came at once because you said you had something important to tell me,' he stroked her breasts, 'and I've missed you, Dorothy, more than I thought I would.'

'Oh, Reggie! Darling!'

She flung her arms round his neck and pressed her body against his. Where once his body had been huge and fleshy against her, now it felt curiously deflated. He held her back away from him.

'And now am I to be told the important news?'

'Now you've come back to me, darling, it isn't important any more.'

Hardness in his voice he said:

'I have to know this news, Dorothy.'

She moved back to him, nestling her head on his shoulder.

'Paul was drunk, he said things.'

'What things?'

'About that night, the night that Harriet Lloyd got murdered.'

His voice dangerously quiet, he said:

'And?'

'Paul saw you there, didn't he, and then,' her voice grew firmer, encouraged by his silence, 'and then you asked that man to your party, that barrister, playing with danger. It had the hall marks of you, Reggie, but I don't care even if you did do it. I love you.'

She moved and pressed her cheek against his. 'Oh darling, no one has ever done to me the things you do, no one has ever said to me the things you say, no one has ever made me feel . . .' She was babbling now like a distraught child. 'You taught me when I was so young, you can't abandon me now. I'm your disciple, your Trilby, darling, your . . .'

He stopped the incoherent flow with his mouth on hers, hard and savage.

'My best pupil, Chinese Dorothy.'

Gratefully she clung to him, seeking his mouth again.

'If I could be the *only* one. Reggie, please stay, love me again like you used to.'

He tilted her head back.

'You really want a man who might be a murderer? How could you trust me? How could I trust *you* not to blazon abroad those poisonous insinuations of young Earnshaw?'

'As long as you stay with me, I'll be happy,' Dorothy said, 'and as long as you stay with me, you can trust me, darling, your secret's safe with me, as they say in the books.'

Ah, the veiled threat, sticking its barb up through the honey. As long as you stay with me.

'Reggie, my body aches for you. It's been torture. sheer hell, you must stay, please.'

He let go of her and turned his back on her.

'Undress.'

'Oh darling!' Frantic, she slipped the dress from her shoulders. He turned and watched her, a look of speculation as well as lust in the cold eyes.

A smile of sensuous invitation curved her mouth. She put her hands in the top of her pants, preparing to slide them down.

He moved swiftly and put out the light.

'Oh Reggie,' she wailed, 'why did you do that? I wanted to watch you undress like I used to.'

'I like the dark.'

'You used not to.'

A niggling fear worried her. Even in the darkness she could see the sagging folds of his once large, fleshy body. He was dieting too much, that was obvious. Now that he was back with her she would make him stop.

'Tell me,' he whispered as he played with her, 'tell me about the things Paul Earnshaw did to you.'

'Nothing compared with you. I never wanted him in the first place.'

'What? A handsome young stud bull like Earnshaw? Most girls would have been frantic for him. What about you, my Dorothy, were you frantic *with* him?'

'Reggie, please darling, don't!'

With a sigh almost of impatience he stopped questioning her.

'Remember this?' she whispered and put her hand on him.

'Black games.'

'The priest and the nun.'

'I've missed all this. Did you with anyone else?'

'Yes.'

'Reggie, dig your fingers into me there. Draw blood.'

Paul Earnshaw would not have recognized his refined, sensible secretary-mistress in the threshing tigress that writhed this night with her lover, her lips mouthing obscenities, her body torn with desire.

When it was over they lay together, drained and exhausted.

'I can never go back to Paul or anyone else now, Reggie.'

'Sweet, you never will,' he promised her. He turned and cradled her in his arms. 'Now plans, my darling, listen carefully. Tomorrow you write Paul a note telling him it's finished. I'll call round to collect it about eight and send it by messenger to him so that you don't have to see Paul, neither will the letter have to go through the post.'

'If it was sent to his office,' Dorothy said, 'I should open it.'

'You won't be going to the office from now on,' Reggie said gently. 'Write the note, don't answer the door to him if he calls.'

'What about my job?'

'You won't need it now. Trust me, darling, leave it all to me. Just write the note and wait till I call for it.'

'Oh, Reggie, I've never been so happy.'

'You'll never be unhappy again, darling,' he said. 'I'll see to that.'

'This operation,' Tabitha said, 'is it inevitable?'

He shrugged.

'If I don't have it, I shall die. If I have it, they say I stand a small chance.'

She stared at him curiously. She thought dispassionately, he has the mark of death on him, I think I've known it ever since we went to Jamaica. All these years we've lived together, gone our separate ways, and now, at last, all of a sudden when he's going to die, we seem close.

'Cancer of course,' she said, her eyes on his yellowing face.

'Cancer.'

'Why did we go haring off to Jamaica if you're so ill?'

'Just say I wanted a last look at some real sun.' He laughed. 'There may not be any sun where I'm going.'

'Look Reggie,' Tabitha said, 'don't you think they might be wrong? The pain, it could be an ulcer.'

He laughed again, shortly, unhappily.

'Blast you, woman! I've had it diagnosed. They know what it is. *I* know what it is. *You* know what it is. You saw how I was in Jamaica, seldom free from pain, and my loss of weight. God, Tabby, you're not that much of a fool that you think I'm like this from guts ache.'

He sat down suddenly. She looked at him in concern.

'Are you all right?'

He laughed again as though thoroughly amused.

'Yes. I had an exhausting night last night, put up quite a good show for a man with the sentence of death on him.'

She shuddered. 'Don't.'

He stared at her speculatively.

'I wonder if you'll marry again?'

'Ugh,' she shuddered. 'You're a cold blooded bastard.' She turned away. 'I have a headache, I don't think I'll dine with you and Paul tonight.'

His sagging body seemed to tighten. He got up.

'You must.'

'But why not here? Why in the London flat with no servants?'

'It's more convenient there. I shall have the meal sent in.'

Petulantly she said:

'I never like the service meals they dish up there.'

'I won't get it from service.'

'Why must you see Paul?'

'On business. I have things to put straight and I want you there.'

'Can't it be done at your office?'

'I don't want it done at an office. Bugger me, Tabby,' he lost patience suddenly, 'call it the whim of a dying man if you like. I'm dining Paul tonight at 8.30 in the London flat. I want you there.'

'But why all the secrecy?'

'Business reasons.'

She indicated through the open door of the study the two small suitcases the butler had just brought into the hall.

'And after dinner we light off to some place unknown, straight from the flat. For how long?'

'Not long, just a short break.'

'Are the police after you?'

He smiled.

'Of course not.'

'Then what is this, Reggie? Some kind of joke, all this melodrama?'

'Another whim of a dying man,' he said with his old sinister smile. 'I shan't be around much longer. It won't hurt you to humour me now.'

She spread out her hands helplessly.

'I have all sorts of appointments to cancel. It was so damned sudden.'

'You've given Sands a list, he can cancel them, say you've been called away suddenly. You didn't tell the servants we were dining in the London flat, did you?'

'No, you said particularly not to. Reggie, what *is* going on?'

'Nothing that need worry you. I have good reasons.'

'You're a devious swine.'

'I know.'

A sudden thought came to her.

'You're not taking me somewhere to murder me, are you?'

He was amused.

'No, not you, Tabby. This may be hard for you to take, but I've been very fond of you.'

Relaxed again, she murmured softly,

'Sometimes you could've fooled *me* darling.'

He laughed.

'You're a cool one, Tabby.'

She bared her teeth at him and gave a mock growl.

'The jungle we live in, darling, survival of the fittest. I learned early.'

His eyes appraised her thoughtfully, travelling over her, sinewy and catlike in her thin white sweater and black velvet pants.

'You haven't changed much, Tabby, since you were the bride of the year.'

'Except that the stars have gone from my eyes.'

'I appreciate all you've done for me, for staying. Sometimes lately I've found myself wishing I'd been different.'

She laughed in amazement.

'God, you *are* ill, aren't you? Spare me the violins, darling, they set my teeth on edge.'

He grinned back at her.

'Yes, that was out of character. I've never dealt in corn, have I, it's too late to start now.'

Suddenly she shot a surprising question at him:

'Reggie, have you ever had children from some other woman?'

He stared at her in surprise, then shook his head.

'Not to my knowledge. Why? Were you thinking of adopting my by-blows when I'm gone?'

'I just wanted to know.'

'No, Tabby, all my ends are neatly tied, like they've always been.'

'Once or twice,' she said. 'Some of your neatly tied knots have almost come untied, just once or twice.'

He laughed confidently.

'But they never did, did they? I've never been one to trip over my own shoe laces. I've been a very skilful operator in my time, there's just this last thing I can't manipulate. It's got me by the throat and I know when I'm licked, but I shall last just long enough to have a bit of a giggle yet, one last giggle.'

As she moved away, he spoke her name sharply:

'Tabby.'

She stopped and turned, eyebrows raised.

'What now?'

'You may have lost the stars, but you haven't gained any bulges. Somehow I never saw you as the spreading, contented matron.'

She laughed mirthlessly.

'So you *did* see me?'

'All the time, in your sleek, cat-like elegance, your fabulous clothes and perfumes and jewels, your cool sophistication, all a man could wish for, but he'd have to be a rich man, Tabby. Married to a poor man you'd have been just another scrawny, carping bitch.'

'So, without money, I'd have been nothing?'

'Well, would you? Feeding squalling kids in some two by four, queueing up at the supermarket, living for Friday's pay packet.'

She smiled thinly.

'You paint a graphic picture.'

'I know people.'

'But you don't particularly like them.' She moved on to the door and turned, 'life with you, Reggie,' she said, 'has been mad, bad and, at times, diabolical, but it's never been dull.'

'I've never been bored with you either,' he said.

She bowed to him mockingly and shut the door.

By the time the meal ended, Paul could see that Tabitha Gunner-Cartwright was drunk. Paul was as mystified as Tabitha was at being summoned so peremptorily to this strange dinner party. Also he was deeply depressed. At home there was the emptiness of life without Katheryn and the twins. At the office today there had been no Dorothy. His attempts at ringing her had met with no reply. Tonight, before coming here, he had gone to her flat, but the door had not been answered, although he had the feeling that there was someone inside. He had imagined hearing someone rustle up to look out of the peephole on the door. While he had been standing there ringing the bell, the girl, Anthea, passed him on her way up to her own flat. She turned round as she ascended, eyeing him curiously, but beyond nodding 'Good evening,' said nothing else. He had been forced to leave then to come to this strange rendezvous with Reggie and Tabitha.

Tabitha picked up her brandy goblet and leaned back in her chair.

'Well, shall I retire now, while you two talk shop?'

'I've changed my mind,' Reggie said. 'We're not talking shop after all. I've dictated tapes which will be sent to my secretary and passed on to Paul in due course.'

'Well, for Chrissake!' said Tabitha, rising and strolling to the window, 'the man's a nut. We come here, hooded and cloaked like Scarlet Pimpernels for a secret pow-wow and now the man says it's out.'

'I've changed my mind,' Reggie said. 'You change yours often enough.'

'I don't bulldoze people to an empty flat for a picnic.' She pressed her face against the window. 'There's a white cat out here, he's staring at me with green sinister eyes. Ugh! I know he'd like to spring at my throat.'

'You're tight, my darling,' Reggie said.

She turned from her morbid contemplation of the cat.

'But not tight enough, my pet. Sober enough to query this sudden flit we're doing.' Her tone sharpened suddenly. 'Who are we running away from?'

'If we were running away, my love,' Reggie said, 'should we stop to dine in London first?'

'Where are you going?' Paul asked, 'and how long will you be away?'

Reggie smiled and gestured with his cigar.

'Sorry, dear boy, can't answer either question. I want a rest and a surprise trip for Tabby. If people don't know where we are, they can't tell anyone. No one knows except myself and Gregson where we're going and for how long.'

'Gregson? Oh God,' said Tabitha, 'are we taking him? Why?'

'He can drive when I get tired.'

Her voice rose aggressively, 'Well, *I* can drive when you get tired.'

'I want you to rest, too.'

'I did rest, in Jamaica, got bored to tears resting. I'm not the resting kind.'

She laughed shrilly. 'This gets more and more devious. Honestly, Paul, I have the strangest feeling that he's going to lure me away and murder me. Or no, perhaps not. Perhaps it'll be Gregson who'll do it. How much have you paid him, darling, to put arsenic in my gin?'

Reggie seemed annoyed.

'Don't talk rubbish.'

Unabashed, she waggled a be-ringed finger at Paul.

'Darling, you may very well be the last person to see the victim alive. Note this conversation well. Trusting wife lured away to second honeymoon only to be foully murdered, strangled with her own tights, held under the water in million-aire's pool, pushed off the cliff, oh darling, there are so many lovely ways.' She turned to Reggie with a high-pitched giggle. 'And will you get your barrister friend, Rackstraw, to defend you, darling? Is that why you asked him to our party, to soften him up for the kill?'

Reggie's smoothness took over again, the thin mouth smiled, the old oily smile.

'Tabby dear, should you be drinking so much? I'd hate you to be ill on the journey.'

She rolled her eyes at Paul and took another sip of her brandy.

'Mark my words well, my young friend, strange deeds are

afoot this night, dark deeds, more than you and I or the world e'er dreamed of.'

'Of course,' Reggie said, 'the boot could be on the other foot. Tabby will make a lovely widow, don't you think, Paul? All sorrowing and mysterious under her veil of black.'

'Wondering about the will,' Tabitha said.

Reggie looked at his watch and stood up.

'And now, my dear wife,' he said, smiling, 'I think the time has come for us to depart.'

Paul said good-bye and let himself out of the flat, still mystified by the strange summons. He shivered with a strange feeling of oppression. They were kooks, Tabby and Reggie, with their macabre conversations. He ran down the one short flight of steps and out into the street, meeting no one. He walked along until he came to the side street where he had parked his car. He thought of calling at Dorothy's again but, on looking at his watch, saw that it was quarter to eleven. He decided against it and drove home.

CHAPTER SIXTEEN

THE morning of the day of the strange dinner party the telephone rang beside Dorothy Trent's bed. The time was 7.30, she was just about to get up. Remembering Reggie's instructions not to answer the telephone, she thought it couldn't be Paul this early in the morning but if it is, I'll hang up again.

It was not Paul, but Reggie. His soft voice sent her flesh crawling with desire.

'Dorothy, my lamb, I'm glad you answered.'

'I thought it might be you.'

'But don't answer it any more today. It might be Paul and I don't want him getting round you. I know these good looking young bucks and their persuasive ways.'

'He couldn't persuade me, darling. I've finished with him.'

'Good. Have you written the letter to him?'

'Not yet. I'll do it after breakfast.'

'Do it soon before you change your mind.'

'I shall never change my mind Reggie. You're all I want, always.'

'Write it then and I'll pick it up when I come tonight. Darling, have you any personal belongings at your office?'

'Only a few, perfumes, indoor shoes, not much.'

'I'll arrange to have them sent to you.'

'I hope Paul won't mind too much.'

'He's young and resilient,' Reggie said, 'and he has a pretty wife. Anyhow, by the time we get back, he'll have forgotten it.'

'Get back? Are we going away then?'

'How would you feel about a spell in the Caribbean?'

Delight almost choked her.

'Oh Reggie, superb! But what about your wife?'

'Let me worry about her. Now I must ring off, don't forget, darling, Paul will probably ring you or call. Don't answer. You have a peephole in your door so you can see if it's him. Oh, and I may be a little late tonight, I may not get to you till about nine but I'll probably send you some red roses to keep you company till I get there.'

'I don't want flowers, darling, only you.'

At 8.30 she went on to the landing to take her milk in. Anthea was just tripping down the stairs off to work. She regarded Dorothy, still in her negligee, with surprise.

'No office today? Thick night?'

Dorothy flexed her arms, the milk bottle in one hand, and arched her back luxuriously.

'I'm blissfully happy, Anthea. There'll be no more office for me from now on.'

'Crumbs! Have you come up on the pools?'

Dorothy shook her head, smiling happily.

'It's a feller then,' Anthea said suspiciously, 'God you're not running away with that god-like boss of yours, are you? You haven't brought it off after all?'

'No, I'm running away *from* him.' Dorothy's eyes clouded briefly. 'I'm afraid he's going to take it rather hard.'

'You've got a new feller?'

'No. Not a new one, my old love has come back to me, my one and only true love. Oh Anthea, I'm so happy.'

Anthea smiled doubtfully.

'Bully for you then dear. I really must go. There's no man in *my* life to rescue me from the dole.'

Dorothy took the milk in and closed the door. The telephone rang several times during the day but, as instructed by Reggie, she didn't answer it. She spent the day tidying her rooms and sorting out her clothes, putting aside those which would be suitable for a holiday in the Caribbean, although she knew, from past experience with Reggie, that he would see she had clothes a-plenty for their trip. Money had never been short. A mean bastard he could be in love, but never with money. She sighed. But he will never be able to leave me again, she decided fiercely, with what I know, he will be *afraid* to leave me again.

Early in the evening Paul called, but she saw him through the peephole and stayed quiet until he left. Poor Paul, if it hadn't been for his tipsy indiscretion, I'd never have got the edge on Reggie.

And Dorothy Trent, in her blind trustfulness, went on with

her dream about the future with her love until half past eight when, after elaborate pains with her toilet, clad only in a foamy chiffon jacket, she went to the window to watch for him. She saw a man turn into the drive, walking, carrying a large cardboard box, but paid little attention until her door bell rang. She got down from the window seat and went to look through the peephole in the door. The man had opened the box and taken out a large bouquet of red roses. Reggie had mentioned flowers and Reggie loved extravagant gestures like messengers delivering flowers out of business hours. She took the chain off the door and opened it. Holding the flowers in gloved hands, the man said 'A message Miss from the Hon. Reggie Gunner-Cartwright.' He propelled the empty cardboard box through the door with his foot. 'If I may leave the box.' He kicked the box right in and quickly turned, kicking the door shut. He threw the roses on the floor and, before she had time to scream, his hands closed round her throat. He lowered her limp body gently to the floor, the scattered roses strewn round it. Then he stepped lightly over her into the sitting-room. There, as his boss had said it would be, was the note addressed to Paul Earnshaw. He drew it from its envelope and read it, his face expressionless. The envelope he put in his pocket. Then he went to the sideboard, still holding the note in one gloved hand. He took the stopper off a bottle of Scotch and took a long swig from the bottle. He replaced the stopper. The note had become creased in this process, he creased it some more, then he went back with it to the girl's body. Raising her a little he placed it under her shoulders. He looked down at her once, as if seeing her for the first time, and quietly left the flat.

Dorothy Trent lay dead amongst her scattered red roses, her dreams destroyed, her lips forever silent.

Paul Earnshaw sat, head in hands, the cup of tea untouched before him.

'Strange dark deeds are afoot tonight,' Tabitha had said. Oh God, how right she had been. Where were Reggie and Tabby? Only they could get him out of this mess. He raised his head and spoke again for the hundredth time his plea to the detective on the other side of the table.

'For God's sake, trace Reggie Gunner-Cartwright and his wife. I dined with them, I tell you, in their town flat that night. Their manservant, Gregson was there. He can confirm that I'm not lying.'

'The town flat has been shut up for some time. Lady Tabitha and her husband and manservant left their country home in the afternoon for a mystery holiday.'

Paul laughed bitterly.

'Mystery's right. I couldn't have killed Dorothy Trent, I tell you I was with *them*.'

'But you were seen at her flat that night.'

'Early on, I tell you. Oh Christ! I didn't even get in, she wouldn't answer the door.'

'Why is that, sir, had you quarrelled?'

'No, no. I don't know why she didn't answer the door.'

'You were not seen to leave the flat, sir.'

'I tell you I rang and rang, but I never went in.'

'I suggest, sir, she opened the door long enough for you to give her the roses and fling her good-bye note back at her.'

'What roses? What note? I've never seen them.'

The detective tapped the paper in front of him with a biro.

'In your statement you admit you were having an affair with Dorothy Trent.'

'On and off, hardly an affair.'

'Enough of an affair for her to write to you ending it.'

'She never wrote to me.'

'We have the letter.'

'Then I never received it. Oh Christ, help me! How much longer do I have to endure this?'

'Until you tell us the truth, sir.'

'I *am* telling you the truth, God help me.'

'Let's go over it again then, sir. You called at Dorothy Trent's flat at what time?'

'Half seven, quarter to eight, something like that. I can't remember exactly. The girl in the top flat saw me, she'll probably be able to tell you.'

'She already has, sir. She also says she never saw you leave.'

'I probably left before she'd even had time to open her door. She must have heard me go downstairs.'

The detective shrugged.

'And you went away without giving Dorothy Trent the red roses and flinging her farewell note back at her?'

Wearily Paul reiterated, 'I know of no note or flowers. I've told you so a thousand times.'

Insistently the policeman persisted:

'I suggest you quarrelled and lost control. Oh it can easily happen sir, you probably never meant to kill her, just frighten her.'

'I didn't, I tell you. I didn't even see her, let alone talk to her. She didn't turn up at the office so I telephoned, got no reply, then I called, got no answer.'

'And after that?'

'I've told you. I went to dine with the Gunner-Cartwrights in their Chelsea flat.'

'Which has been shut up for some time. The service to the flats states that no meal was sent up by them that night to the Gunner-Cartwright flat. As far as they know, the flat was empty.'

Paul ran his hands through his hair.

'We had a meal sent in. The man, Gregson, fetched it and served it. Just find him, he'll tell you.'

The detective smiled tolerantly.

'But he went away that afternoon, sir, with his employers, from the country house. They'd probably left the country by the time the murder was committed.'

'They hadn't, I tell you. They were with me. Oh God! God!'

He beat his fists in frustration on the table. Then, eventually, under the dispassionate survey of the detective, he fell into quiet despair. His eyes were sore through lack of sleep, his stomach lurched with the gripe of a thousand hangovers. There was stubble on his chin now. He felt dirty and old. This poor wretch slouched here couldn't be the same slick immaculate young man who had paid court to Katheryn Scarlett long ago where there was moonlight and music and laughter, before David Lloyd came to live in the cottage by the river, before the whole black business began. Oh God, I'm innocent, can't they see? They have no right to take away my freedom and treat me like a criminal. Into his tortured mind came the vision of that other near-condemned man, David Lloyd. He remembered the quiet, patient despair on the man's face. And I would have let him be sentenced, he thought now, condemned without lifting a hand to try to save him, although Katheryn had lied her soul away for him. What must *she* be thinking now, Katheryn, whom *he* had been allowed to call 'Katie?' Oh God, save me and give me as much dignity to show to her as *he* did.

And then, for the first time in many years, he thought of his mother and father with compassion. How ashamed they must be, how bitterly disappointed in their only son. He wanted them suddenly, he wanted to bury his shame in the comfort of their love.

'Can we charge him?' the sergeant asked.

The superintendent sighed.

'Yes, I think so. He's a persistent cove, though, never changes his story one iota.'

'He wouldn't, would he? That Anthea bird's story certainly doesn't help him.'

The detective-sergeant picked up a paper and read aloud Anthea Potts' statement:

'I saw Dorothy Trent early as I was leaving for work, taking in her milk. She was ecstatically happy because her lover had come back to her. I asked her what about her current boyfriend, Paul Earnshaw, and she looked a little sad and said she reckoned he'd take it a bit hard. She dreaded telling him.'

When questioned further, Miss Potts said she didn't know for sure who the lover was who had come back to Dorothy Trent, but she did know, for a fact, that, at one time, Dorothy had been head over heels in love with Reggie Gunner-Cartwright.

'Christ!' the superintendent said wearily, 'what a crowd! Reggie Gunner-Cartwright and his missus, the lovely Lady Tabitha, nympho mark I, were mixed up in that other murder case some years back down on the river at Marbrook, the one that rocked a few in high places. Now he's involved in this.'

'We don't know for sure that he was the lover the girl referred to,' said the sergeant, 'he's not young any more and certainly no oil painting. Surely a pretty girl like Dorothy Trent . . .?'

The superintendent snorted.

'Does that worry these girls as long as there's money and high-powered technique? I could name you a few big fat oily rich men with pretty young things who stick like leeches, and it isn't always for the money. They got to have odd kicks some of 'em, these days. Straight fornication isn't in any more.'

'Well, she got hers all right, poor bitch,' the sergeant said. '*She* won't break up any more homes.'

'It would have been no use my coming to the airport for you Katie,' Gaynor said, 'my car is too small to take us, the children and your luggage.'

'It was all right,' Katheryn said abstractedly, 'I hired.'

'Paul's parents, how are they taking it?'

'I don't know. I haven't heard from them.'

Katie, Gaynor thought, looks as calm and controlled as if we were discussing a tea party. She remembered that Katie had looked and acted just the same that other time when father had told her David Lloyd had shot himself. Why can't she show her feelings, break down, just for once?

'Katie,' Gaynor said, 'shall I stay with you? I can if you wish, or will you perhaps go to Paul's people?'

Katheryn came out of her abstraction then.

'Why ever should I go to them? No, I don't want you to stay. I shall be all right.'

'I've seen him,' Gaynor said, 'Paul. They let me see him for just a minute. He sent his love to you.'

Katheryn's eyes widened.

'You went *there*?'

'He had to have someone. He didn't do it, Katie, I just know he didn't.'

Katheryn closed her eyes. For a second it seemed that she and Gaynor were young again and there was Gaynor passionately declaring her belief in David's innocence, as she was doing now for Paul. Paul and that girl.

'They were lovers,' she said, her mouth contorting as if in pain.

'Paul loves *you*, Katie.'

Staring across her sister's head Katheryn said:

'He took her to Amsterdam and other places. They were lovers in Amsterdam.'

The pain that was Gary Thompson throbbed in Gaynor's brain.

'Men don't have to love women to sleep with them,' she said bitterly, 'men are different from women in that way.'

Katheryn turned and looked at her sister curiously.

'Men are no different from women that way,' she said calmly, 'I don't have to love to go to bed.'

Sick at heart Gaynor got to her feet.

'It seems,' she said heavily, 'that I've never known *anyone*. I've had my own ideas of people, my dear ones, but these ideas are nothing near the truth. I think perhaps when I get away, broaden my outlook, I may come to a proper understanding of people. I hope so.'

'I shall go away too probably,' Katheryn said, 'there's nothing to keep me here now.'

Gaynor was about to say 'Paul', but the stony closed look on her sister's face stopped her.

'Can Mabel get you some lunch?' Katheryn asked.

'No thanks,' Gaynor said wearily, 'I have to get back. You know where I am if you want me.'

'Yes.'

The sisters walked together into the hall.

'I'm going out too,' Katheryn said. 'There's someone I have to see.'

'Paul?'

'No,' Katheryn said, 'not Paul.'

'Well, I shan't leave England,' Gaynor said, 'until we know for sure how Paul gets on. He's going to need someone besides his parents.'

'He had someone,' Katheryn said stonily, 'it's not my fault if she's dead.'

Gaynor found a vestige of hope in her sister's harsh words. Katheryn was jealous. If you don't care about someone, you can't be jealous. She prayed that Katie wouldn't be too blind to see.

He drew her to him and kissed her on the mouth.

'I've missed you.' He held her back and looked at her. 'Brown as the provincial berry. It suits you Katheryn, gives you an urchin look.'

He drew her down on the settee and sat beside her, holding her hand.

'I'm sorry darling,' he said, 'so very, very sorry.'

'I had to come to you. I hope you don't mind.'

'Of course not. You've come, of course, to ask me to take his case.'

She came out of her icy calm with a jerk.

'No, of course not. Would I ask *you* . . .?' She stopped, seeing him so plainly in Court that time long ago, trying to harpoon *her*, his cold voice so different from the voice he used to her now.

'Why not me?' he asked softly, an ominous edge to his voice.

She shuddered. 'I couldn't ask *you*.'

'Why did you come then, Katheryn?'

She raised her head and looked at him squarely.

'I came because of me, not Paul.'

'Yes?'

'It was good what we did before I went away? You were happy?'

'Very good, my darling, but then I knew it would be. We had all the ingredients, you and I.'

'Then, Derren,' she said calmly, 'will you take me away, me and the children, right away from here?'

Away from it, please, her sore heart cried, away from the intrigue, dreams and nightmares of the cottage, of Paul and his treachery, right away . . .

'I can't get away yet darling. Later on perhaps, we can arrange something, a week or two abroad.'

'I mean now,' she said, 'now for good. I've got money – so have you.'

He was silent, staring at her with shocked eyes. He let go of her hand. His voice, when he spoke, was cold, like it had been in Court.

'You mean, go away together, leave my wife?'

'Yes.'

'And you'd leave your husband, *now*?'

Her mouth tightened.

'He was unfaithful to me.'

He gave a short laugh.

'God, Katheryn, you were unfaithful to *him*.'

'He was unfaithful first.'

Ah, so that was it. That's why she had come to him so suddenly and so willingly.

'And if you'd never discovered his infidelity, you wouldn't have gone to bed with *me*?'

'I was attracted to you. I might have tried to control it.'

He gave a snort of disgust. His hard mouth set in a disagreeable line. It was the face seen often in Court by fearful offenders.

'So you used me to salve your hurt pride?'

'I don't see it that way. You wanted me, didn't you?'

'My God!' He laughed incredulously. 'I thought you were hard that time in Court, when you were very young, but . . .'

'You don't want me then?'

'Yes, I want you, bitch that you are.'

'But not on a permanent basis?'

He gave a hard, ugly laugh.

'No, certainly not on a permanent basis, my darling. Do you seriously imagine I would abandon my poor pathetic wife for a young girl who doesn't love me, who has never given me one real word of love?'

Katheryn remained silent, facing him with stony eyes.

'Can you imagine,' he went on, 'the position when I grow old? Bad enough with a young wife who loves me, but absolute bloody hell with one who doesn't. One who, I may add, speaking from past experience, would lie in her pretty teeth without compunction if it suited her to deceive me, as she has done to me twice already. I'm not that much of a mug, my darling. Living in sin may be paradise for some, but not for me. I'm far too respectable!'

David's words came back to her. 'Believe me, Katie, there's no lasting fun in being wicked, for one as lovely as you.'

'Once,' she said, her voice low and strained, 'I went with my father to visit an old lady of 102. I remember thinking then, how awful it must be to be like a cabbage and not care. I think that's how I feel now, like a cabbage.'

'As long as you can still feel at all, Katheryn,' Derren Rackstraw said, 'there's hope.'

She picked up her cardigan and started for the door. In the
door way she turned.

'I think you've always hated me,' she said, 'I felt it that time
in Court. I think I've always really known it.'

He passed a hand wearily over his mouth.

'Perhaps I have. I've come near to loving you, too, but *he* has
always been between us. That man, that black, rotten spot in
your heart. Get rid of him, Katheryn, without him you may
presently know some peace. With him there, never. Good-bye.'

'Good-bye,' Katheryn said.

She left his chambers, her cardigan flung over one shoulder.
On the steps the hot sun flooded over her, but she felt cold. She
shivered. From his window, Derren Rackstraw watched her
slowly walk out of his life.

Diana Thompson put down the paper.

'So history repeats itself. That lot mixed up in another
murder. And that's the crowd you'd have got yourself married
into.'

'This has nothing to do with Gaynor Scarlett,' Gary said
quietly.

Diana stood looking down at him accusingly.

'It's her sister's husband, isn't it?'

'They're all the same, *I* say,' Edith Bridges said, 'all tarred
with the same brush, all sleeping around, here and there. Can't
think why they bother to get married at all. Too much money,
that's the trouble. Pity it isn't more evenly distributed.' She
turned to her daughter. 'You gonna look at that house tonight
then?'

Diana's moody face brightened slightly.

'Yes. It's next door but one to Bett and Dave. It'd be great to
live near them, wouldn't it Gary?'

'Great.'

Because, he thought, we are just like Bett and Dave, puny
petty wage earners with puny petty ambitions.

'You might sound a bit more enthusiastic then.'

He got up and stretched wearily.

'I'm tired. I've been swotting, remember.'

She stepped forward and kissed him lightly.

'Yeah, but it'll be worth it, love, you see, when you qualify.'

'*If* I qualify.'

She looked at him sharply.

'That's not the attitude to take. Once you was a damn sight more ambitious than you are now.' Suspiciously she added, 'You might almost think . . .'

'Oh, give it a rest, Di,' he said tiredly, 'I do my best, I can't do more.'

She turned from him to her mother.

'Ah well, I'm grateful if *he's* not. I never thought the Council would come up with a hundred per cent mortgage. I'm glad I didn't change my job with the Council after all.'

The two women smiled at each other and Gary remembered the words of the landlord in the pub the night he'd first taken Di for a drink. 'Look at a girl's mum and and there you see the girl herself in a few years' time.' Yes, he could see it now, all right.

'You'll soon be doin' fine, you see,' Edith said.

Yes, Gary thought miserably, doing fine. He had written to Gaynor on hearing of Paul Earnshaw's arrest, but the letter had been returned to him care of his office, unopened. He had telephoned her flat, but she had hung up on him. He remembered how they had stood together in the rain, as kids, as she had passionately declared her belief in David Lloyd's innocence, and her encouragement to him then in his grief over his sister. He wished he could be with her now to comfort *her*.

He had told his father he didn't want to be tied to anyone yet, not even Gaynor. That was true but, given a little more time, he would have eventually settled down with Gay. They rushed me, both of them, he told himself with typical male self-pity and now I'm trapped. Life with Gaynor would have been limitless with her money and connections. He stared at the broad gold band on his wife's finger and hated the solidarity of it. But marriage needn't be permanent, he told himself, one day. . . . Then reality drowned him, sickening, defeating. His father had always been saying 'you see, one day' and where was he now, poor sod, not even bothering to say it any more.

'Gary,' Diana said sharply, 'dreamin' again, are you? Are you ready?'

'Yes, I'm ready,' he said.

Inspection of rabbit hutch, forward.

They had got nearly to the front door when the telephone rang. Edith Bridges answered it.

'Gary,' she called, her voice puzzled, 'it's for you – Marbrook Police Station.'

'Police Station?' He heard Diana's sibilant repetition beside him. His stomach felt as if it were banded with ice. His heart pounded violently in his breast. Gay, had she . . .?

'Mr. Gary Thompson?'

'Yes.'

'Marbrook Police here. Bad news I'm afraid, sir, your father . . .'

'My father?'

'Yes, sir.'

His throat dry, he croaked: 'Is he . . .?'

'Drowned, I'm afraid, sir. You see . . .'

Diana crept up to him and put her hand in his. He was grateful for the warmth of it in the awful coldness that paralysed him.

'Yes, I see,' he said, 'I see. . . .'

Diana waited, watching him questioningly.

Most of the conversation came from the other end.

Finally Gary said, 'Yes, I'll come at once. How is my mother?'

'In hospital, sir, suffering from shock. She shouldn't have to stay in long, she's O.K. otherwise.'

'Thank you.'

He was surprised to find he was not outwardly shaking. He replaced the instrument and turned to his wife.

'Dad's dead. I have to go home.'

'I'm coming with hou.'

He stared at her blankly. He wanted no strangers along to share in his grief.

'I'm your wife, aren't I?' she said softly, removing her hand.

Somehow her being his wife wasn't very important just now. In this family thing she was still a stranger. Dad and Greer and

Gay, all had gone. Mum was all he had left now. It was frightening. He didn't think he could bear it.

'Gary,' Diana said quietly, 'I'm going to pack and then you can tell me all about it.'

He stared at her uncomprehendingly. Why had Mum gone to the river? She never could stand the water. And Dad, Dad couldn't even swim.

CHAPTER SEVENTEEN

THE diamonds glittered at her throat and on her ears and fingers. Her black dress was topless, starting at the rise of her breasts. He looked at her critically.

'Did you think we were having a party, Tabby?'

'No.' She smiled and her eyes glittered strangely. 'I dressed for *you* to show you I can be as glamorous as other women.'

'There's never been any doubt about that.'

'Oh darling, how sweet of you.'

She drained her glass and held it up to him for a refill.

'You're drinking too fast, Tabby, you'll be drunk and there's no more revolting sight than a drunken woman.'

She laughed shrilly.

'Unless perhaps a strangled one, eh? Harriet was strangled and you didn't have an alibi that night, did you, Reggie?'

'I had an alibi the night Dorothy Trent was murdered,' he said calmly, 'I was dining with you and Paul.'

She laughed again, too loudly.

'Harriet, Dorothy, Little Bo Peep.'

'Dorothy Trent was Paul Earnshaw's,' he said.

'Was she, darling, always? I wonder.'

'Can't we drop the subject?'

'No.' She stamped her slippered foot. 'I like inquests. So, taking recent events, we leave Paul to fry, then, when we think he's almost burnt, we come back like they do in films in the nick of time to give him his alibi and free him. Why, Reggie, why did you have to torture him like that? After all, he's kept quiet all these years about seeing you near the scene when Harriet was murdered. I've often wondered, Reggie, whether you killed Harriet.'

'Why didn't you ask me?'

She shrugged elegantly.

'Because I'm afraid of the answer.'

'I could lie to you.'

'I don't think you would. Oh God, Reggie, you're an evil

bastard. All these years I've lived with you knowing you to be the spawn of the devil. How do I go on living with myself?'

'You'll have to soon,' he said calmly, 'or, at any rate, without me.'

Tabitha sipped her drink and sat down.

'Tell me something, if you're so convinced you're going to die soon, why have that Trent girl killed?'

He raised his eyebrows.

'Who said I did?'

She laughed curtly.

'Who said you arranged those other murders, that club manager, that female croupier in Cannes, that . . .'

He interrupted her.

'All scum, bloodsuckers, spreaders of scandal.'

'So they had to die.'

'I detest scandal,' he said, 'I may not have given you much, Tabby, but at least I don't leave you a first class scandal round your ears for your friends to gloat and laugh about. The world knows that you and I and Paul Earnshaw were dining in one part of London, whilst this unfortunate Trent girl was being done to death in another part of London, and our alibi is undeniably supported by the admirable Gregson who served us with the meal, which he obtained from a café nearby, the manager of which will confirm, and, if you remember, Gregson was all the time checking his watch because of our impending departure to France. He has also found us a porter who saw Paul leave our flat.'

'Flushed out by the admirable Gregson? And we stay cooped up, incognito, in a dusty village in Normandy while you let Paul Earnshaw have his first lesson.'

'He may have learnt it, I hope so.'

Tabitha put down her glass, got up and whirled gracefully over to the stereo. She smote her hand on her breast and rolled her eyes.

'And there the poor sod sat, Indian faces leering at him, stewpot at the boil, arrows at the ready, all pointing at his chest, and then, at the eleventh hour, they came, galloping through the trees, trumpets sounding, the bloody rescuing cavalry. Yippee!'

'Very funny,' Reggie said, 'haven't you forgotten the gunboat?'

'Poor young sod,' Tabitha said, 'I bet he's so grateful now he could kiss your feet.'

'He should be,' Reggie said, 'after all, I took him from nothing and now he's a man of the world.'

'Some world,' Tabitha said. She bent over the stereo and the stark, plaintive voice of Brenda Lee filled the room.

'Too many rivers between you and me, too many rivers to cross.'

Tabitha sang softly with the record.

'And when you try to put love back together, there's always a few little pieces you can't find.'

'That song makes me cry,' she said.

She moved, like a lithe, sinewy cat, away from the stereo and topped up her drink.

'To you,' she cried gaily, holding up her glass. 'To you, darling Reggie and twenty-five years of married bliss. Never a cross word we've had, me old man and me, never a cross word. Oh God, I think I *am* going to cry.'

In the police station the file on Paul Earnshaw was tidied up and put away. The case remained unsolved, murder by a person or persons unknown.

'My money's still on Gunner-Cartwright,' the sergeant said.

'Then you've lost your money,' the superintendent replied, 'Gunner-Cartwright always has perfect alibis, all those other murders of people in his employ, he was nowhere near them.'

'He's a clever bastard.'

'And a sick one, too, I hear,' the superintendent said. 'I heard he collapsed at the opera a night or two back, I did hear they don't expect him to get over it. Lady Tabitha's never left his bedside.'

'She's a bit of all right if you like,' the sergeant said.

'Yeah, if you like 'em skinny. Me, I'm a bust man meself.'

'Depends on the performance, I say,' said the sergeant. 'Well, if he's dying her performance won't worry him any more, and we'll get nothing on him now. He's been too clever for us.'

'Trust him to get his punishment from the top brass,' the superintendent said. 'He was always way out of our class.'

'He's had a good run fer his money,' the sergeant said, 'a bleedin' good run.'

'It was good of you to call, Hedley,' Gaynor said. 'I was going to write to you today. Can you stay for a meal?'

He shook his head.

'Sorry, Gay, no. I was in town and thought it a good chance to call and see how you were, but I have a train to catch in half an hour.'

She was still losing weight, Hedley Strong thought. She'd lost entirely now that plump merry look that had been so attractive on her when he'd first known her.

'Paul's just been,' she said.

'How was he?'

'So different, Hedley. I don't think he'll ever be the same again.'

She clasped her hands together and looked at him, pleading in her eyes.

'Hedley, I was going to write to you and ask you to see me. I know now that I can't go abroad. I'm not strong enough to be on my own so far away. I want to be near people who know me, care about me.'

'I'm glad,' Hedley said. 'Let me know what you decide to do.'

'I already have. When I'm through university, may I work near you, where I can see you sometimes? You see . . .' Her lips trembled, 'I have so much need of the kind of friendship you can give me. The other kind . . . love . . .' she stopped and spread out her hands helplessly. She raised her eyes to him in entreaty. 'I could teach school near you, maybe help you in your work.'

'I may move around.'

'Then I'll move around, too.'

He looked at her steadily. It would be an easy promise to make because he was sure that, somewhere along the way, she would find her own strength and cease to need him. Right now she had to have assurance.

'I'd like it, Gay,' he said, smiling his gentle smile, 'because *I'm* a little scared, too.'

She smiled back at him.

'When you're officially made into a priest, may I come to the service?'

'Please. I can't hope that my family will.'

She laughed lightly and a touch of the old merriment lit her eyes briefly. 'Can you see us, Hedley, in thirty years' time? The old priest trundling round the parish and the dried-up old school marm trundling round after him, doing his chores and nagging him?'

'You're not a Catholic, Gay,' he said gently: 'there'll be a limit to your activities.'

Her face clouded.

'Will that matter?'

'It matters only that we shall both love God,' he said, 'and each other.'

'It's been lovely seeing you.'

'The cottage,' he said, 'have you let it again yet?'

'No. I haven't found the right tenant. Maybe I'll keep it for you to go into retreat in. That's what priests do, isn't it?'

He smiled.

'I'm afraid it won't do for retreat. I enjoyed my stay in the cottage so much. I shall never forget it.'

'Katheryn would say,' Gaynor said, 'the cottage liked you, as it liked David.'

'It's no ordinary cottage.'

'No, it lives. It has feelings.'

'Well, Gay,' he said, 'I really must go. British Railways wait for no man.'

He turned in the doorway and looked back at her as she stood in the middle of the room, her eyes brimming now with tears, her hands clasping and unclasping in front of her.

'We aren't saying good-bye, are we, Hedley?'

'No, Gay, never good-bye.'

'Hedley,' she said, 'do you think you were sent to me to help me?'

'Probably Gay. Perhaps *you* were sent to help *me*. Who knows?'

When he had gone she went to the window and watched him walking down the street, a thin, shabby figure in his old rain-coat, and she was filled with compassion for him and admiration, too, for his strength.

As if some telepathy had winged to him from her, he turned suddenly, looked up and waved, a smile lighting his pale face.

She watched him greedily until he was out of sight and there was no one special to her left in the street, only strangers who walked by and didn't know or care. She turned back to her quiet flat and wondered if she would ever stop feeling so alone.

CHAPTER EIGHTEEN

'AND give up the chance of our own home here?' Diana said disbelievingly, 'to go and live with your Mum in Marbrook for keeps?'

'Yes.'

Her mouth set rebelliously.

'I'm not going.'

His voice cold he said, 'Please yourself. I'm going. Sue for a divorce if you want to.'

She stared at him bleakly.

'So that's what you want me to do.'

'No it isn't. It's entirely up to you. My mother can't live alone and she's not bad enough or old enough for an institution.'

'Gary,' she was pleading with him now, 'I can't go and live with your Mum, she doesn't even like me. Besides, what about your job?'

'I've spoken to the partners. I'm being transferred back to London. I shall commute.'

'You treat me like a stranger – it's the sort of thing you should've talked over with me.'

'Well I'm talking to you now about it, aren't I?'

'Yes, now that it's all fixed. *She* knew, didn't she?' Diana added, 'before we left?'

'Yes, I talked to her, said I wouldn't leave her alone.'

'I had a funny feeling,' Diana said, 'when we said good-bye to her; she wasn't sad, she seemed, well, kind of triumphant.'

'Nonsense.'

'I'd hate it, being in the same house as her, sharing her kitchen. She's barmy, Gary; she's ever so funny, she ought to be in a home.'

'She's not barmy,' he said coldly, 'she's just terribly upset. She needs looking after.'

He thought of his poor mum, her pathetic mouth working all the time, the cloudy eyes puzzled as she moved round the house doing her chores like an automaton. He wondered what sudden madness or depression had flooded her brain, sending her running down to the river she hated, to fling herself into oblivion. And Dad, slow to realize her errand and when he had, pounding after her down on to the towpath. Dad who couldn't swim had held her up till help had arrived, then, they said, obviously his heart had stopped beating and there, in the cold, dark water he had died.

'Dad's house protection policy makes the house Mum's,' Gary said, 'with no more repayments. It will, naturally, be mine after her death so we don't need to worry now about a mortgage.'

Diana considered miserably. Freda Thompson must be about fifty. We'll be too old to care, she thought, when that house becomes ours. She looked at him bleakly.

'She might live for donkey's years, yet.'

He eyed her with hostility.

'I hope she will. If you don't want to come, Di, we can call it a day.'

'Oh Christ.' She put her head in her hands. Behind her closed eyes vivid pictures flashed through her brain. A break-up of the marriage, Gary and his mum being taken from the tiny house on Fletchley Estate to a bigger, better place by Gaynor Scarlett, who Freda Thompson liked anyway. They would make a small flatlet for Freda so that she wouldn't be under Gaynor's feet. They'd be so cosy and happy, the three of them. She raised her head.

'I'll come,' she said. She waited for his face to drop, but his expression didn't change.

'Good.'

'But I don't promise. . . .'

'Di,' he said, 'if you make it any harder for her, we're through.'

'You'd stick up for her against me, and I'm your wife?'

'There should be no question of taking sides. We're all civilized people.'

He remembered Gay's bitter words to him – 'the kitchen's never been built that's big enough for two women to share'. This then was his penance. He was tied irrevocably to these two women – his sad, half-crazy mother and his bitter, unloved wife.

'Gary,' Diana was leaning towards him, her eyes entreating him. 'I will try, darling, if only you'll love me, but you must realize it's a bitter disappointment to me. I'd set my heart on that dear little house near Bett and Dave. In Marbrook I'll know no one and she – that Gaynor Scarlett – she lives there.'

'Not now,' he said, 'and if she did, it wouldn't matter. That's all over now.'

Young dreams gone, slain by lust and selfishness. No use remembering any more.

'I'll try then, Gary,' Diana said pathetically, 'I can't do more, can I?'

She rose heavily, almost like an old woman. The vision rose up in her mind of Freda Thompson, suddenly a bowed, untidy, prematurely aged crone, eyes crazed, mouth working like the mouth of an idiot. How will I bear it, how will I live with the dislike I see sometimes in her eyes when they come alive and focus on me?

She put out her hand to him.

'Help me.'

'Yes, I'll help you.'

The misery on her face moved him to compassion. Once he had wanted her so much. If she was going to try, then he had to try too.

'You can get a job in Marbrook, Di, part-time, if you want to, it won't be so bad then, and Mum can be left for a few hours, it's just that she mustn't live alone any more and it solves our problem, too, of a house. We'll have more money to spend now. It'll work out all right, you see.'

She smiled wanly and moved to the door.

'I'm gonna tell Mum now. You better not come. Let me break it on my own.'

When she got to the door he called her name 'Di'.

She turned.

'Thanks,' he said.

'I don't know how he can expect you to,' Edith Bridges said, 'we must get Dad to talk to him.'

'It's no use, Mum, all the arrangements are made.'

'Without consulting *you*.'

'He has consulted me, Mum, and I've agreed. It's the only

thing Gary . . .' – she corrected herself – '*we* can do in the circumstances.'

'Give him an ultimatum, you or her.'

'I know who he'd choose.'

Edith eyed her daughter critically.

'It hasn't exactly bin a flamin' success, this marriage, has it?'

'No, but I intend that it shall be. I shall work on it until he's really settled down, got her out of his system. If only we could've bin on our own instead of having to go and live with this old biddy.'

'I still say you should refuse,' Edith said.

Diana gave a twisted little smile.

'And hand him to her on a plate? He tried to go back to her, Mum, when I had that miss.'

'He never did!'

'She turned him down.'

'Oh Lord,' Edith said, 'the rotten little swine!'

'Don't you see,' Diana said, 'she turned him down then, but she might not later on if he were free of *me*.'

'If you'd got any pride, Di, you'd let him go.'

'No,' Diana drummed her fist on the table. 'No, I shall not let him go. I love him, Mum, without Gary there'd be nothing left for me, nothing left at all.'

'Well if that Thompson woman makes you unhappy,' Edith said, 'she'll have yer Dad an' me to answer to, I swear that.'

'I have a husband, Mum,' Diana said, 'he's the one who's got to look after me from now on.'

'He better had, too,' Edith said darkly. She shook her head despairingly. 'It was a bad day fer us when he come here lookin' fer digs, and I liked him so much in the beginning, too.'

'I loved him in the beginning,' Diana said, 'and I always shall.'

Freda Thompson dusted the picture carefully, speaking her thoughts aloud in the empty house. The faces of Ned and herself in their wedding clothes smiled back at her.

'Hello Dad, knew you was on to a good thing then, didn't you, when you married me. Never had to wait one minute fer yer meals, did you?' Her face creased, her eyes grew puzzled. 'Can't think why you goes out so much these days – them union meetings and Council – seems you're never in. Our Gary and Greer neither. Clean socks our Greer had this mornin', look at 'em now, all black where she rubs one foot against the other, even in the picture you can see the dirt.' She picked up the other picture of Gary and Greer at the school sports. Then she put it down and wandered round the room, flicking at things with her duster, plumping up cushions. Her eyes came to rest on the china birds on top of the telly. Something was different about them yes, she knew what it was, there were no bills stuffed in their beaks, and then she remembered: our Gary took 'em out when he was here, to sort 'em, he said, because Dad ... Dad ... memory returned, sickening, flooding her with sorrow. She sank down on the settee and cried, rocking herself to and fro with grief. I killed him; it was my fault. If I hadn't been so wicked, he'd have been here with me now, poor old Dad, he'd never had much with all his ambitions. Now Gary's coming with that girl – that common, tarty, young girl – when it should have been dear little Gaynor. Round and round in her befuddled brain ran the crazy reasoning. If that girl hadn't got her cheap little hooks into our Gary, Dad wouldn't have had to die. Greer wouldn't have died, either, if she'd kept her socks clean. Always brought up nice, they was – Greer and Gary – always clean and nice. Freda got up off the settee and bustled into the kitchen. Harold Dinfold would be calling soon for Greer. It was Thursday night. He always came at half past seven on Thursdays to take her to the pictures. 'Greer.' The empty room brought Freda's muddled brain suddenly back into focus. Harold Dinfold hadn't been here for a long time because Greer had gone to London and now she was dead. Gary was coming, though, with that girl. Was the room ready? In a frenzy Freda ran upstairs and inspected the room Gary had asked her to get ready for himself and Diana. 'Diana will look after you, Mum,' he had written, 'so try to get along with her, won't you?'

'The dirty thing,' Freda shouted. She rushed out of the bedroom and down the stairs again. Back in the kitchen she crouched thinking of those two on that bed upstairs, writhing, twisting bodies enjoying their lust. She shuddered and trembled while her feverish imaginings rose to a sickening crescendo, then tailed away into a fog. One day, she thought, when it gets too bad and I can't bear it, I shall go down to the river again, where it's cool and dark, and maybe, down there, I'll see Dad.

She went back to the foot of the stairs, calm now, the double bed and the river forgotten, and called up the stairs.

'Greer, come on, you'll be late.'

Greer didn't answer. Freda smiled. Sulking again because I told her off for having dirty socks. There was fog in Freda's brain again now. It came so often these days. She decided to sit down for a while until it cleared.

CHAPTER NINETEEN

PAUL'S tired eyes ranged round the small ward. In spite of the shine of the equipment and the fresh beauty of the flowers, it had the cold hand of death on it, he thought, death in the shape of that mockery of a man in the bed.

'Five minutes, no longer,' the sister said, 'he asked so specifically to talk to you, it shouldn't really be allowed.'

He had seen Tabitha outside where she had gone for five minutes' respite and a cigarette.

'He seems amazingly strong all of a sudden,' she said, 'he asked so insistently to speak to you Paul, better be quick, I'm afraid this spurt of energy won't last.'

He sat down close to the bed. All the hard things he had thought about this man seemed unimportant now.

'She must have had lots of other lovers, Paul,' Reggie said feebly. 'A girl like that gets around, pretty thing, Chinese mother pretty . . . any one of them could have done it; she was always free with her pussy, that one.' His voice trailed off but his eyes grew momentarily brighter. He remembered Dorothy Trent as she had been when he had first taken her, a sensuous, greedy, eager child, but innocent, so innocent. It had been sweet, teaching her. She shouldn't have tried blackmail, though, they all did, silly bitches. He gave a great sigh.

'This is too tiring for you,' Paul said.

'No, I want to talk. Tabby'll be back soon, must get our talking done before she comes.'

On the table beside Reggie's bed stood a small gold clock. Noticing Paul's eyes on it, Reggie smiled.

'Pretty, isn't it? It chimes — got it in Vienna — priceless almost. Funny, all the skill, all the money can't stop death. Makes you wonder . . .'

Soon death would be in this room, ruthless, final, and all these pretty things wouldn't matter to the man any more.

'Reggie,' Paul said, leaning nearer to the sick man, 'you arranged it all, didn't you, that strange dinner party, your disappearance.'

Reggie smiled weakly.

'It was a macabre nightmare for you, boy.'

'It was hell.'

Although bathed, shaved and immaculately attired now, Paul's eyes were still sore with strain and he felt old and dirty. He knew that he would carry the scar always.

From the bed came a hollow chuckle.

'That haughty little wife of yours won't treat you like chicken feed ever again, Paul. You have the mark of manhood on you now. It suits you. Before, you were just a puling boy.'

Paul looked away from the grinning death mask on the pillow.

'Live, Paul,' Reggie said, 'live like I've done. Take what you want, women, business deals, *use* people, don't be scared. You've always been scared, but not any more eh? You have to suffer to know how to live.' He grinned feebly. 'I'm suffering now, and *I'm* going to die.'

'Isn't there anything they can do for you, Reggie?'

'No.'

'You're very calm.'

Reggie's grin died. The heavy-lidded eyes took on something of their old cynical amusement.

'How would you have me? Screaming about the ward, brandishing my repentance for my sins? No.' He gave a low laugh. 'There's no repentance in me, Paul. I've had a bloody good innings and I've enjoyed every minute of it.'

The sick man's eyes closed. Paul thought he had dropped off to sleep, but then he spoke again. 'All these years you've never really known, Paul, have you, about the night Harriet was killed?'

'I think you did it,' Paul said, 'I think you killed Harriet.'

Reggie's eyes opened then. He smiled.

'But you were never sure.'

'No, I was never sure.'

'So you kept silent, just in case.'

'Yes. I knew it would be bad for you if I said I'd seen you coming up out of the woods that night.'

'And David, who they almost nailed for it? You never thought that if you'd mentioned seeing me, it would have helped *him*?'

'Yes, I thought that.'

'But you didn't help him. Why?' The voice from the bed was strong now, it didn't sound like that of a dying man.

'He was rotten. He deserved to be punished,' Paul said.

'Because your Katheryn loved him.'

Weaker now again, the voice of the sick man. 'You are not God, Paul. It wasn't for you to judge him.'

A snatch of subdued girlish laughter drifted in through the open window to the little ward from the courtyard outside as two nurses walked swiftly by.

'I treasure that sound,' Reggie said, 'women's laughter. I've known so many women, all lovely ones, I never had time for the other kind. With my money I could shop around.'

In the distance a car door slammed.

'I treasure that sound, too,' Reggie said, 'even car doors banging, it's a sound of life, so soon to be gone.'

'Surely, even now,' Paul said, 'they could do something.'

'No, I left it too late, wouldn't admit there was anything wrong. For years I've had it, fought it like I fought everything else.' The sick man's voice tailed away into a tired plaint. 'No good now.'

They sat in silence. There was no sound save the quiet ticking of the little gold clock. Then Reggie spoke again, wearily.

'Paul, what were *you* doing near the woods that night?'

Paul passed a hand over his mouth before he answered. His voice was flat and weary too.

'I was too drunk to make love to the girl I'd taken to the dance, so I took her home and went for a walk down towards the woods to try to sober up.'

'Near Katheryn Scarlett's house, although you'd quarrelled with her at the dance?'

'Yes, I suppose so. I couldn't keep away from her.'

The door opened quietly and Tabitha came into the ward.

'Finished chatting, you two?'

'Yes,' Paul said. He got up.

'Cranston came in this morning,' Tabitha said, 'to bring some reports on the Digby-Meade accounts that Reggie asked for.'

'And to say good-bye,' the man in the bed said. 'Always take Cranston's advice, Paul, he's a good accountant.'

'Cranston said he'd got the agency to send you a temporary secretary, Paul,' Tabitha said.

'Yes, I know. I'm going back to the office now.'

'And then go home Paul,' Tabitha said, 'you look so tired.' She put a hand on his arm. 'And Katheryn, how is she taking it?'

He gave a bitter little laugh.

'As if nothing's happened,' he said. 'She speaks to me as if she doesn't even see me.'

From the bed came Reggie's hollow laughter.

'Marry an iceberg, you can't expect flames.'

'You can't win 'em all, Paul,' Tabitha said. 'Good-bye.'

As he walked into his office the new secretary gazed at him with unconcealed interest and handed him the telephone.

'Just in time, sir, your housekeeper is on the line for you.'

'Thanks.'

'Mr. Earnshaw, this is Mabel.'

'Yes Mabel, is there anything wrong?'

'The cottage, sir. Miss Gaynor rang to say it's burned down, vandals they think. It's bin empty since the young feller left to be a priest. Mrs. Earnshaw looked a bit queer when she heard. I don't think she ought to have gone off alone, but she just grabbed her handbag and went.'

'Did she tell you to ring me?'

'No, sir, but I thought . . .'

'You did right, Mabel, thank you. I'll go there at once.'

'Oh, good, sir, I'm glad. Miss Gaynor said she would get there as soon as she could, but she couldn't leave straightaway.'

'I'm going now, Mabel,' he said. 'Good-bye.'

'I have to leave,' he said to his temporary secretary who was watching him curiously, 'I'll be in touch with you later, by phone.'

Katheryn hadn't asked for him, hadn't even thought of him, but then, of course, she wouldn't. The cottage was hers . . . and David's.

EPILOGUE

SHE stood motionless, breathing the acrid, scorched smell of the ashes that quivered in the breeze. All around her there were fragments of blackened glass, grimed bricks, pieces of charred furniture, an odd chair leg intact, a scrap of wallpaper, its pattern of lemon and orange and red nasturtiums ludicrous amidst the macabre debris. A twisted metal bedhead leaned drunkenly over a charred saucepan. Part of the stairs to the balcony hung perilously from a pillar of scorched bricks, unharmed by the fire. These stairs and bricks were all that was left standing of the cottage. There was nothing now, no cloister any more for its ghosts, its memories, just nothing.

Soon the trembling ashes and charred remains would be scattered and trodden into the earth. The snowdrops would spread and grow over what had once been the floor and no-one would ever know there had been a cottage there.

She moved and her foot caught against something. She looked down. It was a part of the wall with the date 1857 carved on it. Beside it lay one of the ornate scrolls that had so proudly adorned the date on the cottage wall.

Picking her way carefully she stepped out of the ruins on to the path. She felt giddy suddenly and the smell of the wreckage was a sickness in her stomach.

'Katheryn,' Paul said, 'are you all right?'

She put a hand out gratefully to his proffered arm.

'Come and sit down over here.'

She looked up at him wonderingly as he led her to a big log and sat her down on it.

'I didn't know you were here.'

'I've only just got here. Mabel phoned me.'

He sat down on the log beside her.

'I think I knew it was going to happen,' she said tonelessly. 'Last night I had a dream, the snowdrops, white and lovely, and then, when I bent to pick them, the red stain of blood, crawling

like wicked flames until they were all red and wet in my hands.'
She shuddered.

'You must come home,' Paul said. 'Come in my car. We'll send for yours later.'

'Home?'

'Yes.'

She stared at him with a sudden new awareness. He'd been in trouble, too, like David.

'Are *you* all right, Paul?'

'Yes, I'm all right, although' – he gave a harsh little laugh – 'it wasn't exactly a picnic.'

Memory stirred like a sharp pain, giving those words vividly back to her, spoken by another man in this same place, so long ago it seemed now.

'It hasn't exactly been a picnic,' he'd said. Everything he'd said that last time by the cottage was written for all time in her heart. There were black shadows under Paul's eyes now, as there had been that day under David's, and lines of strain on his haggard face. Paul was a man now like David. The knowledge gave her an odd comfort.

'Katheryn,' he said, 'did you think I'd done it, killed that girl?'

She shook her head, smiling faintly.

'No, I know you couldn't have, any more than it could have been you who killed Harriet.'

He took her cold hands in his.

'How do you know that?'

'I just do. You couldn't kill anyone.'

'Come on, darling.' He drew her gently to her feet, 'You mustn't stay here, you can do no good now.'

'No,' she said steadily, 'there's nothing anyone can do now. It's gone, all gone forever.'

Her hands still in his, she turned and looked across at the boathouse.

'Someone killed Harriet that night when there were so many stars. Do you remember the stars that night, Paul?'

'Yes, I remember.'

'David didn't kill her,' Katheryn said, 'David didn't. I know.'

Big tears were rolling down her cheeks now. Her little marble face was crumpled with grief. He was strangely glad. He had never seen her cry before. He tried to lead her away, but she pulled her hands from him, turned and gestured towards the wreck of the cottage.

'He's so dead now, so very, very dead.'

'But he's been so long a-dying,' Paul said tiredly. She slipped her hand into his. He looked down at her, desperation in his weary eyes.

'Never leave me, Katie.'

His name for her, but she accepted it now without protest. She gave a tiny sigh, turned her back on the pathetic remains of the cottage and started to walk slowly back up the hill, her husband by her side.

'Katie,' he pleaded again, 'never leave me.'

She caught her breath on a sob and wiped away the tears with the back of her hand, then she put her wet hand back in his. She looked up at him as slowly they climbed the hill.

'It would be funny without you, Paul,' she said, 'it seems you've always been *there*.'

She looked back just once more and then set her face steadfastly ahead. He rejoiced to see that she was still crying.

THE END

A SELECTED LIST OF
TITLES PUBLISHED BY
CORGI BOOKS

All these books are available at your bookshop or newsagent, or can be ordered direct from the publisher. Just tick the titles you want and fill in the form below.

CORGI BOOKS Cash Sales Department, P.O. Box 11, Falmouth, Cornwall.

Please send cheque or postal order, no currency.
U.K. send 19p for first book plus 9p per copy for each additional book ordered to a maximum charge of 73p to cover the cost of postage and packing.
B.F.P.O. and Eire allow 19p for first book plus 9p per copy for the next 6 books thereafter 3p per book.
Overseas Customers: Please allow 20p for the first book and 10p per copy for each additional book.

NAME (Block letters) ....

ADDRESS ....

(Nov 77) ....

While every effort is made to keep prices low, it is sometimes necessary to increase prices at short notice. Corgi Books reserve the right to show new retail prices on covers which may differ from those previously advertised in the text or elsewhere.